CANNIBAL

CANNIBAL

by MICHAEL HARNER
and ALFRED MEYER

WILLIAM MORROW AND COMPANY, INC.

NEW YORK   1979

Library of Congress Cataloging in Publication Data

Harner, Michael.
   Cannibal.

   1. Mexico—History—Conquest, 1519-1540—Fiction. I. Meyer, Alfred, 1935- joint author. II. Title.
PZ4.H288Can [PS3558.A62475]   813′.5′4   79-12939
ISBN 0-688-03499-3

Printed in the United States of America.

First Edition

1 2 3 4 5 6 7 8 9 10

ACKNOWLEDGMENTS

Translations of Aztec poetry and prayer are from the following sources:

Aztec Thought and Culture: A Study of the Ancient Nahuatl Mind, by Miguel León-Portilla. Translated by Jack Emory Davis. Norman, Oklahoma: University of Oklahoma Press, 1963.

General History of the Things of New Spain: Florentine Codex, Book 6—Rhetoric and Moral Philosophy, by Bernardino de Sahagún. Translated (from the Aztec) by A. J. O. Anderson and C. E. Dibble. In thirteen parts, Part VII. Santa Fe, New Mexico: School of American Research, and Salt Lake City: University of Utah, 1969.

The Native Races of the Pacific States: Vol. II, Civilized Nations, by Hubert H. Bancroft. The Works of Hubert Howe Bancroft. San Francisco: Bancroft, 1882.

Quotations, primarily in the Epilogue, are from the following sources:

General History of the Things of New Spain: Florentine Codex, Book 2—The Ceremonies, by Bernardino de Sahagún. Translated (from the Aztec) by A. J. O. Anderson and C. E. Dibble. In thirteen parts, Part III. Santa Fe, New Mexico: School of American Research, and Salt Lake City: University of Utah, 1951.

General History of the Things of New Spain: Florentine

Codex, Book 8—Kings and Lords, by Bernardino de Sahagún. Translated (from the Aztec) by A. J. O. Anderson and C. E. Dibble. In thirteen parts, Part IX. Santa Fe, New Mexico: School of American Research, and Salt Lake City: University of Utah, 1954.

General History of the Things of New Spain: Florentine Codex, Book 10—The Gods, by Bernardino de Sahagún. Translated (from the Aztec) by A. J. O. Anderson and C. E. Dibble. In thirteen parts, Part II. Santa Fe, New Mexico: School of American Research, and Salt Lake City: University of Utah, 1970.

Daily Life of the Aztecs on the Eve of the Spanish Conquest, by Jacques Soustelle. Translated by Patrick O'Brian. Harmondsworth, Middlesex, England: Penguin Books, 1964.

The Aztecs of Mexico: Origin, Rise and Fall of the Aztec Nation, by George C. Vaillant. Revised by Suzannah B. Vaillant. Harmondsworth, Middlesex, England: Penguin Books, 1966.

The Conquistadors: First-Person Accounts of the Conquest of Mexico. Edited by Patricia de Fuentes. New York: Orion, 1963.

The Conquest of New Spain, by Bernal Díaz del Castillo. Translated by J. M. Cohen. Harmondsworth, Middlesex, England: Penguin Books, 1963.

Books of the Gods and Rites and the Ancient Calendar, by Diego Durán. Edited and translated by Fernando Horcasitas and Doris Heyden. Norman, Oklahoma: University of Oklahoma Press, 1971.

The Discovery and Conquest of Mexico, 1517–1521, by

Bernal Díaz del Castillo. Translated by A. P. Maudslay. New York: Farrar, Straus and Giroux, 1956.

Cortés: The Life of the Conquerer by His Secretary, by Francisco López de Gómara. Translated and edited by Lesley Byrd Simpson. Berkeley and Los Angeles: University of California, 1965.

Portions of the Epilogue originally appeared in the *American Ethnologist,* February 1977, and were reprinted in *Across the Board,* June 1977.

NOTE

Although this book has been written in the form of fiction to lend perspective and verisimilitude to the events and practices depicted, it is inspired by both historical and anthropological fact, as the Epilogue makes clear.

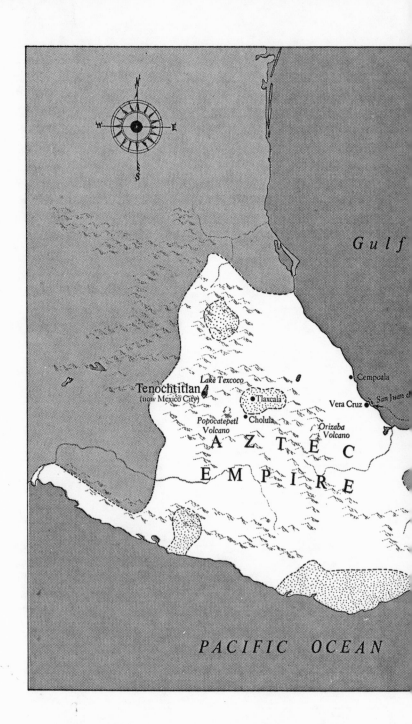

N

W   E

S

Gulf

Lake Texcoco

Tenochtitlan
(now Mexico City)

Cempoala

Tlaxcala

Vera Cruz

San Juan d

Popocatepetl
Volcano

Cholula

Orizaba
Volcano

A Z T E C

E M P I R E

PACIFIC OCEAN

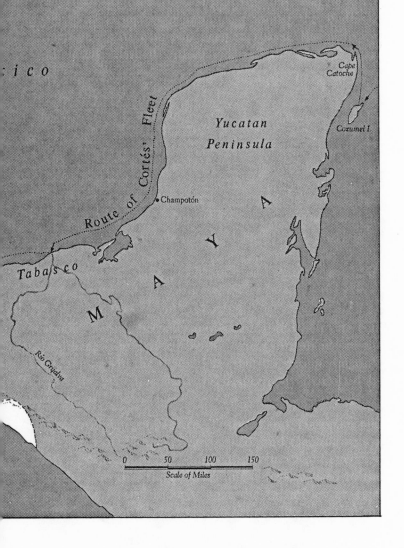

THE AZTEC EMPIRE, 1519

▢ APPROXIMATE AREA OF AZTEC EMPIRE

◈ INDEPENDENT NATIONS ENCIRCLED BY
THE AZTEC EMPIRE

ico

Cape
Catoche

*Yucatan
Peninsula*

Cozumel I.

Route of Cortés' Fleet

•Champotón

A

Y

Taba sco

A

M

Río Grijalva

0   50   100   150

Scale of Miles

PROLOGUE

Atlacol should have gotten up earlier, or waited another day back in the pine copse where he had slept. Better to be hiding among the decoys near the rock *before* dawn, not after. If he had found worms in the earth near the copse, or even beetles beneath the bark of the trees, it would have been possible to wait another day. But there was nothing, not so much as a grub. All he could do was chew on a pine bud, a small piece, not enough to make him start retching.

He stretched his arms, yawned, and reached down into the lake to fill his cupped hands with water. He washed his mouth out, spat into the sand, and shook his grizzled head. It seems like I'm always hunting these days, he thought.

Obviously handsome when younger, even now Atlacol held himself erect, still muscular and slender. His straight black hair was streaked with gray, but no wrinkles creased his tanned face except for the crows-feet at the corners of his eyes. He bore the aquiline, stoic face of the experienced warrior. A man had to be a warrior, a possessor of power, to survive, as he had, for some forty-five years. Among the Aztecs, he was old.

The sun was already high. Its heat knifed through the cold mountain air, warming his arms and shoulders. He turned to the sun and softly sang a prayer. From a pouch at his side he took a maguey thorn. Bowing his head, he stuck the thorn through his tongue and withdrew it, spitting drops of blood onto his hands. He outstretched them toward the sun.

"It is the only offering I have, Lord Tonatiuh," he said. "If I have success today I will give you more than this."

Finished, Atlacol looked up and down the shore of the lake to make sure he was alone. Other foragers could be a nuisance—sometimes even dangerous.

The bleached skeleton of a fish caught his eye. Atlacol turned it over with his toe, and then reached down and picked it up. Probably dry. He snapped the skeleton in two, hoping to find a trace of fluid in the backbone. Sucking each half, he tasted only sand, which he spat out in disgust. Dropping the skeleton, he looked around once more, and then waded out into the lake. When the water reached his waist, he turned northward, walking parallel to the shore. He bent forward slightly, peering into the water, searching for any irregularity, whether movement or object. Yet he did not want to concentrate too much and see things that weren't there. Better to fill his mind with other thoughts, and let his eyes signal his hands directly. That was the way to hunt when you were also going somewhere.

Atlacol thought of the food that he had eaten in the years before the famine. Now the village had been out of meat for months. Ever since the crops had again failed, hunters had combed the mountains for any game, large or small. The animals seemed to have vanished. A duck might be caught, a gopher killed, but little else. No deer, no other large animals seemed to exist anymore. The children cried from hunger, and some died.

He remembered five years ago, before the famine, when he had gone to the great city of Tenochtitlan at the time of the Feast of Huitzilopochtli, the war god. He remembered the maize cakes, beans, turkey, and chocolate. His wife's cousin, Tezcatl, a *pochteca*—one of the empire's traveling merchants—had brought him to the capital to see whether he could arrange for him to become a guard in the palace. A high-ranking noble, jealous of the pochteca's wealth, or so Tezcatl told him, obstructed the appointment. Secretly, he had been relieved, though he never let Tezcatl know it. He felt uneasy in the city, particularly in the Lord Moctezuma's palace with its imposing apartments and the hundreds of people in fine dress who streamed through them all day and, it seemed, all night. He despaired of learning all the signs of rank. But at that time his family had not been hungry. Now he would go back in a moment. As a servant, as a slave—anything. As long as his wife and daughter were fed.

There, something floating. He moved to his left, and reached into the water. What luck! His fingers encased the spongy mass of a water-fly nest. Atlacol thrust the nest into his mouth, sieving the gelatinous larvae through his teeth, and swallowing as deliberately as he could, savoring the odd, pungent taste. Twenty such and he would be content today, provided he got ducks to take home.

Perhaps he could even catch a salamander or two, although it was early in the season. Frogs then, or at least stone shit, if he could find a concentration of the algal scum that sometimes drifted to this side of the lake. He would carry it back over the mountain to his wife and little daughter. She worried him, his daughter. So beautiful, but so quiet, no longer wanting to move around much. The algae might make her smile. And his wife, too, with another one in her stomach. Her face was oily and shiny all the time now. He would gently wipe it when he got back.

He resumed his search, determined not to return home until the netted sack draped on his shoulder contained food. Ducks, frogs—anything. He himself, even if the hunger made him weak and crazy, would eat of nothing he found. No more fly nests. No, not so much as the wing of a fly. Out loud, he solemnly promised this to the sun.

His thoughts settled once more on the city. True, the ceremonies had excited him deeply: the procession of the generals in full regalia, the sudden, dramatic appearance of the Lord Moctezuma, shimmering and befeathered, his litter swaying through the throngs like a canoe on a sea of people, the shuffling of the naked Tlaxcalan prisoners of war as cadres led them to the base of the Great Pyramid, and atop it, the dancing of the black-painted priests, smoke from the Pyramid braziers curling in stark white wisps high into the turquoise sky. Every day since, those images of the capital tumbled across his mind. They came in his dreams, lingering in the morning, came to him whenever he was alone, like a wind from the snowy peaks.

Black and craggy, with green and white traces of guano running down it, the rock protruded out of the water directly ahead. Beyond, his flotilla of decoys, tethered together and anchored by a stone, still rode in the same formation in which he had arranged them late the day before.

Nothing had disturbed them. Shaped like flasks with long necks and covered with duck feathers, the gourds had been weighted with sand so they floated lengthwise. All except one, which did not float, and which he had carefully lashed high on the rock. Though it bore a coating of feathers, a large, circular hole was cut out of one side. In addition, two smaller holes were notched into the upper half of the decoy, on its shoulders, one on each side of the narrow neck. He untied it from the rock, inspected it, and smoothed a feather here and there. Now the wait. He looked across the empty, cloudless sky. Then, placing the gourd over his head, and adjusting it so he could peer out of the two small eyeholes, he lowered himself into the water, and edged ducklike toward the other decoys.

Inside the gourd, Atlacol's head soon started to bake, like a maize cake in an oven. As the day wore on, his scalp itched, and his ears buzzed in the close heat. Below, his hands rested inside his belt, and his feet shifted more often than necessary to rotate his body. The outside world was reduced to a narrow, horizontal band in front of him; he saw, in sequence as he turned, open water, the shore and its shadows, the black rock and its shadow, and open water again. At one point he saw a canoe in the distance, though it stayed well out on the lake, and finally disappeared to the south. His eight decoys bobbed in the foreground, like offspring; most of the time he looked right through them.

The whirr of wings and the splash of ducks hitting the water behind him came suddenly as he was studying the pitted surface of the rock. He counted five splashes, though he knew two or three could have been simultaneous landings. Tense with excitement, Atlacol turned slowly toward open water. Two mallards came into view, four more, yet another. Seven in all. He focused on the one closest to him, a drake with a bright-green head, and inched toward it. Do not go fast, do not go fast, he warned himself. The drake had already begun dabbling, tilting its body forward and downward into the water, ignoring the decoys.

Atlacol stopped as the busy drake came into range, turning this way and that, beads of water dripping from its yellow bill and saucy, iridescent head. He let his arms float up to just below the surface, bringing them together in front of him, his hands like open traps set in tandem. The drake swam into them, doomed.

He grabbed its feet, and yanked it under so swiftly it gave no alarm. In one motion he had it between his legs, pinning its wings with his knees and squeezing. The drake writhed in vain as the other ducks paddled obliviously about. He squeezed more tightly, feeling the bird-heart pumping wildly between his legs, a life-thing to snuff out, lest it retaliate in some dark way. The pumping gradually changed to irregular spasms, and then, after what seemed a long, dangerous time, ceased altogether, the chill of the lake seeping unchecked into the limp, feathered body. He had subdued the force, and was safe.

Atlacol waited a little longer, though certain it had

drowned. Finally he relaxed his legs. Keeping submerged
except for his head inside the gourd, he slowly took a
short length of maguey twine from his waist. Still taking
care not to disturb the surface of the water with his move-
ments, he looped the cord around the drake's neck, and
fastened it to his belt, picking in the process his second
target, that appeared through the eyeholes to be a brown
female.

This time, however, after painstaking stalking, one of
his hands missed, and a kicking, webbed foot slipped
free. Before he managed to submerge the thrashing bird,
it had let out a brief, gurgling squawk. Tripping over
the water, the remaining ducks flashed into flight with
frantic exclamations of their own, wheeling sharply away
from the alarm below. Holding the duck between his
knees, Atlacol fought a throbbing pump once more, forgetting that he could have simply wrung its neck now
that there were no more birds to deceive. But he persisted,
and the pump, soon exhausted, gave out. Victorious again,
he tied the second duck to his belt without surfacing. Let
more of them come, he challenged, as he settled back
into his waiting crouch. Surely more would come.

Atlacol had scarcely completed a single rotation when
he saw it. He froze. His temples began pounding and his
stomach knotted. It was in the water and moving slowly
toward him from the south, a human figure, foraging
exactly as he had done earlier. He could tell by its pace
and by the back-and-forth motion of the head. His eyes
strained as they sought out identity, strength, intention.
He could not tell if it was one of the Mexica, a fellow
Aztec; probably not, he concluded, since it came from
the south. His hand moved to his waist to make certain

the knife was there. Now he could see the man better. He was young, dark, and looked strong. Most important of all, his hair was tied in the kind of topknot worn by an Enemy-of-the-House. Any moment now and he would spot the decoys. The stranger looked up, hesitated, then moved cautiously toward one of the floating gourds. Reaching out, he picked it up out of the water, and turned it over in his hands.

Atlacol did not breathe lest he be heard. If only he could stifle the pounding in his temples, which reverberated inside the gourd like a signal drum. He watched as the man replaced the decoy and moved even closer to examine another. Do not go fast, do not go fast, Atlacol warned himself, as though stalking ducks.

The stranger stopped again, but instead of picking up the second decoy, looked in turn at all the others. And then straight at Atlacol. Had he seen the eyeholes? The figure approached, obviously puzzled, and when he came within arm's length, Atlacol struck. Reaching down like a wrestler, he clasped the stranger's ankles, and pulled them up. The Enemy-of-the-House tumbled backwards into the water.

Freeing himself from the gourd, Atlacol dove forward onto the man just as he began to thrash to the surface. Atlacol quickly locked his arm around his throat, and squeezed, ignoring the desperate clawing. Harder, I must squeeze harder, Atlacol told himself, fighting his own impulse to surface. Finally, Atlacol released the man, propelling himself up for a snatch of air. Before his foe could also surface, he was upon him once more, squeezing again, directing all his strength into his arm. Within a few seconds his adversary went limp.

Ducks are easier, Atlacol thought, relieved that the struggle was over. He stood in the water up to his shoulders, breathing heavily.

The stranger floated facedown, motionless just below the surface, beside one of the ducks that had been torn loose from Atlacol's waist. He recovered the duck and refastened it. Then he took hold of the stranger's body by the hair, and towed it to the lake side of the rock, where he would be unobserved from shore.

Two ducks was not so bad, but this, *this,* he told himself, he had not expected. People these days were always hungry, hungry like ducks. Ducks flew by and, seeing the decoys, were forced by their hunger to drop down and share in the bounty they assumed the decoys had found. He thought how his own hunger made him understand the efficacy of the decoys. He too flocked to a neighbor's house if there was food to be had. How he detected it could vary; smell, sight, rumor, invitation. Though as yet, he reflected, he had not been deceived by anything like human decoys luring him into a trap.

Atlacol worked quickly with his knife, severing the right thigh from the torso. Blood colored the water around the rock. He debated whether he should take the head, then finally decided against it. Too heavy. He opened the chest, and with a yank pulled out the heart. He would offer it at the temple at home. Then he reached one hand into the red water and, scooping it up, tossed it in the direction of the afternoon sun. He uttered a brief prayer to the great daystar, the giver of life.

Soon he waded ashore, the ducks at his belt, the heart in his bag, and the arms and legs tied across his shoulders. In his hand he carried the decoy with the eyeholes. He pictured his homecoming. The image of his daughter, awake and smiling, danced before him. He would wipe his wife's face, and help her prepare the feast. Atlacol wondered if the next child had yet come.

CHAPTER

I

The broiling carcass slowly rotated on the spit over the low fire, its four limbs projecting stiffly from the body. With each rotation, fat dripped from the amputated tips into the red-hot embers, sending flames upward to sear the already browned flesh. The spit, which pierced the length of the body from the mouth to the anus, was cranked at one end by a liveried servant.

A fine-looking boar, thought Marcos de Medina, as he idly fingered his wineglass. But then the Medicis always had the pick of the best game in Tuscany. In fact, the pick of the best of everything in Northern Italy, whether food, women, or mercenary knights such as himself. He turned and surveyed the garden party. He saw his patron, Cardinal Giulio, across the lawn under a blue-and-white striped canopy. The Cardinal was holding court with a fawning group of male and female admirers. Medina could hear their laughter over the whisper of the cascading fountains that surrounded the glade. The sound of the falling water reminded him of the rushing stream behind his family's castle in Castile. Eight years, he thought, eight years since he had left Spain.

"Don Marcos, are you going to stand there alone all day?" a teasing female voice called to him from the side. "After all, this *festa d'addio,* this going-away party, is for you."

Medina turned his head and looked over at the approaching girl. She smiled at him as she tossed her shoulder-length black hair with mock petulance, lifting her long skirt slightly as she crossed the grass. She took his arm, squeezed it coquettishly, and peered up at him with her inviting brown eyes. She stuck her tongue out at him, half-little girl, half-courtesan, and pouted with her sensuous mouth.

"You seem so distant today, Marcos. What fills your head? Dreams of your Spain? Or, more exactly"—she giggled—"dreams of the girls of Seville?"

Medina smiled and half-nodded toward the fulsome breasts partly showing through her webbed bodice. "My dear Caterina, your own outstanding realities far surpass my wildest dreams. And as for Seville, who is telling you such foolish tales?"

"The entire court knows that you are going there. And the Cardinal himself has just admitted as much. But he refuses to say anything more."

"You already know more than you should, little cat."

Caterina stamped her foot in mock annoyance, then stared thoughtfully at the man before her. Don Marcos de Medina, Knight of the Golden Fleece, soldier-of-fortune, cream of the Spanish aristocracy, handsome, tall, and intelligent, was going to disappear from her life. On some stupid, secret errand in the distant west.

"Take me with you," she said suddenly.

Medina laughed and shook his head.

"I mean it," she persisted.

"It's not possible, *mia cara.*" He smiled.

She put her mouth close to his ear. "Then at least come to my chamber tonight," she whispered.

"We'll see, my little Caterina," Medina replied noncommittally.

"If you don't, I'll come to yours. And I'll make you regret you ever thought of leaving." She kissed him on the cheek and gaily spun away to join the party in the pavilion.

Medina pensively watched her go. He had indeed enjoyed her, and the others like her, in the Medici court. He would miss the easy morals and pleasures of the Florentine elite. Yet he ached for action. Masquerade balls, pleasures of the bed, and occasional jousts in tournaments were not enough for his Castilian soul.

Above the mellow, languid cadences of Florence and the murmur of the voices of his own past, he felt he could hear another, wilder call, though he could not identify its source or decipher its message. All he knew was that life's challenges had thus far seemed small to him, and incomplete. No task had yet required of him the totality of effort he yearned to put forth. All his life he had a sense that he was grooming himself; for what, however, he still did not know.

He came from a line of warriors, warriors who had held off the Moors for centuries, and then finally expelled them back across the Mediterranean into North Africa. But now there were no Moors to fight in Spain, and almost a decade ago he, like many other young Spaniards, came to Italy in search of new wars. Medina exceeded even his own expectations on the battlefields, and his single-handed exploits became almost legendary among the Spanish troops in Italy. Then Florence was finally taken, and the Medicis put into power. And now the battles were over here, too.

Peace had been killing him in a way war never could. He was dying a slow death until yesterday, when Cardinal

Giulio had summoned him to his quarters, and informed him that he was to depart in two days for Seville to receive orders from Bishop Fonseca, director of the *Casa de la Contratación,* the official headquarters for Spain's exploration and conquest of the New World.

Medina had asked Giulio the nature of the orders, but the Cardinal only winked and said, "I know nothing except that you will be a lone crusader on a mission of God." Now, thinking the matter over, Medina wondered if the mission had been assigned by the Cardinal's nephew, Giovanni, who thanks to the Spanish-supported return of the Medicis reigned as Pope Leo X. He shrugged. Leave the politics to the politicians. What counted was that he was being saved from the lingering death of court life. Medina felt energized by the anticipation of the unknown. Perhaps, he thought, he would grace little Caterina's bedroom tonight after all. Odd how idle pleasures became sweeter when the prospect of putting them aside loomed so close.

He strode toward the roast boar, which had just been removed from the fire by servants and, with great ceremony, lowered onto a long marble table between baskets of plump, bursting fruit and large Venetian glass vases filled, alternately, with flowers and red Tuscan wine in accord with the tastes of the host. The Cardinal and his friends had already approached the steaming, savory carcass.

By virtue of the crimson brilliance of his outfit, the most conspicuous figure at the table was the Cardinal. It was common knowledge that Giulio designed his own ecclesiastical robes. He prided himself on flourishes of individuality, as he saw it, ordinarily being careful nevertheless to retain some semblance of conformity to the dress code of the College of Cardinals. The robes he donned this afternoon, however, struck Medina as extreme, ostentatious, even foppish. Crimson pennants dangled from his sleeves, and the silver cross embroidered on the front of his surplice had been set—instead of in the traditional vertical position—at an angle, almost a rakish one.

"Don Marcos," called Cardinal Giulio boisterously, "it falls to you to make the first incision."

"With pleasure, Your Eminence," replied Medina, reaching for his dirk and bowing low toward his host.

"Granted," responded the Medici, "first because we are honored by your presence, second because we are famished." He bowed in return only with his head, and very slightly at that. Rank and power in the courts of the Medicis were signaled by increasingly restrained acknowledgment.

"Take care, Don Marcos, not to perform too neatly," piped Caterina at his elbow. "Else the Medicis shall make you labor with their butchers."

"I shall be sure to cloak my sanguinary skills," laughed Medina. In many ways, he thought fleetingly, he already had labored for the Medici butchers. A roar of approval rose as he plunged the blade into the boar's flank with studied clumsiness. Warm, fat-flecked juices ran copiously onto the table. Medina cut a section of flank and, stabbing it with his dirk, offered it to Caterina.

"A pitifully ragged morsel, my dear, guaranteed to offend any master butcher," he boasted. "Yet, I daresay, it is succulent fare. It will give you strength and make a firmer woman of you."

"Scoundrel," she retorted brightly, "you put yourself in great jeopardy by making me any stronger or firmer than I am." Abruptly, she snatched the meat from the end of the dirk with her teeth. Widening her eyes, she emitted an emphatic, suggestive sigh of pleasure, to the great delight of the company.

"My turn," shouted the Cardinal as he grabbed Medina's dirk and addressed the boar. Egged on by encouragement from his underlings, he immersed himself in the task, carving slice after slice of dripping meat. He became heedless of the fat and juice stains that spread rapidly across the front of his surplice, along the edges and up the pennants dangling from his sleeves, and finally inward to the marrow of the silver cross.

At length he paused. Wielding the dirk with a slice of meat skewered on its tip, he turned to Medina.

"Here, Don Marcos," he announced loudly. "This will make you stronger and firmer." Then, amid the uproar caused by his comment and as Medina leaned forward to pluck the meat from the dirk, the Cardinal added, in a whisper, "Make you stronger and firmer not only for Caterina but for Mother Church, Don Marcos."

Whether it was the afternoon wine, the energy of the meat, or the pleasant anxiety of impending change, Medina couldn't be sure. But what was certain was that he could scarcely keep his eyes off Caterina, nor, he decided, his hands. As the party waned, he took her by the arm and led her across the spacious lawn toward the great house.

It was well past midnight before his thoughts turned once more to what lay ahead.

* * *

The streets of Seville teemed with the commerce of Spain's greatest port, booming from its trade with the New World. Medina strode through the busy throngs toward the ancient Moorish fortress that housed the *Casa de la Contratación*. On all sides of him, embarked on a thousand tasks, he saw sailors, soldiers-of-fortune, porters, monks, pilots, captains, drovers, and merchants. The crowd momentarily parted to allow the passage of a small procession of footmen and slaves following an ostentatiously dressed cavalier with a gold necklace and earrings riding a richly caparisoned charger. Near the gateway of the *Casa,* toward which he headed, Medina's attention was caught by a string of stark-naked men, women, and children, linked together by a chain fastened to the iron collars on their necks. From their brown skins and strange appearance, he concluded they were Indians. They looked emaciated and dispirited. One of the women, more attractive than the others, bore bruises and welts on her body. Medina thrust the scene from his mind, thought vaguely of Caterina, and entered the portal of the fortress.

Inside the doorway, Medina's eyes slowly adjusted to the dim light. A sentry came forward and, after a brief inquiry, led him up a dark stone staircase lit only by torches, and through a long corridor to a stone-walled antechamber outside a large oak door. In response to a question from the soldier, Medina handed over a rolled parchment tied with a ribbon, his letter of introduction from Cardinal Giulio. The sentry went in through the door and shortly reappeared, motioning Medina to enter. The guard left, closing the door behind him.

The room was not quite as dark as the corridor. Muted sunlight slanted in from a small closed window, and burn-

ing tapers on two large standing iron candelabra cast
their flickering light against manuscript-laden shelves. A
large crucifix hung on one wall, Christ's wounds garishly
painted in red. Oil paintings of martyrs hung on the opposite side. The air was heavy with humidity and the heat
from the candles. Between the candelabra stood a large
leather-covered desk over which a seated figure remained
bent, apparently reading something before him. The
figure looked up, rose, and waved Medina closer. Medina
saw that Bishop Fonseca was a thin, elderly man.

"Ah, Don Marcos de Medina," he said, "it is a pleasure
to make your acquaintance at last. Do sit down." He
pointed to the chair opposite his desk, and settled himself
again in his own.

"I knew your father," the Bishop continued, "when
we both served at the court of Ferdinand and Isabella.
May his soul rest in peace. He was an illustrious knight of
an illustrious lineage."

"Your Excellency is most kind," replied Medina, wishing that the formalities were over. But his impatience was
tempered by the knowledge that he was in the presence of
one of the most powerful men in Spain, the brains behind
the Spanish conquest of the New World. The white-
haired, sharp-eyed man before him was determining the
destiny of a new empire.

"And you, Don Marcos, you have added nothing but
additional luster to your family's name. Your bravery in
the Italian campaigns is well known."

Medina shifted uncomfortably in his chair.

"I will come to the point, Don Marcos. You have been
recommended to me from the very highest level in Rome,
a level so high that I may not reveal its precise identity.

And the King is in accord with your selection. What you should know, however, is that your services are needed urgently in a task of the greatest importance both to the Crown and to the Church. I must tell you also that the task is dangerous, and could easily be fatal."

Fonseca paused, seeming to wait for Medina's reaction. When none came, he continued. "First let me give you some background. What do you know of the Indies?"

"The usual stories, Your Excellency, of gold and heathen savages, of islands where fortunes can be made in mining and plantations."

"Have you heard of a place called *Yuca . . . tan?*" The Bishop lingered over the word. "The natives of the Indies also call it Maiam."

"No, Your Excellency."

"It lies to the west of the islands under our present control. It may be an island, too, or it may be part of a new continent. We are not sure yet. What we do know is that it is a land with cities of stone containing undreamed quantities of gold. Gold in amounts far beyond anything encountered in the Indies before." The Bishop's voice had risen noticeably.

Medina repressed a smile. He had a feudal nobleman's disdain of the money-grubbing of merchant and Church alike. Sometimes he wondered if the Church was half so interested in saving souls as it was in saving gold. But he said nothing.

"Under the authority of the *Casa*," the Bishop continued, "the Governor of Cuba, Diego Velázquez, sent an expedition westward last year commanded by a Francisco Hernández de Córdoba.

"Twenty-one days after sailing from Cuba they sighted

this land, *Yucatan*. From offshore they could see a large town with tall pyramids somewhat inland. Because of the pyramids, they named the town Great Cairo. The Indians came out peaceably in canoes and, by means of signs, invited Córdoba and his men to visit the town. They accepted the invitation and went ashore, somewhat improvidently I fear, for the heathens had set an ambush, and attacked without warning. In the ensuing battle, Córdoba and his soldiers managed to seize several gold objects from the houses as well as two Indian warriors before retreating back to their ships. After tending to their wounded, they set sail again along the coast."

Medina squirmed slightly, wondering how this tale related to him, but he kept silent. Hernández de Córdoba struck him as a bit of a fool.

"Córdoba and his men landed two weeks later farther along the coast to fill their casks with water, but this time took great care not to be ambushed. A delegation of unarmed Indians came to visit them at the pool where they were filling their casks, and called them 'Castilans.' Obviously they were trying to say 'Castilians.' "

"But how could they have known Spanish words?" asked Medina, with growing interest.

"Ah, that was a mystery, Don Marcos. Not only that, the Indians led our men to a group of temples containing idols covered with blood. Even more curious is that next to the idols stood crosses." The Bishop paused.

"Crosses? Crosses in heathen temples?" The incongruity puzzled Medina.

"Yes. And not only there, but at some of the other places where they landed in Yucatan." Fonseca cocked an eyebrow.

"Córdoba and his men departed rapidly from there, because many Indians were assembling, and sailed farther west along the coast. The casks, however, were leaking and the expedition soon ran short of water again. They had to attempt another landing. Their scouts found a bay beside which lay ponds of fresh water. Although they could see an Indian town, called Champotón, only a league away, their need for water was so great that Córdoba decided to risk the landing at sunset. Well-armed, he and his men spent the night filling the casks. At dawn, as they made their way to the boats to depart, they were attacked by thousands of Indians."

The Bishop paused. "Now what is significant here, Don Marcos, is that the Indians attacked in disciplined formations, like European soldiery. Córdoba and his men had never seen anything like it in all their years in the Indies. Within minutes, fifty of our men lay dead. The Indian troops pursued the landing party to the boats and right into the water. Every Spaniard was wounded, and many died later on board the ships, of thirst and their wounds. In complete despair they set sail immediately for Cuba, reaching it after much suffering. Córdoba, whose wounds had festered, died there."

"It is not like Spanish troops to suffer a defeat at the hands of savages," Medina commented.

"That is the point, Don Marcos," Fonseca said. "We may not be dealing just with savages."

"What do you mean?"

"The two Indians Córdoba brought back to Cuba have since been taught some Spanish. One of them, who has been baptized Melchorejo, is already able to communicate on a rudimentary level. He claims several white men live among the Indians in Yucatan."

"How did they get there?" asked Medina.

"Melchorejo contends they are survivors of a shipwreck. He also says that one of these white men organized both attacks on Córdoba's expedition. Apparently he trained the Indians in European tactics, and personally directed their attack on Champotón."

"That hardly seems possible, Your Excellency."

"I know, Don Marcos. My reaction, too, until two months ago when a caravel arrived here from Cuba. It brought the first report from a new expedition that was sent to Yucatan this spring under a man named Grijalva."

"A new expedition?" asked Medina. "After the disasters that befell the other one?"

"We cannot pause in our explorations, Don Marcos, no matter the odds. The Crown is desperately in need of the gold of the Indies. The mines of Cuba and the other islands are almost exhausted. We must have this new land of Yucatan, this New Spain, if our nation is to pursue its destiny. With enough gold, our King may even become Holy Roman Emperor of all Christendom. This is something that the Pope himself supports."

Fonseca paused and fingered the crucifix hanging from his neck. "We must not fail. Do you know by what right we lay claim to the Indies, Don Marcos?"

"By discovery, of course, Your Excellency. Cristóbal Colón was in the service of our Holy Majesties."

"Yes," Fonseca said, assuming a legalistic tone, "but that right had to be ratified by the Pope, and indeed it was, one year later, in 1493. In the Papal bull, *Inter cae-*

tera, His Holiness granted to Spain . . ." Fonseca hesitated, as though trying to recall the precise words, "islands and mainlands toward the West and South in all their rights, jurisdictions, and appurtenances, excepting only lands already held by Christian princes."

Medina put a hand to his chin, and stared steadfastly at the Bishop. He feared that the old man had started to ramble. What did a Papal bull have to do with that renegade white man, or with the report of that new expedition to—what was it again?—Yucatan?

"But no Christian princes live in those lands," he stated, trying to recapture a sense of the Bishop's logic.

"There *were* no Christian princes," emphasized the Bishop. "At least not until now."

Medina took in a sharp breath. In his mind the outlines of the picture Fonseca had been painting began to take shape. Its enormity, and its implications for his own life, startled him. He watched as Fonseca slowly reached into his desk drawer, reached into it like a man keenly aware of the inherent drama of gesture.

The Bishop withdrew a sheet of paper and laid it on the desk between them. "The caravel from Cuba brought not only Yucatan gold, but also this document, presented to a landing party of our expedition by a delegation of Indians bearing white banners." He turned the paper around on the desk so that it faced Medina.

Medina pulled his chair forward and peered downward. He had never seen anything like it before. Strange red, black, and green figures adorned the edges of the parchment in a completely alien style. Some seemed human, others animal, others combinations of both. At the top

center of the paper was a cross, but again in a style he had never seen before. Below the cross, in large black cursive letters, read a message in Spanish:

Noble Lords—

You have entered the principality of His Highness Martim Braga, Christian Sovereign of these lands of Maiam. In accordance with the 1493 decree *Inter caetera* of His Holiness, Our Holy Father in Rome, you are forbidden further entrance, and are commanded to depart at once, on penalty of death. You are also commanded to inform all Christian Majesties that these lands are not available for conquest, and to inform the Holy Father of Our Allegiance to the Holy Faith.

(signed)
HIS HIGHNESS MARTIM BRAGA
This Year of Our Lord 1519

Medina mulled over the contents of the document before him. Was it the work of a madman? The drumming of the Bishop's fingers on the desk forced him to look up.

"Well, Don Marcos," asked Fonseca, "what do you make of this . . ." he seemed to be searching for the word, and then spat it out disgustedly, ". . . decree?"

"Is it authentic, Your Excellency?"

"You would not have been called from Italy if it were not, Medina," said the Bishop curtly, annoyed at the suggestion. "We have sworn statements from the commander of the expedition, Juan de Grijalva, and from Pedro de

Alvarado, a cavalier who brought the document back to Cuba from Yucatan. Now tell me, do you note anything peculiar about the message?"

"Two obvious peculiarities. First, the year is wrong. This is 1518, not 19. Second, this man's Christian name is spelled 'Martim' instead of 'Martin.' "

"Very good. And what, Don Marcos, would you make of those two facts?"

Medina leaned back in his chair, and considered what the Bishop had already told him. "It would appear," he said, "that this man has been in that country some time. Long enough to have lost track of the passage of years. And the spelling of his name suggests that he is Portuguese."

"Precisely our conclusions, too," said Fonseca, getting up from his chair and walking over to the window. He seemed to think a moment, and then turned to Medina. "It is a fact, although the Crown is not happy about it, that many of our 'Spanish' colonists in the Indies are drawn from the riffraff of all the south of Europe: we number in our ranks Venetians, Greeks, Sicilians, and," he paused, "even Portuguese. Men of all sorts—sailors, soldiers, artisans—are badly needed in the Indies. We cannot therefore afford to question their origins too closely. And women, too. You may not know this, but the prostitutes we formerly placed in convents for rehabilitation are now being sent to the Indies as brides." He smiled ruefully.

"This Martim Braga," Medina interrupted, "he seems perhaps different from most of those you describe. Judging from the document, he is literate and familiar with law. Indeed, he might even be a nobleman by birth. Certainly he seems a capable battlefield commander," he added ironically.

Fonseca nodded. "Yes, you are quite right. As you know, a number of young aristocrats over the years have sailed for the Indies, some attracted by the opportunities for fortune and adventure, others fleeing from political misfortunes or even the Holy Inquisition.

"The important point is," Fonseca went on, "this man seems to be a Portuguese, and has declared the richest known area of the Indies to be forbidden to the Spanish Crown, using a Papal bull as his authority."

"Does Lisbon know of this?" asked Medina.

"As far as we know, not yet. This document has been handled in the utmost secrecy. Only two copies of it have been made by our scribes. One was sent by special courier to the Holy Father in Rome. The other is in the hands of the King."

"Pope Leo was put into power with Spanish arms," commented Medina. "It would not be in his interest to advise the Portuguese of the document."

"That is true, Don Marcos. But like all of Italy, the Vatican is a snake pit of intrigue and espionage. The Portuguese court may already possess this information." Fonseca looked hard at Medina. "Obviously His Holiness is aware of the danger or his uncle would not have sent you to me."

Medina understood. Conceivably, the document could provide Portugal with the opportunity it had been waiting for: the chance to claim a portion of the richest part of the New World. The Papal decree giving Spain a monopoly in the conquest of the Indies contained a glaring loophole. And now one renegade "Christian prince" could provoke war between Spain and Portugal. Medina began to suspect the nature of the assignment facing him. He decided to broach the question directly.

"And what is my role in all this, Your Excellency?" he asked.

"Don Marcos, this man needs to be removed." Fonseca leaned forward. "There is no chance of penetrating inland with a military expedition to destroy him. Our troops cannot even hold the shore. Besides, an invasion of his territory could be interpreted by Portugal as a violation of the Papal bull. Portugal might use such an invasion as a pretext for interceding." The Bishop shook his head. "Braga must be removed discreetly. In fact, secretly. What is needed, Don Marcos, is a deserter."

"Don't you mean an assassin?"

"Yes, but a man who can pretend to have deserted from a Spanish expedition and who can reach Braga wherever he is in Yucatan." The Bishop leaned back in his chair and looked at Medina. "Then our man will have to eliminate this instrument of the Devil."

Medina sat silent and considered the problems of the mission one by one. The assignment seemed impossible. Impossible, and therefore interesting.

"And I am to carry out this mission, Your Excellency?"

"Yes." The Bishop seemed to stare through Medina. "If you accept it, and God Our Lord is willing."

Medina knew that he should have been dismayed, but instead, he felt suddenly alive. Alive in almost a perverse way, precisely because of the odds against him. This was what he had been bred for.

"If I were to accept the assignment," he said, "how would I be landed in that country?"

"From a ship of a fleet that Governor Velázquez is now assembling in the harbor of Santiago, Cuba. The fleet will sail for Yucatan within a few months. It would be essential that you sail with the expedition."

Medina mulled over the problems. "How would I survive once ashore?" he asked. "If the Indians are as hostile as you say, would I really last longer than a few hours? And, besides, how would they know I was a deserter wishing to join them?"

"I have been assured by Velázquez that he would place at the disposal of our deserter the Indian named Melchorejo. This man apparently now knows enough Spanish to act as an interpreter. He should also be able to teach you something of the language. But even so, Don Marcos, this would be a most perilous mission." The Bishop slowly turned a writing quill in his hand.

"Your Excellency," said Medina, "assuming I actually reached Braga, and succeeded in eliminating him, there seems little chance that I could emerge alive from the interior, and rejoin the fleet."

The Bishop nodded. "So it would seem. But Diego Velázquez states in his letter to me that there is a plan."

"And what is that?"

"He did not explain, but said that it had been worked out by the Captain-General of the forthcoming expedition, a man named Hernán Cortés."

"Who is he? I do not believe that Cortés is the name of a noble lineage."

"It isn't, Don Marcos. I am told that he was formerly a mere notary public. But things are different in the Indies. Although perhaps not an *hidalgo*, he has risen to prominence in Cuba. Governor Velázquez, on whom I must rely at this long distance, assures me that Cortés is the best man for the command."

For the first time in the conversation Medina felt irritated. A man of quality, an *hidalgo,* a distinguished knight of noble birth, does not take orders from a commoner. This did not sit well with him.

The Bishop seemed to sense Medina's displeasure. "You would operate in cooperation with this Cortés, not subservient to him. You would bear secret orders from me making this explicit."

Medina sighed to himself. The wars in Italy had been different. There, the officers were noblemen of quality who knew how to fight and how to die. He remembered standing in front of his troops with his officers for three hours under a French cannonade, to set an example. During the last hour they opened a few bottles of captured burgundy, and sipped it nonchalantly as men fell about them in a hail of steel. Two of his lieutenants were toasting each other when both their heads were torn off by a chain shot. That was style. Now he was being asked to serve with a commoner to assassinate some renegade, and among heathens no less. His thoughts were interrupted by the Bishop.

"Well?"

"Very well, Your Excellency," Medina said, "I'll go, with one proviso."

"Yes?"

"I must be provided with letters to Governor Velázquez and to this Cortés making clear three things: that they must assist me in every way possible; that they must keep my mission secret; and that I am independent of all authority in the Indies other than yourself."

The Bishop smiled. "So be it, Don Marcos." He rose. "And you, of course, must never mention the Vatican's awareness of this matter. You will be provided with all you ask on the morrow. A brigantine is at the quay ready to carry you to Cuba as soon as I give the order. May God Our Lord protect you and keep you in your mission." He pointed his finger at Medina, and slowly traced the sign of the cross in the air.

Medina took his leave and went toward the door. Then a thought crossed his mind. He stopped and turned. "Your Excellency, one thing more," he said. "What proof do you require that I have accomplished my mission?"

The Bishop, still standing, pensively fingered the crucifix that hung from his neck. He thought a moment. "His head, if possible, my dear Medina. His head. That would be more than sufficient."

CHAPTER

II

Medina watched the low green coastline of Yucatan rise gradually from the horizon as the galleon trembled under his feet against the offshore current. Only a few hours more, he hoped. He felt trapped on board ship, like a caged animal, even on this six-day sail from Cuba. And the month in Cuba had hardly been enough to make up for the endlessly dull eight-week voyage from Seville.

Below him, on the open deck amidships, a priest in gold-streaked vestments was administering communion to a kneeling group of off-watch crewmen. Medina had come to know the priest slightly during his stay in Cuba. He looked down from the poop deck as Father Olmedo turned away from the field altar, gazed momentarily heavenward, reached into the ciborium, pulled out a piece of unleavened cassava bread, and made the sign of the cross with it. The breeze carried the priest's incantation away from Medina, but he knew by rote the Latin words coming from Olmedo's moving lips. *Accípite, et manducáte ex hoc omnes. Hoc est enim Corpus Meum!* Take ye all and eat of this: for this is My Body! The priest raised the bread above him and proceeded to lay the Body of Christ onto the tongues of the congregation kneeling before him.

It was shortly after dawn in late February, 1519. A vicious gale had dispersed the expedition's eleven ships soon after they left the western tip of Cuba. Now the flagship of Hernán Cortés sailed toward the coast accompanied by only one other vessel, a partially disabled caravel. In the crow's nest high above Medina, a lookout scoured the horizon for a sign of the other vessels. A school of dolphins churned alongside the ship.

A brief shift in the wind carried the priest's words back to Medina. "May the Lord Most High speed us on His holy mission and teach us to endure, even as Job, the hardships, the lulls, and the setbacks the world thrusts upon us."

Following the last *Ave Maria* and while the men stood rubbing their knees, Cortés, wearing an amber velvet cloak, sword hilt glittering in the sun, appeared on deck, and called for a detail of ten soldiers.

"One of the horses is dead," he announced tersely. "The large black."

The flagship carried four horses, stowed in the central hold and rigged in broad leather slings suspended from the overhead bulwarks. They were magnificent animals, with deep-set eyes, flaring nostrils, and thick flanks. A mixture of the Arab and Barb stocks originally brought to Spain by the Moors, they became engines of war at the touch of a spur. But at sea, where their hooves barely reached the planking of the hold, they dangled helplessly like puppets. All were stiff, tense, and off their feed. And one of them had started hemorrhaging the night before.

The detail went below. Moist with sweat, the black stallion hung dead in its sling, its legs splayed, blood still trickling from its nostrils down onto the straw-covered deck.

The men trussed it with line and unbuckled the leather sling. When the corpse came crashing down, it sent a tremor through the ship, as though the vessel had hit a floating log. Four lines leading from a winch and pulley were lowered into the hold, and the soldiers fastened them to the truss.

The corpse rose like a long bale of hemp, its legs akimbo, the lines of the truss creasing into its flesh. Slowly it went up, twisting, swinging back and forth, scraping against the inside edges of the hatch opening. At last the horse lay in a heap on a track of rollers leading to the side. A section of rail had already been removed. Re-emerging on deck, the soldiers undid the line and waited.

The ship's captain came out of his cabin, stepped down to the main deck, and approached the horse. An old hand at burying horses at sea, he took it as neither a curse on his vessel nor a reflection of his seamanship when a horse died on one of his ships. The sea lanes, particularly where they crossed stationary calms in the south Atlantic, were called the "horse" latitudes with reason.

Medina watched from the stern deck as the first mate, the chaplain, and Cortés gathered beside the horse. The captain stepped forward, clearing his throat with a short cough.

"Farewell, poor beast," he intoned, "and the pity of it is that you did not live to carry a Spanish cavalier into the thick of the infidel savages that await us, and so serve to extend the might and grandeur of His Majesty, Charles, King of Spain, Servant of the Lord Almighty."

With that, he pointed seaward and nodded. The soldiers shoved and the horse—still slippery with sweat—slid to the edge and went over, making a thumping splash as it hit the water. Medina watched it bob into the distance, hemmed in by the ship's wake.

The audience dispersed, but Cortés, spotting Medina,

joined him. "Five hundred gold pesos' worth of horse," he muttered, shaking his head.

Medina nodded in tacit sympathy as he gazed toward the Captain-General. The man exuded a strong, almost undeniable presence, he had to admit. Cortés was almost as tall as he, though somewhat bowlegged, and he dressed extremely well. His mild, grave face was adorned with a trim, black beard. But it was the eyes, eyes that blazed intensely, that were his most dominant feature. Eyes dark like a gypsy's or even a Jew's, thought Medina, comparisons that prompted him to wonder about the Captain-General's antecedents. Perhaps in his lineage "new Christians" existed, those who during recent centuries had hastily converted to escape massacre or the Inquisition.

"Now we're down to sixteen horses," Cortés complained. "That is, if the other ships survived the storm." He scanned the coast for the sight of a sail. "It's a good thing that you won't require a horse for your mission, Marcos."

Medina was not accustomed to being addressed by a commoner without the title of "Don." Cortés' constant familiarity irritated him. Yet Medina's assignment depended on the man's wholehearted collaboration. He had to get along with him somehow. He decided to try to appear friendly.

"Do you think the other ships survived the storm, Hernán?" he asked.

"Pilot Alaminos tells me there's an excellent chance. In fact, he thinks that they may already be anchored at the rendezvous at Cozumel Island. I just hope that troublesome Alvarado has had the good sense not to get into a scrape with the Indians."

Medina already knew Pedro de Alvarado's reputation

as an impetuous and ruthless soldier. Alvarado had served with distinction on the two previous expeditions to Yucatan, although he often disobeyed his commanders. This very month he had ignored Cortés' orders, sailing from Cuba for the Cozumel anchorage several days before the fleet itself was scheduled to depart.

"He could jeopardize my mission, Hernán, unless he can be kept under control," Medina said.

Cortés looked in silence at Medina, his eyes flat and level. A half-minute passed. When he finally spoke, his voice bore an almost unnatural calmness.

"Don Marcos, you tend to your mission, and I shall tend to mine." He bowed curtly, and headed for the door to his cabin, leaving Medina alone.

Medina smelled trouble with this gold-greedy upstart. He shrugged and descended to the gun deck to continue his lessons in Mayan, the language of Yucatan, with Melchorejo. He found the Indian standing beside the sand-covered platform that served as the cooking area, watching the cook prepare another crude meal of cassava bread and salt-pork soup. Dressed in ill-fitting soldier's castoffs, Melchorejo managed nevertheless to maintain a serene dignity.

Medina motioned to him to follow, and went to sit on a cast-bronze cannon by an open port. When the Indian joined him, Medina resumed his questioning.

"What is that?" he asked, pointing toward the cooking fire.

"*K'aak'.*"

"*Ka-aaka,*" repeated Medina, trying to imitate the Indian's pronunciation.

"Almost," smiled the Indian. "*K'aak', k'aak'.*"

Melchorejo taught Medina with patience and a simple grace, as he had done in the weeks since they started working together in Cuba. Contrary to Medina's expectations, the Indian proved to be neither savage nor a stupid lout. This perplexed him at first, but then he concluded that Melchorejo must be a most unusual Indian —a rare specimen óf the breed.

They had entered their second hour of work when shouts came from above decks. Medina and Melchorejo went topside to discover that the rest of the fleet had been sighted. All other nine vessels seemed to be there—ships of various types and sizes, and even "the farm," a barge-like vessel laden with cassava flour, half a dozen goats, two pigs, and a chestnut mare in foal—in the small bay at Cozumel, just off the Yucatan coast. Stretches of sandy beach interspersed with thick, ragged stands of mangrove ringed the harbor.

In half an hour they dropped anchor in the midst of the fleet. A small boat put out from one of the other vessels—Medina thought it was the *San Sebastian,* the vessel commanded by Alvarado—and headed toward the flagship. Medina fervently hoped that Alvarado in his ignorance had not botched things with the Cozumelian Indians. Only Cortés knew of Medina's real mission; the others thought he was merely a veedor, an inspector for the King sent to observe the operation of the expedition. While such secrecy had its advantages, it also meant that a hothead like Alvarado could unknowingly commit a blunder and thus threaten Medina's strategy to enlist the help of the Cozumelians.

The entire expedition knew that there were some shipwrecked Spaniards in Yucatan. In fact, the fleet had three official purposes: to trade for gold; to carry the word of God to the heathen; and to rescue the stranded Spaniards. In truth, this last objective had been cooked up by Cortés and Medina to provide an excuse for the planned effort to locate Braga.

Now, as the boat from the *San Sebastian* came alongside, Medina joined Cortés at the spot where the rope ladder had been dropped over the side.

The first man up the ladder was Alvarado, beaming triumphantly, as though bearing great news. Behind him came Pilot Camacho, then the red-haired Father Teodosio Sánchez, and two Indians dressed in white tunics. Alvarado took off his plumed cap with a flourish and bowed to Cortés.

"Señor Don Hernán," he said, "I come bearing the riches of the Indies." He grinned, took off a leather satchel he carried across his shoulder, and dumped its contents on the deck. A dozen gold figurines, some a palm-width in height, shone in the morning sun. Curious in form, half-human and half-animal, they reminded Medina of the figures on the document Fonseca had shown him a little over three months ago in Seville.

"How did you come by them?" asked Cortés evenly, showing neither pleasure nor displeasure.

Alvarado smiled with the impishness of a child. "My men and I rescued them from the heathen temples in the towns." He nodded toward Cozumel.

Cortés did not reply, but simply stared at Alvarado. Before his steady gaze, Alvarado's face slowly lost its smile. Finally Cortés spoke.

"Those were not my orders, Señor Alvarado," he said icily. "Nor were you authorized to depart from Cuba before the rest of the fleet."

Cortés turned to an officer beside him. "Put that man in irons," he commanded, pointing toward Camacho. The pilot blanched, but said nothing. He allowed himself to be led away.

"Now, Señor Alvarado," Cortés resumed, "do you wish to join him or will you hereafter obey my orders exactly?"

Embarrassment and then anger crossed Alvarado's face. But he quickly regained his composure.

"I am sorry, my Captain. My enthusiasm to serve affected my judgment. It will not happen again."

"It had best not—ever." Cortés paused. "Now why don't you, Father Sánchez, Don Marcos, and I go to my cabin?" Cortés said, nodding toward the priest and Medina. "I want to hear what you have discovered. And bring the little treasure, too." He motioned toward the gold figures still lying on the deck.

Once inside the cabin, they seated themselves around the bare table and waited while Cortés peeled a small Cuban orange. As they sat there, Medina found himself studying the priest. He seemed a strange man to be wearing the robes of a priest. He was a huge hulk, brutal in appearance, with the eyes of a fanatic. Medina felt a vague uneasiness.

"Now tell me what has happened here, Alvarado," Cortés said before biting into the orange.

Alvarado squared his shoulders and folded his arms. "The day after we arrived I took a detail ashore. We encountered no resistance. In fact, the Indians fled the two towns we entered."

"Did they flee before or after you looted their temples?" interrupted Medina baitingly.

Alvarado shot an irritated glance at Medina and, as he was about to reply, Father Sánchez interjected, "It is our holy duty to rid them of their idols. Anyway, I replaced them with statues of the Holy Virgin."

Medina knew that the fleet carried several score small plaster statues of the Virgin Mary to be used for just such purposes. Plaster for gold, he thought. The Church does a good business, indeed. He could not resist goading Sánchez, whom he was beginning to dislike.

"It is fortunate that the Devil added to your motivation by making the idols of gold," Medina commented.

Sánchez glanced at him sharply. "A strange way for a veedor of the King to speak. Talk like that in Spain would interest the Inquisition."

"Gentlemen, gentlemen," Cortés said, "calm yourselves. This is not Spain. And we have urgent business. Alvarado, did you engage in combat with the Indians?"

"No."

"Then perhaps we can entice them back into their towns with gifts. Who are the two Indians you brought on board?"

"We seized them when we first landed. But I have had no way of communicating with them," said Alvarado.

"If we are to succeed in finding shipwrecked Spaniards, we must have help," Cortés said. "I will talk with the two Indians through Melchorejo, and send them back to the island with gifts. With luck, the Cozumelians will come out."

"Green glass beads," said Alvarado. "That should bring them out. The idiots think they're a kind of jade. By the way," he added, "we found a peculiar object in front of one of their cursed pyramids."

"Yes?" said Cortés.

"A cross. A stone cross about ten hands high."

"Strange," agreed Cortés.

"Did it look Christian?" asked Medina.

"Hard to say," replied Alvarado. "It was covered with a layer of dried blood."

"A perversity of the Devil," muttered Sánchez, crossing himself.

Two days later the green glass beads, which the Spaniards had hung on trees and bushes near the abandoned towns, brought a group of elderly male Cozumelians to the shore. Taking Melchorejo with them, Cortés and Medina went ashore with an armed guard, and presented the Indians with additional strands of Venetian beads, knives, scissors, and hawk bells. The Indians seemed highly pleased with the "largess." After they and Cortés had mutually professed eternal brotherhood, Cortés came to the point.

"Do any men who look like us, who came from great canoes like these," he asked, motioning toward the ships in the bay, "do any such men live in this land?" Melchorejo translated.

The Cozumelian elders listened and then talked briefly among themselves. One of them stepped forward, and held up his left hand, made into a fist. Then he raised his right hand, also made into a fist except for his little finger, which remained extended. He spoke in Mayan to Melchorejo.

"The *cacique,* the chief, says they hear five men, maybe six, with beards like yours live in Maiam," Melchorejo told Cortés, pointing toward the mainland.

"Tell him that we want to send some beads to those bearded men and a piece of paper for them to read," said Cortés.

After Melchorejo translated, the Indians talked furiously among themselves.

"They say Indians there are *muy bravos,* very fierce. They fear going there," Melchorejo reported.

After half an hour of further negotiation and considerable additional gifts of green glass beads, the Cozumelians put forward one man to be a messenger. He returned to the flagship with the landing party.

That night, in Cortés' cabin, Medina and the Captain-General drafted a letter in Spanish to send with the messenger. It read, in part:

Noble Lords—
I departed from Cuba with a fleet of 11 vessels and 550 Spaniards, and arrived here at Cozumel, where I am writing this letter. . . . The people of this island have assured me that in your country there are five or six bearded men, like us in every respect. . . . I beg you within six days from the time you receive this letter, to come to us without delay. . . . If you will come, we shall recognize and reward the favor. . . . I am sending a brigantine to pick you up. . . .

Cortés signed the letter, rolled it up, and tied a blue ribbon around the tube. Then he put it into a large leather pouch filled with bundles of the magical green glass beads. He leaned back from the table in the hot, stifling cabin.

"Well, Don Marcos," he said, "we'll see if the bait brings the fox out of his hole."

"Even if it doesn't," Marcos replied, "at least the Indian may discover where Braga is located."

In the morning, with the Indian messenger aboard, a brigantine set sail for Cape Catoche on the Yucatan mainland, where Córdoba's expedition had first been attacked two years before.

The days passed with excruciating slowness as the fleet waited for the return of the brigantine. To avoid incidents with the Indians, Cortés allowed the men to go ashore only under the supervision of noblemen or officers, and even then only to trade with the Indians for provisions or to exercise the horses on the beach. The men grumbled at their enforced inaction, but obeyed their orders and kept away from the Cozumelians.

Despite these precautions, one incident did take place. An Italian sailor, who for reasons of an unsavory past went under the Spanish name of José Pérez, managed to smuggle on board the flagship a pubescent Indian girl given to him by her father in exchange for his seaman's knife. Pérez made a special nest for her in the hay adjacent to the horses in the hold. Shipboard life being what it was, however, he was not long able to conceal his treasure. The ship's mate, suspicious of José's sudden solicitude for the condition of the animals, followed him below one evening and discovered his secret.

After a summary hearing, Pérez was chained and consigned to the bilge. The girl was turned over to Father

Olmedo. Undoubtedly José's punishment would have been far more severe had Father Olmedo not interceded, suggesting that José, who served as his altar boy at Mass, unconsciously fulfilled God's will by "rescuing" the girl from the eternal damnation of idolatry. To remove further temptation, Father Olmedo sent the girl to Alvarado's ship where she was placed in the care of Father Sánchez for baptism and instruction. While the baptism was immediately and easily undertaken, the instruction apparently took considerably more effort. At least that was the opinion of the deck watch crewmen who nightly heard moans from Sánchez' cabin.

After a week and a half, the brigantine returned from its mission to Cape Catoche. The captain immediately came aboard the flagship to report. Medina suspected the worst when he saw the officer clamber up over the ship's railing all alone.

"We put the Indian messenger ashore as ordered, sir," he told Cortés. "And we waited two days longer than our instructions, but the messenger never came back. Nor did we see any sign of a Spaniard."

Cortés dismissed the captain and took Medina with him to his cabin. "Well, what do you think, Marcos?"

"The Indian may have been killed or taken prisoner, for all we know, Hernán. We need to find another method of getting to Braga."

"My men are becoming restless anchored here. We must employ them in some way."

"I agree," said Medina. "Suppose you move the entire fleet to the area where Braga's 'decree' was presented to Grijalva?"

"Good. The Indians might appear again, and provide an opportunity for you and Melchorejo to 'desert.'" Cortés paused. "Melchorejo does not know of your plans, I trust?"

"Definitely not, Hernán. He must think my desertion is real. In fact, you and I must stage an argument in front of him so that he will not be suspicious."

Cortés grinned. "A pity dear Father Sánchez is not in command here. I'm sure then that the argument would sound even more convincing."

Medina chose to ignore the remark, his mind staying fixed on Braga. "After deserting, I may need up to two weeks to accomplish my mission, depending on where Braga is located. Can I count on you to keep the fleet in anchorage that long?"

"Two weeks, but no more, Marcos. The men are already too restless for comfort. They are anxious for gold."

Medina knew that gold obsessed Cortés as much as anyone. The Captain-General had sunk his entire fortune into the expedition, and begged, borrowed, and even committed piracy in order to equip the fleet. He was gambling everything on acquiring a huge treasure from the Indians. He wondered whether Cortés would wait even the two weeks he promised.

"Do you intend to employ my plan in getting back to the fleet?" asked Cortés.

Medina knew Cortés' plan but disliked it. For all his peasant cunning, Cortés could come up with extremely simplistic notions. Like the plan. According to it, Medina by some pretext was to lure Braga and the local Indian *cacique,* the ruler or chief, to a lonely place. Then Medina was to kill Braga, seize the *cacique*, and keep him as a hostage to assure his safe conduct back to the fleet.

"I have mixed feelings about the plan, Hernán."

"The Indians view their chiefs and rulers as sacred," Cortés persisted. "Once you have one in your hands, they will not touch you for fear of your harming their chief."

"The problem is that I cannot expect to be able to guard such a hostage day and night. I need a Spaniard to accompany me."

Cortés shook his head. "I doubt if any man in the fleet is prepared to take such a risk."

"There are two who might, Hernán, the two who are in chains below. Each might really welcome an opportunity to desert."

Cortés nodded solemnly. "An inspired idea. The Pilot Camacho and the Italian sailor. Pérez is his name, José Pérez. Have your pick of either. Pérez, however, is younger, stronger, and, I would judge, wilier. He might be better suited."

"Good. I'll talk to him."

"But don't tell him your real plans. He values his busy Italian column between his legs too much to endanger it."

The next day, the fleet departed to course around Yucatan. The second day out, however, a brigantine transporting an important cargo of food for the expedition sprang a leak. Cortés ordered the entire fleet to return to Cozumel so that the ship could be caulked. Shortly after they anchored in the bay once more, a canoe with several paddlers was sighted coming across the strait from Yucatan. It beached near a small landing party from the fleet.

Twenty minutes later the news reached the flagship. Cortés immediately summoned Medina.

"Our landing party reports that a shipwrecked Spaniard has just arrived by canoe." He jerked his head toward the shore. "Let's go."

The officer who had relayed word to the flagship of the Spaniard's arrival greeted them as the dinghy landed.

"Where is he?" Cortés demanded.

Medina stood beside the Captain-General on the tree-fringed beach and surveyed the faces assembled at the landing area. All he could see was the officer and his men, as well as a smaller group of Indians.

"Where is the Spaniard?" repeated Cortés impatiently. But before the officer could answer, a figure standing with the Cozumelians squatted down on his haunches, Indian-fashion. His face was tanned a deep, nut brown, and his hair had been cropped close to his head. He wore a ragged cloak and a shredded, dirty loincloth.

"I am he," he said pitifully, laying a paddle on the ground.

Medina looked down at the pathetic figure, searching for some identifiable feature. As a seaman pulled the squatting figure to his feet, Cortés spoke: "I am the Captain-General of this expedition sent to find you, and I am at your service. May I welcome you back to the company of your countrymen." He said it formally and with great dignity.

The man wept. "Dear God and the Blessed Virgin," he uttered confusedly, his Spanish poorly pronounced.

After calming him, Cortés asked his name. Medina tensed, though already convinced the man could not possibly be Braga. Braga could hardly be quite so abject.

"Jerónimo de Aguilar, at your service," stammered the man.

No sooner had the name come off the tongue than Medina shifted his hopes to simply learning about Braga. He stayed close to Aguilar and listened as Cortés extracted the castaway's history.

Born in Ecija, a small hamlet in western Spain, Aguilar sailed for Cuba shortly after taking holy orders and becoming a minor prelate. Eight years ago—"or perhaps nine," he vacillated—he and fifteen other men and two women had left the colony of Darien at the southern end of the Isthmus of Panama, bound for Santo Domingo. Their ship ran aground and, hoping to reach Cuba or Jamaica, they set out in the ship's boat. The currents drove the craft onto the shores of Yucatan, where the Indians took the Spaniards captive, and divided them among themselves. Most of the men either died from disease or were sacrificed on the altars of the Indians and eaten. The women, too, quickly succumbed. "From overwork," explained Aguilar, "for they were made to grind corn, and to toil like draft horses."

Intended for sacrifice, he managed one night to escape, fleeing to another community where, to his good fortune, a *cacique* of that town took him in. Of all the people in the original party then, only he and one other had survived. "The one I went to get."

Medina, anticipating Cortés' next question, shaped it in his mind: "Who was that?"

But Cortés, bent on his own course of inquiry, asked instead about the country and the towns. He wanted to know about gold.

"I know little," answered Aguilar, still downcast. "As a slave, it was not given to me to travel through the country. I know only about hewing wood, drawing water, and digging in the fields. But one day I was given a load to carry to another town, maybe four or five leagues distant. The load overwhelmed me, however, and I could not finish the journey. Even so, I think there are many towns and many people in them."

Medina decided it was time to get to the point. He interrupted.

"Who is the other survivor?" he asked.

Cortés gave him an annoyed glance, but allowed the question to stand.

Aguilar looked pained and haggard. He rubbed his eyes deliberately, as though trying to clear them. At last he spoke, his voice quavering.

"He would not come, he would not come." It came out like a chant.

"But what is his name?" repeated Medina.

Aguilar, his face troubled, turned to his new interrogator.

"Braga," he replied. "Martim Braga."

In addition to seven or eight curious Cozumelians, the group standing around Aguilar included Alvarado and Sánchez. But only Cortés and Medina knew the significance of the news. Cortés glanced at Medina and smiled ironically.

Before Medina or Cortés could resume the questioning, another boat landed on the beach, and a sailor approached with an armful of clothing. He and Aguilar withdrew behind a clump of trees where Aguilar donned drawers, shirt, doublet, cape, and sandals. When he returned, Aguilar marveled demonstratively at his new garments, though the impression he made was more that of an Indian impersonating a Spaniard. He still held in his hand, wrapped in its old cloth, the Book of Hours he'd carried with him during his captivity.

"Tell us about Martim Braga," asked Cortés, resuming the interview.

"When the messenger showed me the beads and the letter," began Aguilar, "I was overjoyed, and thought at once to set out to where Martim Braga lives. It is five leagues distant from my own village. I took the beads thinking to give them to the *cacique* there, as the letter suggested. It was wonderful to read Spanish words. How strangely soothing to my eyes."

Emotion welled up in Aguilar again, and he shook his head in disbelief. "You are really here, aren't you?" he asked, his voice tremulous.

"Yes, Aguilar. We are here," replied Cortés kindly. "But go on. I am anxious to know about this other man. What is his nationality?"

"He is, or was, a Portuguese," replied Aguilar hesitantly.

Instead of looking at Cortés, Aguilar stared down at the ragged cloth containing his beloved book. He seemed not to want to continue.

"Speak, man, speak," demanded Cortés.

"It pains me to tell," said Aguilar.

"What is it?"

"When I showed Braga the letter from you he answered me thus: 'Brother Aguilar,' he said, 'I am married and have three sons. Look, how handsome these boys of mine are!' It was true, and they hung on to their father with great affection and respect. Then he said, 'My face is tattooed and my ears pierced. I am a *cacique* and war leader. You go, and God be with you; this is now my home and these are now my people.' Oh, Braga is a *cacique*; this too was true. And he carries himself nobly and is strong in his arms and shoulders.

"Then his Indian wife spoke up very angrily. 'What is this slave coming here for, talking to my husband? He is a prince, married into a ruling lineage.' She said to me, 'Go off with you, and don't trouble us with any more words.' And so I left."

"What did he mean when he said he was a war leader?" asked Cortés.

"That is the worst of it," Aguilar replied. "Two years ago when Spaniards came ashore from three vessels at the eastern end of this land, it was at his suggestion that the Indians attacked."

"Jesus Christ!" exclaimed Alvarado. "That was at Cape Catoche. The Córdoba expedition!"

"He was there himself," continued Aguilar, "in the company of the *cacique* of the large town. Then he did the same at Champotón. He commanded the attack. He has vowed to oppose all landings and attempts at settlement by the Spaniards. He has made alliances between the towns throughout the land for this purpose."

"Good Spanish soldiers died from wounds received in that attack," muttered Sánchez.

"What despicable arrogance," seethed Alvarado, "and a traitor."

"Not exactly a traitor," said Aguilar. "He is a Portuguese nobleman by birth."

"He has become an infidel!" declared Sánchez. "A henchman of the Devil!"

"Not exactly, sir," said Aguilar deferentially.

"What do you mean, 'not exactly'?" demanded the priest.

"He has converted his wife's father, Nachankan, the ruler of the town of Chetumal, to Christianity. At least in a way."

"In a way?"

"Well, Braga introduced Holy Communion there." Aguilar hesitated. "But it isn't too different from what the Indians do anyway."

"What do you mean?" asked Cortés.

"The Host. Instead of bread, they distribute pieces of sacrificed prisoners."

"Holy Mother of God!" shrieked Sánchez. His face turned crimson with rage, and the veins in his temples bulged.

"I wish I had him in my hands," Cortés said quietly.

"Or beneath your feet," added Alvarado.

Medina entered into the questioning again. "Where is this town of Chetumal?" he asked.

Aguilar turned to him. "Not far. But it does not matter. He will not be there. He planned to leave with several thousand warriors for Tabasco, to the west. He intended to organize some new allies for an attack against you."

While his companions bridled with outrage, Medina contemplated the fact that it would now be necessary for the fleet to make landings on the Tabascan coast if they were going to smoke Braga out. It was clear that the expedition should again set sail. By nightfall, he convinced Cortés.

In the weeks following its departure from Cozumel, the fleet doubled around the tip of Yucatan, and cruised slowly along its northern coast, heading west. The route followed approximately that of the earlier Grijalva expedition, many veterans of which were now signed on with Cortés—including Alvarado and the chief pilot, Alaminos. The weather held beautifully, the officers scrutinized the coast from dawn until dusk, and the men cleaned and oiled their weapons.

Before leaving Cozumel, Cortés had landed the troops and horses so he could review them in parade, see them as a single unit, and judge their strength. Though small in number, it seemed at the time a potent force, though as yet untested. In addition to a cavalry of sixteen horses, he counted forty-five musketeers, thirty-two crossbowmen, and several platoons of foot soldiers. For artillery he had managed in Cuba to assemble three heavy cannons, a dozen falconets, ten lombardy pieces, and more than a ton of powder.

Ecclesiastic forces included Fathers Olmedo, Díaz, and Sánchez, but was not limited to them. Cortés himself— eloquent and persuasive—assumed he could champion the Gospel as effectively as the priests. In a position of high command, he regarded it a sacred duty to work as hard for Christ as for gold. Medina remained skeptical.

Soon the fleet reached the mouth of a large river where Grijalva's expedition had earlier engaged in a profitable trade with the Indians. The region, Grijalva's men had learned, was called Tabasco, and the natives spoke the Mayan language of the rest of Yucatan. On Spanish charts, the river was now named after Grijalva.

On his expedition, Grijalva had succeeded in obtaining more than 16,000 ducats worth of gold and jewelry, in trade for glass beads and various other Spanish trifles. The sight of this modest treasure later in Cuba helped stimulate the formation of the Cortés expedition; that and rumors of even richer towns lying some distance beyond Tabasco, those aligned with a people called the Mexica.

According to Alvarado, who rarely tired of recounting his adventures, the Tabascans were friendly and cooperative, having grumbled only when Grijalva suggested they throw over the worship of their idols, and embrace the pale god of the Christians.

Cortés, then, was somewhat surprised, upon anchoring, to see thousands of Indian warriors emerge from the mangroves behind the beaches, shaking their weapons angrily at the ships. They wore fanlike feather headdresses, and their faces shone black and white, painted for war.

"That damnable Portuguese troublemaker is responsible for this, I wager," muttered Cortés to Medina.

Medina surveyed the beach and quickly formulated a strategy. "Send Melchorejo and me ashore with a small landing party under a white flag of truce. The flag may mean nothing to the Indians, but if Braga is present he may honor it and come forth to talk. It's worth a chance."

"And if Braga appears?"

"I'll try to capture him and use him as a hostage to get back to the ship. If I can't capture him, I'll have to kill him."

Cortés rubbed the bridge of his nose.

"What if he should fail to appear?"

"I'll try to 'desert' from the landing party, taking Melchorejo and that Italian sailor, Pérez, with me."

"Very well. Two boats should suffice," said Cortés.

"And, Hernán, have Pérez released from chains and provided with weapons. I've already told him I plan to desert. I think he may go with me and Melchorejo. Are you ready to stage our 'argument'?"

While Cortés issued orders for the release of Pérez and the organization of the landing party, Medina searched for Melchorejo. He found him on the forecastle attentively watching the shore.

"I take you there," Medina said slowly, pointing to the beach. "I tell Cortés."

The Indian looked puzzled.

When Medina saw Cortés returning to his quarters, he motioned for the Indian to follow.

Once inside the Captain-General's cabin, with Melchorejo beside him, Medina announced to Cortés his intention to go ashore and to take the Indian with him.

"The Devil you will!" declared Cortés.

"I'll damn well do what I please!" shouted Medina. "You don't give a Knight of the Golden Fleece orders, you *sin vergüenza!*" Somewhat to his surprise, Medina found that he was enjoying himself.

"Why you bastard, you insufferable snobbish prig, you damn well go ashore and stay there for all I care!" Cortés, too, was getting into the spirit of the exchange with an almost suspicious alacrity. The Indian looked utterly astonished.

"Better with heathens than with a shipload of common thieves!" Medina found himself yelling. He realized he

had better get out of there before it was too late. He
grabbed Melchorejo by the arm and bolted out the door.

As he did so, he collided with José Pérez, almost
knocking him over. Pérez, who could not have helped
but overhear the exchange in the cabin, stared at Medina
with open-mouthed awe.

"To the Devil with that scurvy dog," said Medina to
José, making the most of the situation. Medina waved him
forward, and the three of them climbed down to the waiting boats. Back on the ship Cortés remained in his cabin.

As the two boats pulled away from the flagship, Medina
took inventory of his small command. Besides the six
sailors at the oars of each boat, he had six musketeers
and eight crossbowmen. Pérez and he were also armed
with swords and bucklers. If necessary, he could call upon
the sailors, who had cutlasses stowed beside them. Everyone, including Melchorejo, wore metal helmets and the
heavy padded cotton armor that the Spaniards adopted
from the Indians. On the bow of each boat stood a small
cannon—a falconet—all of them loaded with grapeshot
and powder. A white banner flew from a tall pole above
the falconet of Medina's boat.

As they neared the shore, Medina breathed a sigh of
relief. The Indians lining the beach fell silent, watching
the two boats approach. Then a large canoe suddenly
emerged from behind a line of palm trees marking the
sandbar that partially hid the river's mouth. It made
directly for the two boats. Medina ordered the sailors to
rest at their oars.

Melchorejo, who had been studying the canoe closely
from his seat beside Medina, spoke up. "All old men.
Want to talk."

"Tell them to come close," whispered Medina.

In response to Melchorejo's arm signal, the canoe came to within a hundred yards. As the paddlers, about twenty in number, steadied it in the water, one of the white-tunicked elders, resplendent in a tall headdress of quetzal feathers, yelled a string of words.

"They kill us if we enter town," Melchorejo reported.

"Tell them that we are their brothers, that we bring gifts." While Melchorejo relayed the message, Medina stood up, and displayed several dozen strings of the alluring green beads.

The fortune in green beads produced the desired effect, for the white-clad elders engaged in a lengthy conversation among themselves. Finally the spokesman called out again.

"He says they take gifts and talk more. At beach," said Melchorejo, pointing to the palm-lined sandbar at the mouth of the river.

Medina appraised the situation. The strand seemed relatively free of Indians compared to the beaches on either side of the river mouth. This parlay might be his only opportunity to effect his plan. He decided to take the chance.

"Tell them yes." As Melchorejo called out in Mayan, Medina watched the canoe intently. Without apparent command, the paddlers started it moving and headed it toward the palm trees.

Medina ordered the sailors to row toward the shore, and turned to Melchorejo. Speaking in his faltering Mayan so that the other men in the boat would not understand, Medina said, "Chief Cortés is very angry with me. He will kill me."

The Indian nodded, with a serious expression on his face.

"You and me leave," Medina continued. "We go away from Cortés. We go live with your people there." He pointed to the shore. "Now."

Melchorejo looked at Medina calmly.

"Do you understand?" asked Medina.

"Yes," Melchorejo nodded.

"When we get there, you tell old men I join them. Tell them my chief angry with me. Tell them I help them fight Castilians."

Melchorejo grinned.

Their large canoe securely beached, the elders lined up in a formal greeting formation. Medina ordered the sailors to point into shore about fifty yards to the right of the Indians. Now he turned to Pérez, seated behind him in the stern.

"Remember, José, what I told you. Stick right beside me and do exactly what I say."

The Italian managed a halfhearted smile and picked up his shield. The boats jolted to a stop as they ground onto the beach.

"All you men stay here in the boats with your weapons ready," Medina shouted. "Do not leave the boats except at my command. Melchorejo and Pérez, come with me."

The three dropped into the waist-deep water, Medina taking the lead with a load of the green beads raised high in his right hand.

Just as Medina emerged from the water, arrows suddenly studded the sand around him. A line of screaming Indians rose up from behind the string of palm trees and raced toward him and the boats, shooting arrows and throwing spears as they ran.

Glancing to the left, Medina saw the group of old men disappearing behind the palm trees. Following them ran Melchorejo, throwing away his Spanish helmet as he raced along the beach. In that instant, an irony struck Medina. Melchorejo was proving an even better deserter than Medina had bargained for. He tossed away his own helmet and shield, calculating in almost a detached way that this would allow him greater speed and also make him appear less Spanish to the attacking Indians. Then he chased after Melchorejo, and still carried the strands of green beads in his right hand. Behind him he heard the muskets open fire.

Suddenly Medina felt a smashing jolt to his head. He pitched forward. He saw the sand coming up toward him. Then the sand changed to total blackness.

When he regained consciousness the masts and yard-arms of the flagship rose above him. He experienced difficulty in breathing. Each inhalation took an effort. A tingling sensation ran up and down his arms and legs. But, he soon realized, he was alive. Faces peered down at him. He recognized Cortés, Father Olmedo, and José Pérez.

The priest crossed himself as Cortés nodded paternally. "You'll be fine, Medina. Just rest and try not to move."

Medina lay there a few minutes and then slowly sat up, with the assistance of the onlookers. His breathing came much more easily now. Oddly, he felt no pain.

"What happened?" he asked Cortés.

"One of their slingstones hit you just above the temple. An inch lower, and you'd be dead."

"How did I get here?"

"You can thank Pérez for that," said Cortés, nodding toward the sailor. "He picked you up and carried you to the boats before the painted devils could reach you."

Medina looked at the sailor. "I am in your debt, José. I thank you."

Pérez grinned and shrugged. "We sailors are used to carrying cargo, Don Marcos."

Medina rose to his feet unsteadily. He turned to Cortés. "Melchorejo?"

"Vanished. Completely disappeared."

"Damn! Well, what do you suggest now, Captain-General?"

"I was thinking of attacking tomorrow," said Cortés.

"At this stage, I can offer no alternative," replied Medina, rubbing his throbbing head.

Early the next morning, more than 400 heavily armed Spaniards in boats equipped with cannons plied up the river, and established a beachhead on a small island away from the concentration of warriors on the mainland. By late morning, the first skirmishes began, and the clap of gunfire echoed among the palms and vines fringing the Río Grijalva.

The few officers and men held in reserve on the ships cheered when they heard the volley of musketfire. They longed to be ashore and fighting. Among them, on the flagship, stood Medina, eager for action, almost fully recuperated. It now seemed impossible to employ the strategy worked out in Seville to get to Braga. A wave of emotion surged through the sultry air. For the first time, he identified with the expedition, rather than his mission, and yearned to contribute to its success. The brotherhood of war had begun to exercise its dominion.

In spite of the swampy, stream-laced character of the land and the numerous log barricades erected by the Tabascans, the Spaniards managed by nightfall to fight their way into the town without suffering significant casualties. The bite of their muskets and the arrow-proof padding of cotton armor gave them the day. But once in the town, an eerie sight greeted them. The settlement lay brooding and empty, abandoned by its inhabitants. Ignoring the mud huts on the outskirts, the soldiers systematically searched the better buildings clustered in the central quarter, those built of stone and lime. Even here they found little beyond items of clothing, wooden utensils, and clay cooking pots. Only in the recesses of the main temple, where it appeared Tabascan priests lived, did they uncover a few gold objects, most in the shapes of small, fantastic animals—scant reward for the exertions of the day.

"Put on a double watch tonight," Cortés told Alvarado. "This silence is disquieting. I doubt the Tabascans intend to give us their town so readily."

By the following morning there had still been no sign of a counterattack. The lull made Cortés uneasy. He preferred not to be forced to fight in the cramped spaces of the town. Where were the Tabascans? He dispatched two separate parties to reconnoiter, one headed by Alvarado who was accompanied by Aguilar. In the meantime, Cortés ordered the wounded men to be removed to the ships and the reserves to be brought ashore. When he learned of the order, Medina saw to it he was in the first contingent of reserves to go in.

Cortés noted his arrival with a curt nod. "I'm putting you in charge of a company of foot soldiers under the general command of Diego de Ordaz."

"I'm a horseman and accustomed to greater battlefield responsibilities," Medina protested.

"I know, I know," said Cortés, "but we are desperately short of horses. Besides, I already assigned that command to Ordaz. He and his men would resent it if I suddenly put you in charge."

Medina shrugged and saluted. As he turned away, Cortés called after him, "There shall be other battles, Don Marcos."

Medina was annoyed, but also a professional. He immediately set about organizing his men.

Toward evening, Cortés' suspicions were confirmed when the first reconnaissance party came back breathless and alarmed.

"The whole country is up in arms!" exclaimed Alvarado, leaping from his horse. "Thousands upon thousands lie in wait outside the city."

"All Tabascans?" asked Cortés, trying to keep himself calm.

"No," broke in Aguilar, also now dismounted. "They have been joined by warriors from many towns throughout Yucatan, judging from their various standards."

"Why haven't they attacked?" asked Cortés.

"Perhaps they wait for even more warriors," suggested Aguilar.

When a courier rode up a short time later, Spanish

prospects seemed dimmer yet. "We have found Melchorejo's Spanish clothing hanging from a tree."

"That bodes ill," murmured Cortés, "very ill. He may
be alive. If so, he will provide them with information
about us, a fact that will give them additional courage."

Learning that the Tabascan forces lay camped at the
far side of a broad plain, Cortés formulated his battle
plan and, within the hour, communicated it to his lieutenants.

"We must not sit idly by and wait for them to move, but
instead carry the battle to them," he explained. "We shall
attack at dawn, and engage them on the plain to make
best use of the cavalry. It would not go well for us to fight
here in the town. Ordaz will lead an assault with foot
soldiers straight on, musketeers and crossbowmen leading
the way. The cavalry will circle and attack the enemy
flank." The plan seemed sound, and none of the more
experienced officers could improve it.

"God will see us through," said Cortés, concluding the
meeting.

The bulk of the army bivouacked in the central square,
spread out around the temple-pyramid that dominated it.
The soldiers slept on the ground, clutching their weapons
close to them. Medina found a place to sleep near the men
of his company, all of them strangers, having shipped on
two of the smaller brigantines. It was impossible to sleep,
the anticipation of battle making his mind race. As he lay
there, he could smell the stench of the putrid blood caked
on the massive staircase of the pyramid. Attracted by the
smell, mosquitoes kept Medina and his men awake most of
the night.

Long before dawn the army rose and groped into formation. As they ate the rations they carried with them, Father Olmedo said an abbreviated Mass at the base of the temple. He kept his voice low.

The officer in charge of artillery gave the first signal to move. Pushing and pulling, his men began to haul the guns out toward the southwest. Next to leave was the cavalry, the elite unit, led by Cortés and Alvarado. The horses seemed to Medina unusually formidable, draped in their dyed, quilted armor. In the faint light, the sight of them passing the temple and disappearing among the stone buildings and mud huts to the east—a procession of civilized modernity weaving through an ancient, pagan landscape—struck him as awesomely beautiful. The horses and their riders looked like moving sculpture. But what lent a terrible depth to that beauty were Cortés' final instructions to the other cavaliers: "When we charge," Medina had overheard him say, "aim your lances at their faces."

Finally the word arrived from Ordaz to advance. Medina mustered his men, and led them to join the companies beside which they would fight. After a brief period of confusion as to the order of march, the company fell in behind the crossbowmen, following them out along the same path taken by the artillery. As they passed through the edge of town and entered the patchwork of maize and cassava gardens, the sky grew bright with characteristic tropical suddenness. In front of them meandered a wide stream, its water coppery. A set of logs had been thrown across to accommodate the movement of the guns. Medina's company waded the shallow stream and thirty minutes later caught up with the rear elements of the artillery, which had been slowed by a labyrinth of drainage canals running through plantations of cacao.

"We are near the plain," one of the gunners relayed back. Medina took his sword from its scabbard, and warned his men to keep tight ranks. Ahead, musketeers and crossbowmen had already deployed, forming two phalanxes on either side of the point at which they entered the plain. Ordaz, grim and harried, had stationed himself there and positioned the units as they marched up. Medina's company was assigned to the left, or east, flank.

"Hold it well," encouraged Ordaz. "And remember, the cavalry may appear there first. Hold your position at all costs until it arrives."

Medina broke into a run with his men following him onto the plain. As they moved down along its edge, Medina glimpsed the enemy on the opposite side. What he saw matched any challenge he had encountered in Italy. The mass of Indians stretched to the horizon. The Spaniards were outnumbered at least a hundred to one. Just as Medina placed the company and turned to face the enemy, a high-pitched wail split the air. Then, for an instant, the sky seemed to darken.

"Shields up!" shouted Medina.

The battle commenced. Most of the arrows fell short though several found their mark. Within a few seconds of the Indian volley the first of the six Spanish guns boomed out, and made the earth tremble. A vast hole suddenly appeared in the Indian ranks, followed by a loud chorus of shrieks. Looking to his right, Medina could see the musketeers advancing, step by step. Then, still in line, they stopped, set their firearms onto their aiming forks, peered, and fired, jets of flame darting sharply from yawning muzzles. Beyond, the crossbowmen, on their knees, launched a systematic sheet of high-velocity arrows. Where the Indian missiles rained down in graceful arcs, the Spanish arrows, tipped with steel, shot out horizontally, their flights level and deadly.

For almost fifteen minutes the battle raged at a distance, with only one new element. To conceal the devastating effect of the Spanish fire, the Indians had started throwing dust and leaves in the air, creating a dense, yellow cloud before them.

As yet, there had been nothing for Medina's unit to do except ward off arrows and slingstones as best they could. Despite this, his men showed no signs of cowardice. In fact, in the din, an aggressive badinage sprang up among them. They wagered how many Indians each would kill before the end of the day, and made light of the incoming arrows, going so far as to hurl an occasional taunt across the battlefield. Medina wished Ordaz would give the order to advance. Where was the cavalry? It seemed to him by now long overdue.

All at once he sensed a stirring among his men.

"They're moving, sir," a soldier warned him.

Medina looked. Across the way, the Indian flank opposite had begun to swing forward. "Stand ready," he ordered, strolling back and forth in front of his men. All down the line of infantry he could see preparations being made, swords and lances at the ready. Combat at close quarters seemed at hand.

As the Indian flank continued to move forward, the

musketeers shifted their fire to the left. Two of the heavy guns were readjusted, their range shortened, and they also were shifted in the same direction.

For the first time Medina could see the terrible result of the Spanish barrage. Body parts skittered insanely through the air when a ball struck the densely clustered Indian line and exploded. Blood rained down. The Indians who survived dripped with it, became lurid, crimson warriors.

But still they came, in waves, moving inexorably forward, closing in.

Medina looked to his right, searching for a command or signal. It was obvious that if the infantry was to advance, now was that time. They couldn't wait idly until set upon. Yet no signal came.

He made up his mind, drew his sword, and gave the order to charge.

Though he commanded only seventy men, the impact of their sudden thrust forward reverberated through almost half of the small Spanish force. Immediately the entire line of which his company was a part stepped out.

"Santiago! Forward for Saint James!" Medina shouted, walking at a measured pace toward the Indian line. Behind him the cheers of the Spaniards rose in a crescendo.

At this moment he had no concrete thought either of dying or killing. His action resulted from the context of circumstances rather than hatred or animosity; it was the product of logic, not emotion. As he advanced, his mind emptied, and he felt an almost mystical calmness.

Out of the dust, three nearly naked warriors charged toward him. They carried feather-adorned shields and swordlike clubs whose edges glinted with razor-sharp blades of black volcanic glass. Having already singled out Medina as the leader, the Indians converged upon him. The first to reach him, Medina noticed coolly, was splattered with blood. The Indian swung his sharp-edged club at Medina's throat. Medina slashed diagonally upward with his Toledo broadsword, catching the club in mid-arc and deflecting it. Their shoulders crashed together. In that split second, Medina suddenly felt a surge of power.

Before he could follow up with a sword-thrust, the two other warriors were upon him, one striking him across his padded back, the other slashing at his legs, but missing. The jolt to his back knocked Medina forward, and he took advantage of the momentum to somersault over the Indian he had knocked down. As Medina came up on his feet, sword in hand, he spun around and faced his attackers. They charged him simultaneously, swinging their weapons. Medina waited until they were almost upon him, then suddenly dropped to one knee, thrust his sword upward into the abdomen of the attacker on the left and released his grip on the weapon. The man pitched past him, the sword sticking out of his back. Without pausing, Medina grabbed a handful of dirt and jumped up, throwing it in the face of the other attacker. In the instant that the Indian was unable to see, Medina pulled out his dirk, lunged at the Indian and ripped open his throat. Grabbing the Indian's club without waiting for him to fall, Medina spun around to locate his third attacker. He saw the man, weaponless, starting to run away, raced after him, and with a two-handed swing of the club, partially severed his head. Spurting blood, with his head lolling to one side, the Indian took a few more steps and grotesquely fell in a heap.

The glass-edged club still in his hand, Medina looked swiftly around, and saw that the rest of the Indian line was also withdrawing. He went over to his first victim and pulled out his sword. The Spanish charge—brief but severe—had repelled them, at least temporarily, for there were too many of the enemy not to think that they would quickly regroup, and forge again toward the Spanish flank. There could be little doubt that the small Spanish force would crumple before another such advance. Moreover, it would soon occur to the Indians that, in close, the lethal Spanish artillery became useless.

Still, the soldiers celebrated their momentary victory. Strident and vulgar insults followed the retreating Indians, and as the gap between the two sides widened, the guns resumed their bombardment, though more sporadically than before. Ammunition was running low.

"A brave charge, friend," yelled the captain of the company adjacent to Medina's.

But Medina refrained from acknowledging the compliment, for he could see that the Indians had chosen not to pause for long. Augmented by large reinforcements, they had formed another huge phalanx and started to advance again.

"Stand ready," he commanded once more.

The guns stopped. Then, from the left, a different rumble shook the field. Cortés and Alvarado, their lances in position, charged into the Indian flank like a whirlwind, followed by a dozen other cavaliers. Stunned, the Indians turned in confusion, uncertain where, or even if, to strike these monstrous apparitions, more fearsome to them than the guns.

Yet, all did not go according to plan, for one sizable

group of Indians in the near flank refused to panic, and blocked the run of the cavalry along the length of the Indian line. They regarded the horses coolly as they approached, and swung their obsidian glass-edged clubs at their legs.

As his company edged closer to the action on the Indian flank, still awaiting a legitimate order to charge, Medina beheld a horrifying sight. A stroke from one of the Indian clubs severed the foreleg of Avila's chestnut mare, the one that had foaled at sea. Somehow, Avila managed to extricate himself and fall free as the mare rolled over, neighing shrilly. At the same time, six more Indians swarmed about Montejo. But instead of attacking his horse, they wrestled him off as though wanting to take him prisoner.

"To Montejo," shouted Medina, sprinting toward the fallen cavalier, his company in pursuit, and slashing at Indian warriors as they went. Reaching the embattled Montejo, Medina brought his sword down across the shoulder of one of the assailants. The Indian turned toward Medina and snarled. Before he could retaliate, Medina thrust home through the man's chest.

To defend themselves, the remaining Indians released their hold on Montejo. Then, seeing themselves outnumbered by Medina's company, they ran.

At that moment a stern Indian command rang out. Medina looked through the gunsmoke and dust. One of the savages had brazenly mounted Montejo's gray and now pranced back and forth in the dust. To Medina it seemed he was trying to rally his fleeing forces. But, as the horseman turned and flashed down the main line of Indians, obviously seeking to stiffen their resistance, he produced exactly the opposite effect. Mistaking him for a

Spaniard, or worse, the entire line fell back on his approach. Now free of any further obstacle, Cortés and the remainder of the cavalry plunged ahead. With the Indians already scattering before them, their ride turned from an attack into a victory procession.

The battle was over. With his strange rider, Montejo's gray had disappeared. Beaming, Cortés assembled his army beneath a copse of palm trees skirting the plain, and together they offered up thanks to the Almighty for giving them the battle against a numerically superior force. After the thanksgiving rite, the army buzzed. If many of the Indians saw the rider on the gray horse as a supernatural entity, the same was true for the Spanish army. "It was the Apostle himself," the word ran around. In the opinion of the soldiers, Saint Peter on horseback had galloped through the dust clouds trampling the enemy right and left to assure a just Christian victory.

Only Medina knew otherwise. He had seen the man, seen his long limbs, not unlike his own. And he had seen his tattooed forehead and the ornaments in his nose and ears. It had been an ordinary man, one who wore the black beard of a European.

Three days after the battle a delegation of the defeated *caciques* arrived at the Spanish camp, bearing a few gold ornaments, and bringing twenty young women as gifts. Although the women were attractive and a welcome sight to the Spaniards, the quantity of gold proved disappointing. With the aid of Aguilar, Cortés made clear his dissatisfaction. But repeated interrogations yielded the same story from the Indians. There was no more gold. The little they had came from a place far richer in the substance, a place in the north and west which they called sometimes "Culhua" and other times "Mexico."

"You should go there for more gold," said one of the chiefs, pointing toward the sunset.

"Perhaps he just wants to be rid of us," said Cortés to Aguilar.

"No, I think he tells the truth," said Aguilar. "I heard the same words many times during my captivity."

"Ask him how to get there," prompted Cortés.

"In your floating pyramids," answered the *cacique*, pointing to the ships. "You can journey north along the coast, and reach the eastern edge of that country. Our traders have often done the same in our canoes, for the way by land is difficult and filled with swamps."

"If you want to help us now, why did you attack us a few days ago?" asked Cortés.

"We were accused by our relatives at Champotón of being cowards for welcoming the Castilians who came before you. Besides, the white war chief of Chetumal claimed he could show us how to push you back into the sea."

"That bloody heretic," muttered Cortés. "Aguilar, tell them I want Braga turned over to me."

Aguilar relayed the command and the chief answered. Medina listened and understood enough of the language to realize the reply was discouraging.

"He says," Aguilar translated, "that the white chief has fled west into the swamps with some of his men from Chetumal. The white *cacique* declared he was going to Culhua to find braver men, men who could better fight Castilians."

Cortés grinned at Medina. "It seems as if the Lord has something for each of us in this Culhua, this Mexico. Gold for me, Braga for you."

Medina nodded in silence.

CHAPTER

The Lord Moctezuma, Emperor of the Culhua-Mexica, ruler of all the *Aztecatl,* ate alone behind an ornamented gold screen at one end of the huge palace dining hall. The day was cold, so a fire of charcoal made from aromatic wood had been built a few feet away in a receptacle in the floor. He sat on a low cushion covered with soft animal skins, and another, larger, cushion draped with a pure white cloth served as his table. The bowls and dishes were fine ceramics imported from Cholula, and many of the goblets were gold and silver, or fashioned of mosaics of seashells.

The Emperor had no appetite. Before him sat exquisitely prepared delicacies of game, fish, and fowl procured from the far reaches of the empire. The red snapper on one dish had been brought freshly caught by relays of runners from the eastern coast more than two hundred miles away, but he had not touched it. Even the Emperor's choicest dish, the roasted hindquarter of a young boy in a chocolate and peanut sauce, held no attraction for him.

This year, Thirteen Rabbit, was foretold to be inauspicious, he was thinking. First the wooden box containing the strange clothing had been washed up on the coast. Then Nezahualpilli had brought him the prophecy of doom in the middle of the night. And now, his counsels told him, there were bearers of omens awaiting an audience with him.

He could manage no more than a few dipperfuls of frothy chocolate from a goblet. He motioned, and two young women came forward to wash his hands in a bowl of water. When they finished, his steward stepped forward with an already lit pipe filled with tobacco and liquid-amber.

The Emperor sat quietly thinking as he inhaled the smoke alternately through his mouth and nose. He was a slender, fortyish man with a scanty beard fringing the lower part of a narrow, almost sharp face.

Why, he wondered, could his sorcerers bring nothing but discouraging omens and bad dreams? Were they in some kind of plot to demoralize him, to cause him to flee the capital? If so, who was behind it? Or was this his worldly fate, his true *tonalli*, to meet disaster?

Preoccupied, he rose and passed through a series of rooms and gardens, finally reaching his audience chamber. There he found his lords-in-waiting and secretaries standing respectfully beside the high-backed throne. Upon his entrance each knelt, touched the floor with his right-hand fingers, and touched his lips before arising. All were careful to keep their eyes averted from his august presence. Two valets approached the Emperor, and fastened a blue robe over his shoulders. Another, bowing down, presented him with a turquoise demi-miter. Moctezuma ascended his throne and sat down.

"Where is the *Tlamacazqui*, the sacrificial priest, Molotl?" he asked quietly.

"I am here, Lord Great Speaker," came a voice from the side of the chamber as a thin, hawk-faced man in a long, black, cowled robe stepped forward.

"I presume you have already screened these visitors yourself?"

"Yes, my Lord. I deem these persons to bear significant tidings for your consideration."

"Very well. Let us proceed. Who do you have for me?"

"There are two men, commoners from the village of Cococ just beyond the Fiery Mountain. They bring something to Your Lordship."

Molotl went to the doorway and motioned the two peasants into the room. They were awed to find themselves, for the first time in their lives, so suddenly in the presence of the Great Moctezuma, the earthly personification of Hummingbird God, Lord Huitzilopochtli, the eater of human hearts, the great hunter of men. They fell on their knees.

"Speak," commanded Moctezuma.

Staying on his knees, his eyes averted, the one on the right said, "Great Lord, Great Speaker, we captured this man near our colony in the hot country to the east."

Molotl called to the guard at the doorway, who immediately came in. On a rope behind him limped a short, ugly man in the rough maguey cape and bare feet required for all subjects in audience with the Emperor. Moctezuma immediately felt a chill in his spine: the ugly little visitor had no ears, thumbs, or big toes. Already a bad omen.

"Why do you bring *this* to me, Molotl?" complained the Emperor, somewhat puzzled.

"I apologize, my Lord," said Molotl, shoving the little man into obeisance before the Emperor, "but this demon-child comes from the eastern coast. These commoners," he said, motioning toward the peasants, "thought he would be an amusing addition to the court. But we found, from questioning him in his own language, that he has special knowledge."

"Of what nature?" asked Moctezuma.

Molotl motioned a male slave forward. The slave spoke briefly in Totonac with the dwarf, and then translated.

"Oh, Tlatoani, Great Speaker, Great Lord Moctezuma, I come from beyond the Fiery Mountain. I was walking on the shore of the Eastern Sea when I saw a round hill floating on the waters. It moved toward a point of rocks down the coast." He paused.

"A floating hill! What else? What else?" the Emperor asked.

"No more, my Lord. I ran."

Moctezuma considered this. Then he said, "Molotl, have the demon-child caged until we know if he speaks the truth."

After the man had been led out, the Emperor turned to one of the younger nobles. "Go immediately to the Eastern Sea, and discover the truth of this matter. And tell the governors of the provinces there that they must keep me informed."

The noble nodded assent, and backed out of the chamber, his eyes focused on the floor.

"Now, Molotl, what else do you have for me?" demanded the Great Speaker.

"A special omen, my Lord." Molotl nodded to the guard, and two humble-looking men came forth. Between them they carried an oblong, covered basket. They kneeled, touched their hands to the floor, kissed them and, keeping their eyes down, carefully opened the basket. They gently lifted out the body of a bird resembling a cormorant. Around its neck hung a collar with a metallic disc attached. Strange markings covered the disc, which bore a hole in the center.

A hush fell over the room. None of them had ever seen such a disc before.

Moctezuma took command of the situation. "You have done well. The bird with the disc appears to me a messenger from the Lord Tezcatlipoca, He of the Smoking Mirror. It seems that I am to look into this mirror to see what will come to pass."

He motioned to Molotl. "Bring the bird to the Black Room at midnight. Make the necessary preparations for me to read the mirror."

That night Molotl brought the bird and some ointment to the Emperor in the Black Room, a secret chamber inside the Great Pyramid. First he had to climb the steep 114 steps up the side of the Pyramid, then pass down the secret trap door behind the idol of Huitzilopochtli, following the narrow, twisting stone stairway, lit by copal torches, down halfway into the center of the Pyramid. There he found the Emperor stripped naked and squatting in prayer in the bare room, whose glasslike walls were constructed of polished obsidian blocks.

Molotl remained silent until the Emperor roused himself from his meditation.

"Rub my body, Molotl," he said, "until it is hot. I will be able to absorb the ointment better."

Molotl took out a small jar of dark ointment, made from pulverized *ololiuhqui* seeds and the ashes of poisonous insects. He rubbed it all over the Emperor's body, including his genitals. Then he placed the dead bird, with its disc upward, before the Emperor, below a copal torch.

"Now, my Lord, you shall see."

"Yes, Molotl. Yes, Sacrificial Priest. It is beginning. I am starting to enter the mirror. I am beginning to see. I am traveling beyond the Fiery Mountain. I fly. I fly. . . ." His voice trailed off. Then he collapsed on the floor.

Molotl left him alone and went up the staircase to the top of the Pyramid. Pulling a blanket about him, he sat waiting for hours. Then shortly before dawn, he heard a noise behind him. It was the Emperor, still naked, staggering out from behind the idol.

"I have seen what is beyond the mirror. Men coming in mass. Men coming as conquerors. Men coming in war dress. They are riding deer." He leaned against the wall of caked blood in the temple and said no more.

Molotl wrapped his blanket around the Emperor, and slowly helped him down the Pyramid steps in the darkness.

CHAPTER

IV

Cortés gazed at the shore as the ship beat northward against the wind. From the battle at Tabasco, he had learned some significant military facts, and these paraded through his mind. One, the ferocity of the Tabascans was undeniable. And from his interrogations of the defeated *caciques,* he knew the warriors of "Mexico" would be doubly fierce. Two, he might everywhere expect to find himself up against armies far superior to his own in numbers. Nevertheless, the strength of his firepower might neutralize that disadvantage. Three, his most potent weapon, tactically and psychologically, appeared to be the cavalry, whose sudden presence on the enemy flank had routed the Tabascans who apparently had never seen a horse before. "They thought we were centaurs," Alvarado had chuckled to him after the battle. Yet, thought Cortés, one group of Indians had successfully cut down Avila's mare and unhorsed Montejo. Before long, other Indians would learn that, far from being gods, horses bled and horses died.

"Good morning, Don Hernán."

Cortés turned around and looked into the gray face of Jerónimo de Aguilar.

Cortés, ever the opportunist, greatly valued the repatriated Spaniard's proficiency in Mayan. Though the fleet was headed up the coast where a different language was said to be spoken, Cortés felt that Aguilar's knowledge of the language of Yucatan might be of further use. Accordingly, the Captain-General had appointed him expedition interpreter and kept him on board the flagship.

"Yes, Aguilar?"

"Don Hernán, I've been watching the shore. I think we are being spied on. Every time I look I see a canoe keeping parallel to us. There, just this side of the surf," he pointed. "You can barely make it out."

"I know," replied Cortés, casting his eyes once again at the canoe, which seemed to have a crew of at least half a dozen paddlers. Cortés too had been watching, impressed with the men's endurance.

"Are they Tabascans, Aguilar?"

"It is difficult to tell, sir, but I suspect that they are. What bothers me is that if they are Tabascans they are far out of their territory."

"You mean they are up to something?"

"Well, sir, a single canoe like that would venture this far north only if it were bearing traders or envoys. And I think it is unlikely that they are traders, for if they had any cargo they could not keep up that speed."

"And if they are some sort of envoys or messengers? What would their mission be?"

Aguilar shrugged his shoulders. Both men lapsed into silence as they watched the canoe near the shore. Aguilar decided to change the subject.

"Speaking of Tabascans, sir, I have been talking to some of the girls that they gave us. One of them seems to be originally from Mexico and of noble birth. She says her people are the *Aztecatl*, in her language."

Cortés murmured affirmatively, though plainly preoccupied.

The ship, moving to windward, had been tacking in

toward shore and was preparing to come about. Cortés momentarily thought he could see a man standing in the prow of the canoe, but as the ship tacked away from the coastline, the canoe disappeared behind the crests of the distant waves.

That afternoon, José Pérez decided he had reached his limit. The Tabascan women were driving him mad. His groin ached and he had, perforce, to refrain from relieving himself in the usual way. For in a fit of sincerity, he confessed to Father Olmedo that he resorted to self-stimulation several times a day to, as he put it, "uncork" the demons within.

"How many times?" asked Father Olmedo, leaning forward in the makeshift confessional in his cabin.

"Seven usually, Father," replied José.

"Indeed!" exclaimed the priest incredulously.

"I must be unnatural," said José, half believing it, bowing his head penitently, but at the same time wondering whether the good Spanish Father ever resorted to such means.

"My son," said Olmedo kindly, "it is truly a black, unchaste act in which you indulge. Guard yourself against its necessity through prayer. Such matters are sometimes difficult to contend with, particularly at sea. But we must quench these base urges that swirl so much around us like tropic vapors, and tempt us, and lead us away from God's radiant purity."

"Yes, Father. Forgive me."

"The rocking of the ship probably also has something to do with arousing these unholy impulses."

"Yes, Father."

"Now then, for penance say twenty-eight Hail Marys."

"Twenty-eight, Father? Penance is usually given in round numbers."

"Four per unclean act, my son."

"Still, that is fairly stiff, Father."

"Very well, let me soften it. Two per act. Fourteen Hail Marys and your soul will be sufficiently presentable. A rather heavily used soul, I daresay, but, in God's merciful eyes, yet presentable."

"Thank you, Father."

"One thing more, my son. God works in mysterious ways. The health of the body often reflects the health of the soul."

"I feel pretty good, Father."

"But in the long run, you should know each—how shall I put it—each, ah, *eruption* shortens a man's natural life."

"Then I should be dead by now, Father."

"Yes, well, the mathematics pertaining to these things are not precisely clear. Nevertheless, I can promise you, my son, each eruption also has a spiritual effect, and, should you die unshriven, the, ah, boisterousness of these 'demons' as you call them, will cost you dearly. Mind those demons, my son. Mind them ruthlessly, for they are the shadows of the Devil. Now, go in peace."

The confession scarcely troubled José, since Father Olmedo appeared to condemn only imaginary intercourse, not the real sort. Or at least that is the way José chose to interpret it. The health aspects he regarded as academic, since anyone who wanted to live a long life would not have signed onto the expedition in the first place. Or come to New Spain at all, for that matter. So much for health.

Anyway, half the men on board, as everyone knew, helped each other with their sexual tensions in the time-honored ways of men long without women. Even the Captain-General was known to engage in a little of this kind of fun, and the men privately joked about the time he had been caught in bed with Governor Velázquez back in Cuba. So it was with a relatively clear conscience that José decided to obtain one of the Tabascan women, and find a suitable place in which to endear himself to her. Both tasks, as affairs stood, presented formidable problems.

In the first instance, Pedro de Alvarado had made it abundantly clear when the women were first turned over to the Spaniards on the beach at Tabasco that they were to be regarded as the private property of the nobles. These gentlemen, with the help of Cortés, would sort out who belonged to whom presently.

"Nor, on pain of death," Alvarado had announced that day, "shall these women be molested by any word, deed, or action. Furthermore, I don't mean an ordinary death," he added emphatically. Here the men perked up their ears, for they knew Alvarado's forte. It was cruelty, but cruelty with a certain dash, interesting actually, so long as you were not its object.

"I propose—no, I guarantee—that the man who violates these standing orders shall, within one minute or less of his apprehension, discover his left testicle pinned to the port side of his ship, and his right to the starboard side. And I don't mean gracing the bowsprit either, but there, where the ship is beamiest." The men howled and cheered, daring each other to test Alvarado's word; but the message took. In everyone, that is, except José, who regarded it as so much bombast. He knew Cortés couldn't afford to lose a single able body, not if he could possibly help it, and particularly not where the offense was one of form rather than substance. Still, José thought, he might as well be careful.

The second task, finding a private love nest, seemed even more insurmountable. Privacy for a sailor, soldier, or other low-born type such as José did not exist on a crowded Spanish ship. Rubbing elbows was the way of life while eating, sleeping, or working—even, frequently, while defecating. No, you were never alone, not even on the midnight watch, which Cortés had ordered to be as populated with lookouts as possible. From his unfortunate experience at Cozumel he had learned that the horses' hay, however comfortable, was not a safe place for a tryst. Even so, José reflected, he could always slip away with his prize to one of the holds where the weapons were stored, or go even deeper into the bowels of the ship. But both these places stank, whether from the paraffin coating the weapons or, in the bilge, from dead rats and who knew what else. "*Pssh*," he remarked to himself. "I can do better than that!" He was right. Nor did he have long to wait.

Late that afternoon, Cortés, after consulting with Antonio de Alaminos, the expedition's chief pilot, ordered the fleet to anchor in the lee of San Juan de Ulúa, an island that almost touched the mainland, and which they now rapidly approached. The island had been named by Grijalva on his earlier expedition. Alaminos, who had also served Grijalva as pilot, knew the island would shelter them from the late northerlies that could still pile in even though winter had ended.

The sun was high overhead when the ships glided, one by one, into the bay formed by the proximity of the island to the mainland. Across the water hundreds of Indians silently stood watching on the jungle beach as each vessel furled its sails, the rattle of anchor chains breaking the tropical stillness.

After the near-disaster at Tabasco, Cortés could take no chances on the Indians' intentions. He ordered that the dinghy be sent to bring Alvarado from the *San Sebastian* for a conference. While the boat was being lowered, Father Olmedo and Aguilar asked permission to ride in it to visit the seven Tabascan women on Alvarado's ship. Cortés agreed, and at the last minute Medina decided to accompany Aguilar, with whom he had been working on Mayan. When Medina dropped down into the dinghy behind Aguilar, a familiar face grinned at him from among the oarsmen. It was José Pérez, now such a fully reinstated seaman that he even again functioned at Masses as Father Olmedo's altar boy.

When the dinghy reached the *San Sebastian*, Medina conveyed Cortés' invitation to Alvarado. A delay of several minutes ensued while Alvarado prepared himself to visit the Captain-General. José, who had clambered aboard the ship to stretch his legs briefly, overheard the bosun mention that Alvarado did not plan to return until after dawn of the following day. A plan took instant shape in José's impassioned brain. He called down to his fellow oarsmen that Father Olmedo had asked him to stay on board the *San Sebastian* to assist at services and to so inform the officer of the watch on their return to the flagship. With that, José disappeared below.

Shortly after, the feisty, well-accoutered Alvarado emerged with Father Sánchez. The two of them descended into the dinghy, and it shoved off.

Meanwhile, José caught a glimpse of Father Olmedo going along the passageway toward the cabins aft, and after a brief interval he followed. He found a bored sentinel sitting near the end of the passageway. He explained to the guard that he was Father Olmedo's assistant, and that Alvarado had requested that he, José, personally deposit a document, religious in nature, in Alvarado's cabin. Could he please have the key, which would be returned at once? Without fuss, the guard complied, and José entered the cabin.

Though small, it bore the stamp of Alvarado's appetite for opulence. A Moorish carpet covered the floor, and a bright feathered headdress taken from a Tabascan warrior hung jauntily from a peg on the wall. On Alvarado's massive sea chest sat a large silver basin and pitcher, two bars of soap, and several crystal vials containing perfume, hints of which made the cabin faintly and pleasantly aromatic. An ornate writing desk stood against one of the cabin walls, and a stunning blue-and-white Italianate quilt covered the bunk.

Placing a copy of the *Letters of St. Augustine,* surreptitiously borrowed from Olmedo, on the bunk, he withdrew, returning the key to the guard, but having left the cabin door unlocked. He perspired in anticipation.

Medina, meanwhile, sat alone on the ship's gun deck waiting for Aguilar to return. Medina, like Cortés, saw Aguilar as a person of great value, especially since the disappearance of Melchorejo. Although the fleet was now sailing away from Yucatan and Tabasco, he wished to learn all that he could of the Mayan language from Aguilar. Even if the language should not be of use in Mexico, its study exercised his mind.

Aguilar's command of Castilian had deteriorated badly during his eight years among the Indians, and he, for his part, was delighted to have a companion with whom to converse daily. As Medina had no shipboard duties, he was able to apply himself to the study of the language every morning and afternoon. Both men looked forward to their sessions.

This particular day, however, Medina had something on his mind besides a lone, educational conversation with the engaging Aguilar. He wanted—in Aguilar's presence, of course—to question the Indian woman who Aguilar claimed spoke the language of Mexico as well as Mayan. Through her, he might begin to learn something of the new language. Aguilar had gone to ask permission to interview her from the nobleman to whom she had been assigned. In order to qualify for sexual intercourse with a Castilian, she, like the other women, had been hastily baptized before they had left Tabasco. Her new name was Marina.

The seven Indian women, when not in the service of their new masters, lived in a large compartment amidships. Less than ten minutes after Aguilar left with Marina, José appeared at the door, peering brazenly in.

The guard eyed him suspiciously. He did not like this dark, facile whelp with the Italian accent. He had airs and, working as he did for the chaplain, too many privileges for his own good.

"Father Olmedo wants to see one of the women," José announced superciliously.

"Our translator must be a busy man," replied the guard.

"What?"

"Aguilar has just taken one of them. To talk with Don Marcos."

"I know," said José, collecting himself. Thank God, the lout had cork for a head. "The Father merely wants to compare dialects. The tall one there will do," he concluded peremptorily.

José could scarcely contain himself. He had gotten the woman out of the harem, taken her past the old guard in the officers' section without challenge, and, unnoticed by the same guard, now guided her into Alvarado's cabin, closing the door softly behind him.

Medina found it difficult to keep his mind on the language lesson. He was on the gun deck with Aguilar and Marina. Aguilar and he had often worked well together in such situations, but somehow today seemed different. The girl, although only about eighteen, had the elegant look of an aristocrat. The men on board the *San Sebastian* had even taken to calling her *Doña* Marina, an unheard-of compliment to an Indian woman. He found himself staring at her, forgetting to concentrate as she repeated words at Aguilar's suggestion. The girl, Medina thought, had an attractive tranquility of disposition. Despite her alien surroundings, she remained cool and poised. He wanted to bore into her, know everything about her, consume her. No longer listening, he found himself leaning deliberately toward her, took in the unfamiliar musk of her clothing. Abruptly, he stood up and began pacing back and forth. A sensation of warmth suffused his body. This is another man's woman, he told himself. And, even worse, an Indian and a slave. He stopped, looked hard at her for a moment, then addressed Aguilar.

"That will be enough for today, Jerónimo. Excuse me."

He walked stiffly to the door, and went down the passageway where he turned a corner and came to a halt. I've been too long in these forlorn Indies, he thought. Confound Fonseca and confound the King's hunger for gold that brought me here. Then, from the cabin beside whose door he had stopped, came sounds that transfixed him.

"Now, my dear, lie back. Here, let me put the pillow under that smooth little bottom. Oh, it is so round and soft. So royal, my little princess, so very royal. Ah, that curious navel. Permit me, my love. Let me be the first Italian to plant his Christian lips on that delicate little nub. Ah, my dear, I have never seen a woman so brown, and ripe, and warm. Now don't be afraid. This is just a little soap."

Medina could not bear to stay. He strode down the passageway, climbed up the ladder to the deck, and looked quickly around. Then he took off his outer clothing, dropped it in a pile, and, keeping his underwear on, approached the rail. Under the startled gaze of the helmsman, he climbed it and dove into the water.

The dive was clean, straight, and thorough. Down he went into the cool waters of the Gulf of Mexico. Deeper and deeper, the light bluing, then darkening. Arching his body, he leveled out, found his vertical bearings, and then kicked and stroked his way upward toward the globular, shimmering goal of light above. He crashed through the surface like an eruption, gulping hungrily for breath. God, it's pure, he thought. He dove again, less deep, gyrating underwater like a tumbler, somersaulting, twisting, pirouetting. Coming up, he tossed his head to clear his ears. The salt taste began to seep through his lips and onto his tongue. Orienting himself to the ship, he swam off in the opposite direction. I want to swim forever, he exulted, losing in the rhythmic motion of his churning arms and heaving diaphragm all sense of who he was and where he was going.

He was unaware of the boat in the distance that was plying toward the ship. It was Alvarado, returning prematurely.

Having rummaged in Alvarado's sea chest and finding clothing as fine as he had ever seen, let alone worn, José sat next to his brown pagan princess dressed like half a peacock. It was a miracle, he thought, that the Tabascan woman had not long since fallen insensible from the sheer dazzle of his outfit. A rich hat with a long, trailing plume sat cocked on his head. He wore a shirt of deep-red silk bursting with ruffles on the chest and along the sleeves, and, thrown across his shoulder, was a thick, broadweave Turkish cape, dark-brown in color and embroidered with a pair of postured silver birds. A wide patent leather belt girded his waist. The rest of him, excepting only a pair of soft, sealskin boots—or bootlets, really, since they came closer to hosiery than to anything one could tramp in for very long—was conspicuously bare. The air in the cabin, moreover, was positively fuliginous, since José, in attempting to create a proper atmosphere, had splashed the contents of the perfume vials to and fro rather too liberally. The woman, who at first had been scared out of her wits, now lay back smiling on the quilt, the pillow still propping up her buttocks. After some thought, José had filled the silver basin with water from the pitcher, taken a bar of Alvarado's soap, and, for reasons touching both on sexual foreplay and hygiene, proceeded to lather his Tabascan princess from head to foot. "We higher class Neapolitans are fastidious," he told the uncomprehending, but giggling, woman as he slid the wet bar of soap languorously around her breasts, down her tummy, and in between her legs. She had just pulled him to her, and he had just dropped the soap into the basin and lifted one leg preparatory to mounting her, when the door burst open.

"Mother of God," stammered Alvarado in disbelief.

"What in the name of God have you done with my scents, you dirty *sin vergüenza?*" he demanded, striding in and fanning the air in front of his nose with his hand.

Numb with terror, José closed his eyes and began reciting the *Confiteor* to himself.

"Disrobe that scum and toss him over the side," Alvarado said crisply to his lieutenants standing in the doorway behind him. "As for the woman," he added, suddenly inspired, "leave her where she is."

Leering, the men moved in. They stripped the now audibly chanting José and, stealing parting glances at the Tabascan woman, led him roughly from the cabin.

"At least his own lust has saved your balls, José," whispered one of the men sympathetically as they reached the deck. It was Fernández, a drinking companion from Cuba.

"Saved them for the sharks, is all," muttered another of the men. "We do have to chuck him, Fernández, don't we now?"

"Stop that tongue of yours, worm," snapped Fernández. "He's right, though," he said, turning to José. "We're ordered to throw you over."

"I can't swim, man," protested José, starting to struggle.

He was no match for the men, who picked him up by his wrists and ankles, and began swinging him back and forth.

"A priest, a priest," shrieked José. "Before I die, I must confess. You must let me confess."

The men exchanged glances and put José down, keeping a firm grip on him. Fernández disappeared belowdecks and in a few minutes emerged with Father Teodosio Sánchez, Alvarado's chaplain. The six foot plus Sánchez strode over to the crewmen, a broad grin stretching across his freckled face. He was readily recognized by everyone on the expedition because of his immense size and the tangled mass of red hair that ran across his forehead down to his powerful shoulders.

Sánchez rarely absented himself from matters touching on the discipline of Alvarado's troops. Although he kept his personal history a secret, it was rumored that he had been a soldier of fortune in the Mediterranean before clothing himself in the robes of a priest. In any case, when he found Alvarado, he found a man after his own heart.

"Help me, Father," croaked José pathetically.

"I intend to," replied Sánchez. He approached and took José's chin in his hand and squeezed. His fists were like oaken gnarls.

José screamed with pain.

"You are a foul little runt," snarled Sánchez, exhaling his garlic breath into José's face. Still holding him by the chin, Sánchez lifted José a foot in the air and then hurled him forcefully backward. José crashed heavily to the deck.

"Cowards," said Sánchez, turning to the men. "Were you simply going to let him swim about? You, Fernández. Go below and fetch a ballast stone."

Fernández disappeared down the companionway. Clutching his crucifix, Sánchez began pacing back and forth.

"God hates it," he fumed, "God hates it when a legitimate order is carried out so haphazardly."

"And as for you," he said, standing over José, "you are about to die. But don't think that's the end of it. Oh no, my friend. No forgiveness, do you hear? Your soul will leave this earth as black and as naked as your filthy body."

"Then you aren't a priest," gasped José, blood from a cut on his scalp beginning to soak through his hair.

"You execrable dog!" exclaimed Sánchez. His kick caught José in the testicles. José shrieked with pain and doubled up on the deck.

Fernández returned and the men strapped the ballast stone around José's waist.

"No, no!" screamed José. "For the love of God, no!"

With Sánchez looking on approvingly, the men unceremoniously picked José up, propped him on the rail for a moment, and then shoved with a concerted grunt. He dropped like a plummet into the water and disappeared, leaving only a circle of white foam.

José, choking with water, thrashed desperately, sank, fought his way to the surface, gurgled a cry for help, sank again, thought he saw the Blessed Virgin, felt his chest caving in, then lost consciousness.

A grinning Alvarado was just removing his underwear to take care of the unfinished business that lay before him, when there was a sharp knock at the cabin door.

"The flagship is signaling for you to return, sir. Immediately," a sailor's voice called.

"Damnation!" yelled Alvarado, but he hastily struggled back into his drawers. In a rage of frustration, he slammed out of the cabin, buckling on his sword as he rushed up the gangway. As he strode across the deck he caught sight of two long canoes filled with natives who paddled fearlessly toward Cortés' ship.

"Lower the dinghy," he ordered. "And call Aguilar. Cortés will need an interpreter."

From belowdecks Aguilar brought with him the girl, Marina, hoping that her knowledge of the language of her Aztecatl people might help if the Indians were on a peaceful mission. In their haste to step down into the dinghy, neither Alvarado nor Aguilar thought to call for Medina. Within a few minutes they reached the nearby flagship and were aboard it before the Indians got close.

As the dinghy bearing Alvarado and Aguilar pulled away from the starboard side of the *San Sebastian*, Medina, hidden from view and still in the water, grasped the anchor cable on the port bow of the ship. In one hand he held the long black hair of the chaplain's assistant.

"Hallo," he sang out. A head quickly popped over the bow.

"My God, what've you got there, Don Marcos? Is that José? Is he drowned?" It was Fernández.

"No, not quite. Can you get him up?"

"I can't. I mean, well, he's *executed.*"

"Executed?"

"Yes, by order of Captain Alvarado. He was caught in his cabin with one of the Tabascan women. If Alvarado knows he's alive he'll run him through for sure," said Fernández, lowering his voice.

"I can't hold him much longer," said Medina, exhausted. "Get me a line."

"Yes, sir." Fernández disappeared, returning a few minutes later with a length of rope which he lowered to Medina.

Medina tied it around José Pérez' chest. Half-conscious, José was in no condition to assist.

To Alvarado's disappointment, the Indians who approached the ship were far from hostile. Bearing no arms, they indicated their desire to come aboard with a variety of gestures, some of them bewildering, but all of them unmistakably friendly. Once on board, they proved about as fierce as playful children, chattering amiably, smiling, even curiously touching the beards of those Spaniards who wore them, and who allowed it. Alvarado did not.

In all, twelve Indians stood on deck, each with deep-bronze skin, smooth face, high cheekbones, and pitch-black hair and eyes. They wore white cotton tunics girded at the waist with cord. Alvarado found them arrogant and repulsive, while Cortés thought them handsome, intelligent, and malleable.

Apparently sensitive to his carriage and the behavior of his subordinates toward him, they fell to their knees in front of Cortés, touching their fingertips to the deck, and then to their bowed heads. Embarrassed by the obeisance, Cortés helped one of them to his feet. The others followed suit and stood up.

The purpose of their visit was circuitously unraveled by Marina and Aguilar. She translated from Nahuatl, the language of the Aztecatl, to Tabascan Mayan; he, in turn, from Yucatan Mayan to Castilian.

"Where do you come from?" their elderly spokesman asked.

"Spain. Far across those waters," answered Cortés, pointing to the east.

"Who is your lord?"

"A wise, powerful monarch, Charles."

"We have our own all-powerful monarch, the Great Lord Moctezuma. Why do you come here?"

"To trade, and to tell the people of Mexico, of Culhua, about our God, who is greater than our monarch, and greater than all things."

"We have our own gods. Tlaloc, Huitzilopochtli, and many others. They, too, are great."

The translation process was halting and arduous. Still, the Indians pushed what appeared to be their most urgent question. The elder's eyes narrowed as he asked it and waited for the answer.

"When will you leave?"

"When we have delivered a message we bear from our monarch to yours, this Moctezuma," replied Cortés, beginning to weave the necessary diplomatic fabrications to justify a march inland, should he decide to make one.

"He is a great and powerful lord, our Moctezuma." The emissaries bent down, and touched their fingers to the deck and then to their foreheads at the mention of his name.

"Where does he live?"

"In Tenochtitlan, a large and strong city on a lake in the highlands far from here."

"How far?"

"Four days."

"That is not far."

"That is far. We are good runners. To walk is ten days or more."

"Are you people of Mexico?"

"No, but the Mexicas, the Aztecatl, rule over us. They are a mighty people."

"What do you carry in your canoes?"

"Gifts."

The latent tension of the interview eased as the gifts were passed aboard. In exchange for gold ornaments, flowers, and maize cakes, the Spaniards doled out glass beads, holland shirts, and red wine. The Indians seemed pleased, so too the Spaniards. With the gold. As for the maize cakes, they had a strange and disturbing pungency to them that only a long drink of wine could dissipate. Some of the Spaniards suspected that the offending ingredient was human blood, though, for the sake of appearance, nothing was said.

When Medina finished lashing the rope over Pérez's shoulders, Fernández whispered down to him. "Alvarado will kill not only José but me if he's brought on board, Don Marcos. Can't you take him somewhere else?"

Medina had not planned to spend the day towing a hundred and thirty pounds of bait in shark-infested waters, but he nodded to Fernández, and peered under the bow at the flagship about two hundred yards away. The Indian canoes and Alvarado's dinghy were tied alongside the ship and empty. He did not see any lookouts on deck. He could discern some bobbing heads amidships, but it appeared that everyone there was busy among themselves. He decided to pull Pérez to the flagship. After all, the little Italian had saved his life at Tabasco.

Swimming quietly with a sidestroke, and pulling José by his hair with his free hand, Medina reached the anchor line of the flagship unnoticed. He lashed José to the hawser, using the rope tied about his chest, so that the sailor's head was well above water. Then he swam over to the boarding ladder and climbed up onto the ship. The first meeting between Cortés and the envoys of the Aztecs was proceeding on the deck in a manner resembling a gay, colorful party. No one seemed to notice the dripping Medina circling around them to his cabin.

A few minutes later, after promising the Spaniards food and informing them that their own chiefs would visit within a few days, the Indians descended to their canoes and began paddling toward shore. Night had begun settling in. Looking back toward the ship, they saw José hanging limply halfway between the deck and the waterline.

"That is their way with prisoners, I think," said the elder sagely to one of his companions.

The morning following the visit of the twelve Indians, the Spaniards disembarked. Men, guns, and horses poured slowly ashore. The soldiers began constructing crude wooden shelters in the lee of the dunes. Though he expected a friendly reception, Cortés was taking no chances. The guns were placed in a defensive perimeter around them. Alvarado took charge of the horses, and shortly after noon led a small reconnaissance force through the surrounding country.

As picturesque and safe as was the harbor, the shore proved barren and uncomfortable. The heat was stifling and the insects from the neighboring jungle and marshes bore mercilessly in on the new supply of nourishment, both human and equestrian. Still, Cortés became encouraged, for one after another, the natives living nearby shyly appeared and, before long, fell to helping the men in their work. In addition, they brought fresh water, live birds, and bolts of cotton cloth to serve as awnings.

Though grateful, the men—at least the more enterprising—soon learned to communicate what at the moment was as important to them as food and shade: those shimmering gold ornaments. Did the Indians have more in their houses? A discreet but lively trade sprang up as the Indians slipped between their small village and the Spanish settlement, bringing what gold they possessed, and returning home with costume jewelry and Spanish underwear.

Technically such trade was illegal, for all expeditions operated under the rule of "the King's fifth," by which the Crown automatically reserved to itself one-fifth of the volume of all transactions, whether these involved trade or more direct means of acquisition—plunder, for example. To ensure that the Crown received its due a Royal

Notary accompanied each expedition, and made it his business to audit whatever treasure came its way.

For the moment, Cortés tacitly approved the bartering going on in the new settlement, and failed to notify the notary of its existence. Not only was its scale modest, but it also allayed the restiveness that had increasingly overtaken the men. Partly they were apprehensive about the size of their force compared to what they gradually learned about the strength of the Aztecs. Partly, too, those in the expedition who considered themselves loyal to Velázquez, the Governor of Cuba, the man who had given Cortés his commission, had begun agitating for a return to Cuba. They openly pointed out that Cortés was not authorized to settle and create a colony, as he was apparently bent on doing. They also urged that the expedition stores could not support a prolonged stay, and that more than thirty soldiers had already been lost in the battle at Tabasco and by illness.

The Velázquez faction included several captains as well as two priests, including Father Sánchez. Their intrigues now began to alarm Cortés seriously.

On board the flagship, José awoke and found himself in Medina's cabin. He groaned, his body stiff and sore.

"That rotten son of a whore," he mumbled.

"Alvarado?" said Medina, sitting at a small table with a dish of dried plums in front of him. "I would watch how you speak, my friend. You've already offended him beyond redress."

"I mean that red-bearded carrot, Sánchez," said José. "He had no call to strap that stone to me."

"Have a plum," said Medina, tossing one across the room to José.

"How come you were in the water?" asked José.

"An afternoon swim."

"What a strange form of recreation!"

"Somewhat more acceptable than yours."

"There isn't an officer or nobleman on this expedition who doesn't screw whenever he has the chance," replied José bitterly.

"But you are neither one nor the other."

"No, just a man."

"An exceedingly brazen one."

"Damn! Father Olmedo will dismiss me as chaplain's assistant."

"Your problems are far stickier than that."

"Yes," replied José with a sigh. "I suppose I will have to go live among the Indians after all."

"Become an assistant to one of *their* priests," said Medina with a smile. He felt oddly drawn to this outspoken commoner who wasn't the least bit intimidated by rank or status. Moreover, Medina could not forget how the Italian had risked his life for him.

"They probably don't serve wine at their services," José bantered.

"I'm told they serve stronger stuff."

"Let them. I'd rather have good Christian wine."

The two men fell silent as their thoughts turned to the problem at hand, Alvarado's decree. After his experience at Tabasco, José had no intention of turning himself over to the Indians. Instead, he began to plan on making his way to one of the smaller ships. With luck, he could hide there, for weeks if necessary. Besides, this Medina was obviously going to be helpful. At least it didn't appear he would turn him in to the Captain. With this comforting realization, José turned and smiled at his benefactor.

"It's time we went to see Alvarado," said Medina, standing up.

José's eyes opened so wide that his scalp moved noticeably toward the rear of his head. "He'll kill me! He'll cut off my balls!"

"That might be good for you. Anyway I think I can persuade him to acquit you," said Medina.

"You can't—I know. Sánchez won't let him. He's the only one Alvarado really listens to."

José, who had been lying in Medina's bed, threw off the covers and leaped to his feet. Seeing Medina's sword propped up in a corner, he began edging toward it.

"Stay where you are," said Medina in a low, level voice, perceiving José's intention.

The command affected José deeply. There it was, the ancient, loathsome, inescapable thrust of authority. He stopped short, a wave of resentment welling up in him. With hate in his eyes, he glared at Medina who stood stock-still in the center of the cabin, returning the gaze unwaveringly.

Then, his face softening, Medina walked to the table, picked up the dish of plums, and offered them to José.

"Here, have another plum," he said cheerfully.

José knew he was beaten. He meekly took a plum. Preserving what dignity he could, he carefully selected the largest one.

Medina arrived on shore alone in one of the boats, and

made his way to the Captain-General's tent, by now a rambling affair reminding Medina of the gypsy encampments he'd seen in the Castilian countryside when he was a small boy.

"I was planning to send for you," said Cortés, inviting Medina inside. "I need your advice."

The men entered the tent's main chamber, and seated themselves on a row of cushions fashioned out of sacks of cassava flour. Cortés reached into his leather satchel and removed a letter, which he placed next to him.

"You realize, I think, that there are those on the expedition who insist we return to Cuba," he began.

"Yes, I've heard," replied Medina. "Those loyal to Velázquez."

"Where do you stand, Marcos?"

"I don't know, Hernán. What do you have in mind?"

"I want to go to Mexico, to this city of Tenochtitlan. I want to see Moctezuma. I want to feast my eyes on him, and on his empire."

"Only sight-seeing?" Medina smiled sarcastically.

"That, and trade," replied Cortés. "You've seen what riches these Aztecs possess. There is more gold there than lies in all of Europe."

"I am not interested in gold, Hernán. I came to eliminate Braga."

"But the King is, and the *Casa de la Contratación.*"

"Yes, that is true."

"You are important to the expedition, Marcos," said Cortés. "First, we must find a way to legitimize ourselves. I should like to be answerable to Bishop Fonseca and the King directly rather than to Velázquez. I therefore propose you join us in petitioning the King for authorization to found a colony, and I plan to send with that petition physical evidence of the quality and abundance of gold found here. As you are an educated man, and joined the expedition on a mission of the Bishop and the *Casa,* your endorsement would be most useful."

"It will take months for a petition to reach Seville," Medina said. "Besides, you have little gold at present, as far as I know."

"The gold will come in due course, rather sooner than later, I suspect. As for the petition, yes. It will take a separate voyage to convey it, a voyage that will have to bypass Cuba. Nevertheless, as soon as you agree to my proposition, and as soon as we come by sufficient gold, I will organize such a voyage. Meantime, I have decided to dissolve the present expedition."

"Dissolve it?"

"Yes. If I dissolve it, I dissolve the claims of Velázquez. I will resign as Captain-General."

"What then?"

"Then the men will take matters into their own hands, and found an honest Spanish town right here on these miserable dunes. Elect a mayor and so forth." Cortés smiled.

"And you will stand for municipal Captain-General or Chief Justice, or both, I suppose?"

"I suppose," replied Cortés, proud of himself. "But I also need your help in another way."

"I see. How is that?"

"As an interpreter of Mayan. Aguilar tells me you are making excellent progress in learning the language of Yucatan. If we march on Mexico we'll need you and Aguilar to act as intermediary translators with Doña Marina, since she can only translate this Nahuatl language of the Aztecs into Mayan. If anything happened to Aguilar," Cortés added, "you would be absolutely essential to our survival, let alone our success."

"It sounds as though you intend to mount an invasion rather than a trading expedition."

"Don Marcos, I intend to go to Mexico in as friendly a fashion as I can. But I intend to go, come what may. Therefore, I must be prepared."

"Your force is meager."

"Which is why I shall be friendly, and why I need the ability to communicate successfully with the Indians."

"Why didn't you already consider my knowledge to be at your disposal?"

"I was uncertain how you stood with respect to Velázquez. Now, tell me. Do you accept my proposals?"

Medina paused to think. A mosquito buzzed along one wall of the tent.

"I don't know whether I accept," he said quietly to Cortés. "If I were to, however, two conditions would have to be met. Help me find and eliminate Martim Braga if he has fled to this Mexico, as the Tabascans claimed."

"Agreed. What else?"

"And fully pardon the chaplain's assistant, Pérez."

"I know a little about it, and it sounds like a trifling business. Done."

CHAPTER

V

Riding the sorrel gelding, Alvarado headed north. Twenty soldiers and eight horsemen accompanied him, along with Father Sánchez, his shoulders thrust back and his flaming, bearded chin jutting high in the air.

After moving along the shore for half a league, the party turned inland and followed a narrow, winding path through the jungle. With the offshore breezes choked off by the dense foliage, the horses quickly lathered up, their nostrils expanding as they sucked in the stagnant air. Around them moths fluttered densely through mottled shafts of sunlight.

Within the first half-hour, one of the men walking in advance of the horses unwittingly brushed past a hive hanging pendulously from a low tree branch. A squadron of huge, downy bees shot out and attacked him, his face swelling grotesquely in seconds.

They pressed on, having sent the stricken soldier back to camp.

Sánchez, riding directly behind Alvarado, wrinkled his vast nose at the reek of wet soil and rotting vegetation. Still, he felt good. Nothing appealed to him more than the challenge of a military patrol, where individual prowess and initiative replaced the more abstract strategies of the battlefield.

Shortly after the bee onslaught, they encountered some Indians on their way to the Spanish camp to barter. Wary of the horses, most of the Indians vanished into the safety of the jungle. A few, however, gamely held their ground at the side of the trail as the patrol approached in single file. They watched, fascinated.

Soon the trail widened perceptibly and ceased to meander. It ran straight through a series of garden patches and past rows of thatched huts, terminating at a squat, masonry temple. A roughly pyramidal structure with a flat top, it occupied the geographic center of the village. A set of steps—cracked and sprouting shoots of vegetation here and there—led to the summit and down the other side where the trail resumed, leading past more huts, more gardens, and back into the jungle.

As the Spaniards entered, the villagers scurried about. The women disappeared with their daughters into the huts, and only a few old men and boys lingered near the temple, curious rather than defiant.

Alvarado and Sánchez rode to the temple-pyramid and halted. Glancing about, Alvarado pointed to a pile of bones lying nearby, mostly human skulls and thighs. Several dozen skulls had been mounted at the ends of short sticks stuck in the ground. Unafraid, an old man, apparently a priest, stood rigidly near the bones. His tunic was ripped and dirty, and in his hand he clutched the crumpled body of a dead parrot.

"Just what I expected," grunted Sánchez contemptuously. "I told you they were beasts."

Pulling his crucifix from his sash, he raised it aloft, and uttered a brief prayer of exorcism.

"May the good Christ help us rid the earth of such foul Satanic creatures," he concluded, his knuckles blanching as he squeezed the crucifix and pointed it threateningly at the unblinking Indian priest.

Alvarado watched with satisfaction, relieved that Sánchez rode as his chaplain rather than Olmedo or any of
the other priests he had known in the past year. They
always sided with the natives, he recalled bitterly. Sánchez
appreciated that enemies, no matter how weak or helpless,
deserved to be crushed, not coddled. As for the present,
he reflected, he would gladly sack this piddling village,
burn it to the ground, and permit Sánchez to do whatever
he cared to do with the wretched old pagan witch. That
might prove amusing. Only the order from Cortés that
morning to refrain from unprovoked attack or plundering
prevented it, he told himself; plus his guess that little of
value, monetary or sexual, was to be found in the village
anyway.

"Leave it be," he said gently to Sánchez. "As you say,
they're nothing but animals."

Taking a deep breath, Sánchez replaced his crucifix.
Alvarado gave the signal and the patrol resumed its
march, moving slowly around the temple and through the
far side of the village. The old Indian priest absently
plucked feathers from the parrot as the Spaniards rode
away. He imagined himself atop the temple, waiting as the
men of the village led the red, furry one up the steps.

For the rest of the day, the patrol traveled in and out of
jungle, gradually shifting its direction northward. They
crossed numerous streams and rivers, and occasionally
caught glimpses of a snow-capped mountain looming
distantly in the west. Surprised at the large number of trails
crisscrossing the path they followed, Alvarado observed
that the larger and most worn of them lay along an east-
west path.

"Straight west and over the mountains we'll find old

Moctezuma and all his gold," he cheerfully told Sánchez during one of their frequent pauses.

The priest nodded without commenting. Unused to riding, his hips and back now ached miserably. Moreover, talk of marching on the Aztecs annoyed him, even when it came from this likable fool, Alvarado. Loyal to Governor Velázquez, Sánchez regarded such talk as treasonous, though he carefully concealed his reaction from the impetuous young officer with whom he rode.

The patrol passed through several more villages, each poorer than the first and similarly clustered around a central temple. Hunger and the tropical heat having added to his misery, Sánchez no longer bothered purifying the temples by waving his crucifix.

In what appeared to be the last village they would journey through before reaching camp, the Spaniards reined in their horses in front of a crudely built wooden cage sitting close to the temple. A lone Indian sat squatting on his haunches inside it.

"Release that man," ordered Alvarado, knowing the Indian was destined for sacrifice. While he felt nothing akin to Christian love for the prisoner, Alvarado took pleasure in upsetting pagan applecarts whenever he could.

Several of the soldiers quickly hacked open the door of the cage, and motioned the Indian out. As in the other villages, a handful of Indians gathered, though they kept their distance from the Spaniards, not daring to interfere.

The prisoner didn't budge.

"Prod him," snapped Alvarado.

One of the soldiers stepped into the cage. Taking hold of the prisoner's arm, he tried to raise him to his feet. With a snarl, the prisoner wrenched free, and sprang to the farthest corner of the cage, facing the Spaniard in a low, defensive crouch.

"He doesn't want to get out," said the soldier, shrugging.

"God help the coward," screamed Sánchez suddenly, coming out of his stupor with the energy of a thunderstorm. Leaping from his saddle, he strode toward the cage with hunched shoulders and clenched fists. The soldier scrambled quickly out of the way.

Stooping, Sánchez entered the cage, grabbed the Indian by the throat, and dragged him roughly out.

"When Christians mean to save your wretched life, they mean to save it, you sotted vermin," raged the priest. "Now get up and run, damn you. Run!"

With powerful pushes, Sánchez propelled the Indian toward the surrounding jungle. After having twice been sent sprawling, the Indian finally broke into a trot and disappeared down a small footpath.

"Run, you cur, run," shouted Sánchez after him.

The villagers murmured to one another, and the members of the patrol watched in silence as the priest, muttering to himself, walked stiffly back to his horse.

"They don't even care for their own lives," he announced to no one in particular.

Without a word, Alvarado spurred his mount, and the Spaniards filed out of the village, the banner of Saint James, Santiago—patron saint of the expedition—raised once again by the weary guidon bearer.

Within minutes of their departure, the prisoner walked resolutely back through the village. The fierce, red stranger almost cheated him of a dignified death, he told himself; one he'd prepared for all his life. The shame of having been forced to flee sent a shiver down his back.

*　*　*

It was nearly nightfall before the patrol reached the outlying sentries and entered the Spanish camp. Cooking fires lit up pockets of the shore, and the smell of roasted fish eddied over the dunes.

Leaving the horses in the stable area, Alvarado headed toward Cortés' tent with Sánchez to report on the day's patrol.

Skirting one of the fires, Sánchez noticed a few Indians lounging around it.

"What are *they* doing here?" he asked disagreeably.

"Watching the way civilized people eat," replied Alvarado, glancing absently toward the fire.

Sánchez stopped suddenly.

"Alvarado," he whispered in astonishment. "Do you see that?"

Alvarado paused, his attention drawn to a figure standing near the fire with his arm around one of the Indians.

It was José, bargaining for a gold amulet.

"He's alive, is he?" observed Alvarado sardonically.

Without answering, Sánchez approached the fire to make certain his eyes hadn't deceived him.

When he saw the priest, José withdrew his arm.

"Good evening, Father," he said brightly. "Happy Easter's Eve!"

The priest stared for a moment without replying. Then, abruptly he turned on his heel and rejoined the waiting Alvarado. "We have a gifted, devilish cheater among us," he said simply.

While Alvarado completed his report, Sánchez sat beside him fidgeting, still perturbed. Also, he had seen

Marina, the Aztec interpreter, slip out of the sleeping section of the tent a few minutes before Cortés himself emerged from it. Truly, sin and treachery had infested every quarter of the expedition, he thought darkly. Even the expedition commander indulged in miscegenation.

"Excellent," responded Cortés. "Then the horses should experience no difficulty moving west."

"Nor the cannon," added Alvarado, "though the mountains may be a bit rugged."

"We'll need more manpower," said Cortés, the logistics of a major campaign stimulating every cell in his brain. "And we'll get it from the local Indians," he went on eagerly.

Sánchez could contain himself no longer. "The expedition is clearly not authorized by Governor Velázquez to move inland," he intruded dryly.

Cortés stopped pacing and looked hard at the priest.

"Nonsense," Alvarado intervened. Though he liked Sánchez, he bristled at the thought of being curbed by anyone, particularly by an absentee authority like Velázquez, whom he regarded as a coward.

"Of course, you're right," said Cortés to the priest after a long pause. Unlike Alvarado, who trusted Sánchez and naively assumed his comment to be cautionary, even academic, Cortés saw it otherwise. He had hoped to forestall a while longer the political confrontation he knew would inevitably arise within the ranks when word of his resolve to keep the expedition in Mexico was made public. Now it was too late. He chided himself for speaking so openly about a possible march inland.

"You will have to forgive the enthusiasms that possess us occasionally, Father," said Cortés ingratiatingly. "I have every intention of proceeding only within the good graces of our Governor."

Alvarado looked quizzically at his chief, but decided to hold his tongue.

"We shall see," said Sánchez, knowing perfectly well that Cortés meant not a word of it. Having raised the issue, however, he now backed off, wanting to consult first with others on the expedition loyal to Velázquez. "Another question I wish to bring up involves discipline," he said, getting to his feet.

"Discipline?"

"Yes. A flagrant violation of a standing order requires swift retribution. And when that retribution is thwarted, the violation is compounded and justice cheated."

"What on earth are you talking about?" asked Cortés, genuinely perplexed.

"He's talking about Father Olmedo's assistant," interjected Alvarado in an aggrieved tone, "the one I ordered drowned. Somehow, he managed to survive, expressly contrary to my orders."

"Ah, yes. José Pérez," said Cortés, relaxing. "I understand you yourself were not present at the execution," he added, a faint smile playing on his lips.

"It was hardly necessary," retorted Alvarado, peevishly.

"But you are quite wrong, my friend," said Cortés. "The royal code of arms requires the presence of a military officer at all military executions."

"*I* was certainly present," said Sánchez.

"You are a *former* officer, Father, which hardly qualifies."

"Then we shall simply reexecute the scoundrel," said Alvarado triumphantly.

Cortés shook his head. "I'm afraid that won't be possible."

"So we come to the heart of the matter," said Sánchez. "Am I to understand you have pardoned that would-be fornicator?"

"You are," replied Cortés, growing irritated with the priest's officiousness.

"Do I dare inquire the reason?" pursued Sánchez, his voice heavy with sarcasm.

His first impulse was to order the priest to leave. After reflecting, however, Cortés decided to mollify him instead. It was not the time to bring matters to a head.

"We need every possible man, Father," he answered, "even to keep our garrison secure. As an old military commander, you can appreciate that. In addition, Don Marcos de Medina, whom we are privileged to number among us, interceded on José's behalf. I am in the habit of honoring requests that come from the nobles and officers of this expedition, provided they are reasonable. Since Don Marcos rescued the man in all innocence, and the execution proceeded in such precipitous haste, I therefore chose, as commander-in-chief, to grant the pardon. Had I known the subject troubled you so deeply—and you too, Alvarado—I would not have acted as I did. But it is done, and irreversible."

By emphasizing his rank, Cortés effectively squelched further discussion. As commander-in-chief, he had decided. Period. Sánchez wrinkled his brow, his mind now racing.

"And now, gentlemen, excuse me. Tomorrow is Easter and it will be a busy day," announced Cortés. "I have received word that we will be visited by an Aztec delegation."

When they left the tent, neither Alvarado nor Sánchez thought about the impending visit of the Aztecs.

Though piqued that an order of his had been countermanded, Alvarado admired Cortés too much to resent it. Instead, his hatred settled petulantly on José and Medina. He would deal with both in good time, he promised himself. That was the only way to save face.

Eager for supper, he struck out toward the beach area where his men were bivouacked.

Sánchez, too, left the tent resolved to square accounts with José and Medina. But his mind, unlike Alvarado's, rambled down larger avenues. To be sure, José Pérez was nothing but an insect to be trampled on with scarcely a thought. But that Medina was something else again. Why did Cortés refer to him with such apparent deference? And why did Cortés risk alienating Pedro de Alvarado, his top lieutenant, by granting the pardon? Because he, Cortés, was currying Medina's favor? What could the Captain-General hope to gain by it?

Suddenly it struck him. The Crown! Cortés had few options. Either submit to the authority of Velázquez or outflank the Governor by going directly to the King. That the first option grated on Cortés was common knowledge. And he himself knew with certainty that Cortés had decided to stay in Mexico. That left only the Crown. Cortés intended to use Medina in influencing Bishop Fonseca and the court.

Ignoring the hunger pangs and the soreness of his body, Sánchez decided to seek out at once his fellow priest, Juan Díaz, also unshakably loyal to Velázquez. The time had come to act and cut Cortés down to size. And the way to do it—apart from, perhaps even in addition to seizing the ships outright and sailing back to Cuba—was to deprive Cortés of his trump card, Marcos de Medina.

"*Don* Marcos, that is," he corrected himself aloud as he marched decisively toward the group of tents where Díaz was quartered.

The moment the Aztec delegation appeared the following morning, the Spaniards realized they were no longer dealing with poor, isolated villagers. The inferences they had drawn from the high artistic level of Aztec goldwork, from the stories Marina related of the Mexican capital, and from information gathered by Alvarado's patrol, all held up; these were emissaries from a tightly organized and self-confident society. Condescension, the favored Spanish modus operandi, flew temporarily out the window.

The impression created by the Aztecs came partially from their clothing and grooming. They wore neat, white tunics emblazoned with featherwork and various pieces of jewelry. Coal-black, each head of hair had been combed and arranged with obvious care, every one in a distinctive style. Most of the Spanish soldiers, and even a few officers, felt dirty and grimy compared to the spotless Aztecs.

The impression also came from their bearing. Teuhtlilli, the local Aztec governor who headed the delegation, entered the camp like a European king: proud, self-contained, and unhurried. His manner left no room for doubt that he expected to be entertained, fed, and conferred with at the highest level.

Cortés obliged with pleasure. Before a word was exchanged, he ushered Teuhtlilli and his attendants to a natural amphitheater formed by a ring of sand dunes. As soon as they were seated, Father Olmedo began singing

Easter Mass. Listening impassively, the Aztecs gazed now and then at the huge wooden cross erected on the highest dune.

Following Mass, Cortés took Teuhtlilli and a few of his attendants to his tent where, in the company of Cortés' most loyal officers, an expansive luncheon was served, replete with red wine and a variety of Spanish confections. Awkward smiles and numerous little head bows passed between Cortés and the Aztec governor during the meal as they sized each other up.

At length, the tables cleared, Aguilar and Marina entered, and the conference began in earnest. Cortés explained, as he had to the Indians who boarded his ship shortly after it anchored in the harbor, that he was the subject of a great king who lived across the sea. Recognizing that Moctezuma was also a great king, the Spanish monarch desired to communicate with him, and had therefore sent Cortés as his envoy.

"I have a message," said Cortés. Then, more bluntly: "Exactly when and where will it be possible for me to meet in person with the great Moctezuma so that I might deliver it?"

Teuhtlilli yawned after Marina finished conveying the question. The wine and the slow translating process made him sleepy. Had he heard correctly? He asked Marina to repeat the question, for he had detected in its gist a certain audacity.

As Marina complied, one of the Aztecs stood and moved toward Cortés. Stopping a few feet short, he studied the face of the Spanish commander for a moment. Then, pulling from his shoulder bag several sheafs of a paperlike material, a brush, and a small pottery vial, he sat down and began sketching a likeness of Cortés.

The question came back unaltered. It was true. The Spaniards had only just arrived, and already they insisted on meeting with Moctezuma. Teuhtlilli raised his eyebrows as a haughty look came over his face.

"It is not possible," he replied coldly. "Moctezuma is a very great king, a god; only *he* can initiate meetings."

"But will you ask him?" pressed Cortés. "Surely he knows we are here?"

All of the empire knows you are here, thought Teuhtlilli. And Moctezuma can't sleep, he is so anxious to hear news of you and look at your portrait.

With feigned reluctance, Teuhtlilli finally agreed to send word to the capital, to Tenochtitlan, that Cortés wanted a meeting.

"A reply will come shortly," he promised, "though I hope Moctezuma is not angered by the forwardness of the request."

Later that afternoon, the Aztecs withdrew, taking with them an assortment of gifts for Moctezuma, including an ornately carved armchair. They left behind enough gold to make the camp buzz with avaricious excitement. Even some of the followers of Velázquez began to have second thoughts about supporting an immediate return to Cuba.

Satisfied by his meeting with the Aztecs, Cortés turned his attention to consolidating the strength of his own command among the Spaniards. He took in the effect of the gold as fresh reports reached him that Sánchez and Díaz had started conducting secret meetings with other partisans of the Governor of Cuba.

Within a week Cortés made his move, catching the conspirators off guard. One morning he announced his resignation as Captain-General, an act that not only effectively dissolved the expedition as a quasi-military entity, but also removed the authority technically exercised over it by Governor Velázquez. Within the hour, the civil machinery Cortés had secretly engineered beforehand swung swiftly into motion. By noon he had been duly elected Captain-General and Chief Justice of Spain's newest municipality, Villa Rica de Vera Cruz, "The Rich Town of the True Cross," as it was promptly named. Though merely a stretch of beach studded with dunes and make-shift tents, its incorporation and his election made Cortés answerable to its citizens and the King of Spain rather than to the Governor of Cuba. At least in theory. It only remained for Cortés to petition the King for a bona fide charter. And to support that petition he knew he could rely on the persuasiveness of Mexican gold as well as the good offices of Medina.

Confronted by a *fait accompli* and reacting bitterly, the leaders of the Velázquez faction soon denounced the civilian structure as a patent fraud.

"It's illegal," railed Sánchez to the rebels in a hastily called meeting. "Besides, it constitutes a transparent usurpation of the legitimate powers of Don Diego Velázquez, Governor of Cuba."

For a while that afternoon civil war threatened as the two sides showered each other with invective whenever they met.

Finally, Cortés had heard enough. His own arguments having failed to sway the rebels, he arrested them, invoking his freshly granted authority. Clapped in chains, they were ferried to the flagship, and placed in the hold where, as Cortés put it, they would have sufficient time to reconsider the wisdom of their position.

Yet Cortés had no intention of keeping them locked up. They were too substantial a force, and he couldn't proceed without them. Accordingly, through cajolery, gilt-edged promises, and, in some cases, outright bribery, he succeeded over the next few days in convincing his prisoners, to a man, to cast aside their support of Velázquez and commit themselves instead to helping him carve out an empire, in which they would share handsomely. If he harbored any doubts about their sincerity, he kept them to himself, particularly as a mood of reconciliation swept over the fledgling town once the rebels obtained their release.

The last rebel to come back ashore was Sánchez, rumpled and red-eyed after four sleepless nights. Alvarado greeted him expansively.

"Welcome back to the fold," he said with a grin.

"Thank you. I'm glad you're here, Alvarado. I've had some time to think."

"But apparently little time to sleep."

"Sleep is the brother of death, my friend."

"We've missed you on our patrols, good Father."

"Listen, Alvarado. Now that we are on the same side, I think there is some business we need to attend to."

"The quality of expedition food?"

"The chaplain's assistant and his high-born friend."

"I've thought of that myself. What do you propose?"

The two men walked side by side along the beach. When they parted, they knew they would be satisfied soon.

* * *

After selecting a piece of land a few miles north with a more defendable topography, the Spaniards woke up one morning and said goodbye to the hot, flea-infested sand dunes that had been their home for more than a month. With four hundred Indians helping, they packed their bags, struck their tents, and moved Villa Rica de Vera Cruz up the coast. The ships preceded them with the heavy cannons.

On reaching the new site, all hands fell to work constructing the rudiments of a proper town: a fort, a granary, an administration building, a church, and, on the outskirts, a gallows large enough to accommodate three felons at a time. Again, the Indians helped, providing stone, lime, timber, and sun-dried bricks in addition to their labor.

Cortés, for the present, had every reason to feel smug. The town rose rapidly, the struggle with the Velázquez faction seemed safely behind him, and the new community had agreed to pool the gold already collected, and permit him to forward it to Spain, along with his petition, to make a strong impression on the King.

The "petition"—actually a long letter—took shape slowly even though Cortés spent a minimum of an hour each evening writing. In it he recounted not only his difficulties with Velázquez but also every significant event that had occurred to the expedition since leaving Cuba, including the founding of Vera Cruz, which he presented as the culmination of spontaneous pressures originating from within the ranks. He planned to conclude by asking both for confirmation of the town's status, and his authority as its chief executive, as well as for permission to proceed with colonizing the country on whose threshold he now felt himself firmly planted.

"When I finish," he told Medina one morning, "I would like you to read it, and give me your legal opinion of its composition."

The two men had come to terms, Cortés even agreeing to help Medina to find Braga on the return voyage of the expedition past Yucatan if they failed to locate him in Mexico. Medina, for his part, agreed to serve as a backup Spanish-Mayan interpreter with Marina in case Aguilar became unavailable. Now the letter was the thing, and Medina promised a pleased Cortés he would support it.

By this time two more Aztec delegations had come and gone. Though each brought with it lavish gifts of gold, fabrics, and featherwork, the messages they bore from Moctezuma were all negative, politely suggesting that the Spaniards go back home.

Having assumed the interior of the country to be solely inhabited by Aztecs, or Mexica, Cortés was therefore astonished to see five new visitors, distinct from the Aztecs in dress and manner. Bright blue lapidary hung from their ears and nostrils, and finely wrought gold pendents were fastened to their underlips.

"What have we here?" he asked Medina rhetorically.

With his help and that of Marina, he quickly discovered them to be Totonacs. A recent defeat had put them under the domination of the Aztecs, a condition they found demeaning and oppressive. Though none of the five acknowledged it, they had come to the Spanish camp to explore the possibility of securing an ally.

Cortés could smell as much. He could barely conceal his elation. Here at last was the wedge he sought. Far from a homogeneous, united power, the Aztecs were evidently vulnerable from within.

"Are there," he asked shrewdly, "other peoples or nations also discontented with Aztec rule?"

"The Tlaxcalans," came the reply, "though these, like the Aztecs, are a deceitful, arrogant, warlike race."

God in Heaven, thought Medina; provincial jealousies. It's like Italy with all its contending duchies and petty kingdoms.

Overjoyed, Cortés arranged at once to visit the chief of the Totonacs in their capital, Cempoala, not far distant.

A few days later, he marched to the town in force, and soon confirmed what the five Indians had told him. The Totonacs feared and resented the Aztecs, not only for the excessive tribute exacted by them, but also because the Totonacs were required periodically to provide their conquerors with large numbers of young men to be sacrificial victims, and young girls to be slaves.

Dire though the Totonac complaints sounded about relinquishing their sons and daughters, the Spaniards felt little sympathy. They had all noticed that the sacrificial pyramid in Cempoala itself bore evidence of heavy use. Foul-smelling dried blood caked the central staircase and the temple on top of the pyramid. Piles of hundreds of human skulls lay stacked near its base.

Suppressing his revulsion, Cortés concentrated instead on gauging the extent of Totonac resources. The town, he judged, contained about thirty thousand people.

"We have thirty such towns," the chief explained to Marina. And, when asked how many warriors he could muster in the event of war, he replied proudly, "One hundred thousand."

One hundred thousand!

Cortés ran his tongue around his teeth as he envisioned a vast army under his command marching irresistibly westward toward the Aztec capital, Tenochtitlan.

Too good to be true, he thought, looking hard at the Cempoalan chief. Tall and corpulent, the man wheezed even while seated. Alternating rings of gold and fat encircled his thick, bullish neck, and his pudgy fingers played idly with the labret dangling from his underlip. Did he exaggerate the number? Probably, thought Cortés. Still, even half that amount represented an undreamed of enlargement of the Spanish forces.

Cortés suddenly broke into a broad smile.

"Tell him," he said to Marina, "that together we shall throw off the yoke of the Aztecs."

The Cempoalan chief gurgled with pleasure when he heard the words. Yet he failed to commit himself, postponing further discussion. It was obvious to Cortés that the Totonac was weighing his own options, uncertain whether to defy the powerful Aztecs. Though he showered the Spaniards with gifts, and ordered four hundred of his men to assist in moving their base up the coast, he still equivocated when it came time for Cortés to return to his garrison.

Not until a second visit a week later did Cortés succeed in obtaining a formal alliance, though he had to resort to a fancy piece of diplomatic skulduggery to get it.

A group of Aztec tax collectors made an appearance in a Totonac town where Cortés was meeting with the fat chief. Blatantly ignoring Cortés, the Aztecs roundly excoriated the Totonacs for aiding the Spanish, demanded that the practice cease at once, and announced that, as a penalty for disbursing the unauthorized help, the usual Totonac tax was forthwith doubled. In addition, twice as many candidates for sacrifice were to be drawn from among the Totonacs.

As they vented their wrath, the Aztecs strode disdainfully about, sneering at Spaniards and Totonacs alike.

Cortés bristled. When Marina conveyed to him, through Aguilar, what the Aztecs wanted, and why, he decided to intrude. Infuriated by the Aztec demands and the haughty manner in which they were made, Cortés at the same time sensed an opportunity to force the Totonacs to rebel.

He took the Totonac chief aside.

"Resist them," he ordered.

Shaken, the chief merely wheezed, shifting his gaze apprehensively from Cortés to Marina to the still strutting Aztecs.

"I order you to," insisted Cortés. "You are either my ally or my enemy."

"Very well," agreed the Totonac chief reluctantly.

With short, waddling strides, he walked to the temple courtyard where his warriors were gathered. He gave them the order.

Accustomed to deferential treatment and fawning behavior from all non-Aztecs, the tax collectors could scarcely believe what now befell them. Immediately they found themselves surrounded by Totonac warriors. Then, relishing their assignment, the warriors began systematically knocking Aztecs to the ground. After a few moments of verbal and physical abuse, they were picked up, lashed together, and forcefully pushed toward the courtyard.

The spectacle of the arrest threw the Totonac audience

into a state of near-panic. So brazen an affront to the dignity and authority of the Aztecs, they knew, guaranteed full-scale retaliation. Moreover, since the insult occurred in a Totonac town, the brunt of it would undoubtedly fall on their own heads rather than on the Spanish.

One of the women began wailing. Her cry, low and mournful, was shortly picked up by several others. Dazed, the Totonac men looked at each other ominously.

Cortés, meanwhile, sat down on his portable camp stool and waited. He already planned to release two of the Aztecs covertly, and inform them that the Totonac chief had instigated their arrest rather than himself. That way, he reasoned, Moctezuma would be less inclined to sever all communication with the Spaniards, leaving open the possibility that Cortés might still reach Tenochtitlan without overt hostilities, no matter if he had allies or not.

He didn't have long to wait. Within thirty minutes the Totonac chief waddled slowly toward him. Huge drops of perspiration slid down his globular cheeks, and his labret glinted in the sun.

He had made up his mind—or so he thought—to become an ally of the Spaniards. In reality, his obeying of Cortés' order had foreclosed any other choice.

Nor, as the Totonacs soon discovered, did an alliance with the Spaniards come cheap. For among the terms spelled out by Cortés was a requirement that the Cempoalans give up their gods, halt all forms of human sacrifice, and embrace the Christian faith.

Horrified, the Cempoalans refused. Perhaps life under Aztec rule was not so bad after all. If only they could somehow erase the blot made by the arrest of the Aztec officials. Possibly by rescuing them from the Spaniards?

Reading their mood, Cortés once again seized the initiative. He passed an order to his troops. Standing by in the temple courtyard, they prepared themselves for an all-out assault, brandishing their weapons.

The Cempoalans wavered, and finally capitulated. They would do what was required.

Immediately a small contingent of soldiers under the direction of Father Sánchez raced up the pyramid steps and toppled the two wooden Totonac idols standing in front of the temple on the summit. Crashing to the ground, their shattered remnants were promptly set ablaze.

As the Spaniards gathered around the glowing fire, Father Sánchez, still skeptical about the necessity of converting soulless heathens, suggested that Cempoalans—indeed, all Totonacs—be prohibited from wearing their characteristic facial jewelry.

"The custom revolts me," he exclaimed, "and probably revolts God, too."

Cortés said no.

For the rest of the afternoon, the Cempoalans scraped and scrubbed the grime and blood from the steps of the pyramid and afterward applied a fresh coat of stucco to the temple walls. Finally, Father Olmedo placed a small, garlanded plaster statue of the Madonna on the summit, solemnly blessed it, then returned to the courtyard below where he celebrated a special evening Mass for the benefit of the assembled Cempoalans. Before leaving the town the following morning, Cortés assigned an older Spaniard to stay behind and superintend the security and maintenance of the reconsecrated temple.

From Vera Cruz, Alvarado's patrols fanned out in ever

widening sweeps as they probed the surrounding country. Most of the villages they entered belonged to their new allies, the Totonacs, though a few proved to be independent—isolated little pockets too poor to interest the larger Mexican powers, and too weak to resist the patrols, whose members freely expropriated whatever they found, whether food, chattels, or women. Though Cortés forbade any form of looting, Alvarado pointedly looked the other way when it occurred. To his mind, a patrol, once it set out, became an autonomous entity, exempt from all social —and most military—rules of conduct. It became a movable tyranny, a kind of wandering storm, free to rage when and where it chose. Which is why he exulted in leading patrols, and why Sánchez took every opportunity to join him. Each man felt an unquenchable lust for the compact, freewheeling power patrols bestowed.

Though it took Alvarado a few minutes to recognize it, late in April he and Sánchez found what they had been searching for: a strong, unaffiliated, hostile village. Even before the Spaniards could approach it, sentinels loosed a flurry of arrows at the patrol vanguard, mortally wounding two Spanish soldiers.

"Mind your clothing, Sánchez," fumed Alvarado, launching into prebattle rhetoric. "For the vapors of savage blood will rise to the heavens in such volume as to saturate them. Tonight's rain will have a stench to it, I promise you."

"Hold off," cautioned Sánchez. "Don't be rash."

"Mind you, Father. I intend for us to ruin the place."

"No, wait," the priest urged. "You'd be a fool to try. You have no idea how fortified that village is. Besides, perhaps it will prove useful to us in another way."

Alvarado tried to restrain himself.

"In God's name, Sánchez," he said. "Those were two good men and deserve to be avenged."

"I know; I'm thinking of two others, far less good."

At last the priest's meaning penetrated—he had in mind a way of dealing with Medina and José. His anger seeping slowly away, Alvarado signaled the patrol to withdraw. Sánchez was right, he thought. Besides, no telling what lay in that village.

That night they bivouacked nearby, and buried the two soldiers, Sánchez reciting a brief requiem.

Through most of the next day, elements of the patrol attempted to scout the village from a distance, keeping well under cover, and avoiding another shower of arrows. Despite their probes, however, they learned little; only that the village sat on a low, level plateau, was protected by a palisade, and contained the typical pyramid topped by a temple.

"It's a small fortress," concluded Alvarado after the scouts reported back. "We won't be able to enter without a fight. But Cortés specifically ordered me not to get into a major engagement. What do you suggest, Sánchez?"

"I think it's time to bring Medina and Pérez out on patrol," the priest said. "Show them this village and acquaint them with its amenities."

Shortly after the patrol returned to Vera Cruz, Cortés received a request from Alvarado. At a table in the still incomplete administration house, Cortés sat planning the voyage that would carry his letter and the King's gold to Spain.

"I want to take more men on my patrols," said Alvarado without preliminaries.

"Sit down there on the cot, Alvarado," replied Cortés. "Just move the cloak aside."

"Too narrow a bed for two, it seems to me," Alvarado remarked salaciously, as he moved the cloak.

"You aren't two," riposted Cortés. "I find it adequate enough. Now, tell me. What about more men? I thought you preferred a small unit on reconnaissance."

"I do," came the reply. "But it seems to me it would be in our interests to familiarize as many of our men as possible with the country. Clearly, we are here to stay."

Cortés studied his lieutenant for a moment, then broke into a smile.

"You astound me, Alvarado. So impulsive one moment, so sensible the next. It's an excellent idea."

"Good. Then I'll begin at once."

"When will you leave?"

"In the morning. First light."

"Who are the extra men?"

Alvarado stiffened. He recalled Sánchez' words of that afternoon. "Whatever you do," the priest had coached, "don't tell him you want Medina and Pérez on the first patrol. Seek blanket approval."

"I'm not certain yet," he answered Cortés evasively.

"Then I have a suggestion. Take Don Marcos."

Alvarado blinked.

"Medina?" he stammered.

"He's restive and bored. I think he needs action."

"Anything you say," said Alvarado, now playing his little game.

"But with this proviso," Cortés went on. "I want him safe. Follow a reliable route. Do you know one?"

"Yes, the northwest."

"Totonac villages?"

"Mostly."

"Couldn't be better. He takes an interest in the language of the natives."

"His interest will be amply fueled," said Alvarado, getting up to leave. "That I can assure you."

Cortés rose and walked Alvarado to the door.

"You were right, my friend," he said, touching his lieutenant's shoulder.

"Right?"

"Yes. About our being here to stay. God has been good to us."

When Alvarado left the administration house, he swaggered more than usual. He already rehearsed mentally his next meeting with Cortés. It's a dangerous land, he would tell him, full of treachery and violence. We both should have known that. By the time he found Sánchez, the explanation to Cortés for Medina's disappearance was pat in his mind.

"Well?" said Sánchez.

"A tricky and difficult business. The Captain-General is no fool."

"What is the outcome?"

"Better than expected. I not only persuaded him of the extra men but convinced him Medina should be among them."

"You *told* him?" asked Sánchez incredulously.

"I thought it a more effective ploy than what you

suggested," said Alvarado, enjoying his lie. "He approved, of course."

"Well, no matter," said the priest. "The point is, a delicious prospect awaits us."

Finding José hard at work helping to put the final touches on the framework for the church, one of Alvarado's men curtly informed him that he and Medina had been assigned to patrol. Suddenly queasy, José flung down his rasp, and ran toward the waterfront, searching for Medina.

He found him near the shore sitting beneath a tree, engaged in language lessons with Marina and Aguilar.

"Patrol," he blurted out breathlessly. "We're scheduled to go on patrol."

"Calm down, José," said Medina. Excusing himself, he took José by the arm, and led him close to the water away from Marina and Aguilar.

"What are you talking about?" he asked quietly.

"I've just been told. We're to ride with Alvarado tomorrow morning," he replied, his face ashen. "He intends to murder me, Don Marcos, I know it."

"Nonsense," said Medina impatiently. "The pardon stands. You're immune." He looked out at the ships, reflecting. Cortés had acted more quickly than expected, he thought, recalling his own conversation with the Captain-General two days before in which he had argued for an opportunity to get away from Vera Cruz for a short period.

"Did Cortés authorize our part in this patrol?" he asked.

"That's what Alvarado's man said," replied José.

"Well, then, cheer up, José. If Cortés is responsible for

assigning us to patrol, then he means for us to return safely."

"What does *he* know?"

"More than you, I can promise," replied Medina. "Besides, I asked him for the chance to venture out."

"You're mad."

"And you're impudent," snapped Medina, offended by José's testy familiarity. "Go, get ready," he ordered brusquely.

"The deer-men have returned," uttered the sentinel, breathless from his sprint back to the village. Quickly the alarm spread, and the warriors of the village, armed with bows and arrows, clubs, and spears, posted themselves at their stations inside the palisade. At the same time, a small group of select warriors slipped out a hidden opening in the palisade and, like stalking jaguars, fanned out toward the east, the direction from which the approaching intruders had been sighted. Each man acted independently, and each disappeared into the forest at a different point.

"The gods are hungry, and they are thirsty," muttered a priest to an acolyte as he watched the last of the ten warriors scurry out of sight.

After arriving at this Aztec colony with his family, Atlacol, the hunter, had been accepted among the warriors of the council. Though not among those who attacked the deer-men the first time they rode near the village, he participated in planning a strategy for defense in the event the deer-men returned.

Now Atlacol wound his way stealthily through the forest, keeping well off the paths running through it. He headed directly toward the area where the sentinel had spotted the deer-men. They were seen traveling on the main trail that came from the sun-coast, a trail he already knew as well as the lines on the insides of his hands. Soon the deer-men would reach the shallow stream where he himself had set salamander traps only two days before. No, now was not the time to look after those traps, or after those he set for lizards on a flat rock slab along the trail outside the village.

He no longer dwelt on his traps, for now a different thing started gnawing at his mind as he neared the stream. The same number as before, the sentinel had reported. Perhaps one or two more. Why didn't the deer-men come back with more of their own kind? Surely the first time they came they must have learned how strong the village was. It puzzled him deeply. Why did they come back at all? What did they want?

Do not go quickly, he warned himself. Slowing, he tried to listen to the forest. The sounds that came to him told him nothing. All he heard were leaves rustling in the wind and the stream splashing over rocks. Reaching the water, he turned and moved warily downstream toward the trail-crossing. If they continue to come, these deer-men, they will come that way. Ha, they do not make good quarry, he laughed, for they do not hide but show themselves, as though daring those that might hunt them. If that is their way, he, Atlacol, would accept it. His eyes danced with expectation.

As he neared the crossing, he stopped abruptly. On the opposite side of the trail he saw Mazatl, another warrior. Ah, Mazatl, the older man thought, I recognized you to be as clever a hunter as myself when I first laid eyes on you in the village. They acknowledged each other without movement or sound. They thought alike. A moment later, the two warriors vanished from sight.

Alvarado rode into the stream and reined in, letting the thirsty animal beneath him drink its fill. The rest of the patrol followed his lead though some of the men, including José, dismounted, and walked upstream several paces to obtain water for themselves, leaving the horses on their own.

It had been a long, barren day. By design, Alvarado avoided taking the patrol into any villages whatever, a tactic he employed to frustrate Medina. Eager and filled with questions and observations shortly after the patrol set out that morning, Medina grew increasingly sullen as the hours passed with little or no distraction. He came to anticipate Alvarado's terse command when a village or town lay ahead: "We must bypass it. Too dangerous." The first few times Medina protested, for he was eager to view village life for himself. But Alvarado remained adamant, brushing aside Medina's protests with an air of sanctimoniousness.

"I am under rigid orders not to endanger your person or, of course, those of the rest of the patrol," he replied at one point when pushed by Medina.

"These are pagan territories," Sánchez chose to add, "and we must trust our experienced captain." He said it in the voice of a sycophant.

The horses drank as much as they could, snorting and shuddering.

"We shall pause here and then head back," announced

Alvarado, loudly enough to be heard by Medina. "I judge it redundant to visit the village ahead of us again."

"I must agree, Captain," Sánchez chimed in, "but what a pity. I found it a colorful place. Filled with disgusting Indians, to be sure, but colorful."

"What village?" asked Medina, suddenly roused.

"Oh, one not too far ahead," replied Alvarado casually. He returned his horse to the bank and dismounted, as did Sánchez and then Medina.

"López," called Alvarado to one of his officers, "take the rest of the patrol back along the trail to that large clearing we passed. Set up a bivouac and start a fire. My stomach complains of a vast emptiness."

López mustered the others, commanding them to remount.

"Hold it," cried Medina as López started back. "José, stay here," he ordered.

With a look of surprise, José wheeled his mount around, and faced the three men on the shore. Inclined to question the order but seeing Medina's face clouded and tense, he held his tongue instead, and slid obediently off his horse. Lashing its reins to a tree, he sauntered to the water's edge, picked up a handful of pebbles, and began pitching them across the stream toward a large boulder. On it his imagination emblazoned the ruddy features of Father Sánchez.

"Now tell me about that village," pursued Medina as López and the rest of the patrol rode away.

"A busy, jabbering place I would say," replied Alvarado, straining to describe a village he had never actually entered. "The usual temple, a marketplace, and, in my opinion, a large number of itinerants. Travelers of some sort. But the inhabitants seemed remarkably docile, didn't they, Father?"

"Yes, rather like soft clay," beamed Sánchez. "Malleable and stupid, that is."

"Are they hostile?"

"Is clay hostile?" grinned Alvarado.

"Then why don't we proceed?"

"Medina," sighed Alvarado wearily, "I have reconnoitered it once already, as I think I mentioned earlier. Besides, I find myself somewhat fatigued, and wish to return to Vera Cruz early tomorrow."

"Jesus save us!" exploded Medina. "We haven't seen anything today. Nothing but trees, vultures, and the tails of one another's horses. Good God, Alvarado! Do you call this a patrol?" His face flushed, he stalked off several paces, tugging hard at his vest.

Alvarado stole a glance at Sánchez, and the priest nodded approvingly.

"Calm yourself, Medina," said Alvarado. "Anger does not become you."

Medina turned sharply to face Alvarado again. "I want to know how far away that village is," he said flatly.

Alvarado studied him, his eyes narrowing.

"Perhaps a half-hour, at a walk."

"On this trail?"

"Yes."

"I am going."

"You may not, Medina."

"One moment, Captain," interrupted Sánchez, as though on cue. "Perhaps it will do no harm for him to see that village. If I were you, I would consider it. After all, he is right. It has been a gruelingly uneventful day."

Medina said nothing, but continued to glower, his hands on his hips.

Crack!

For the first time, José hit the target. His missile shattered into numerous pieces.

"Very well, Father," answered Alvarado after a thoughtful pause, "but you are my witness. Should anything befall this restless man you must testify that I expressly forbade his venture."

Sánchez looked toward Medina.

"It is still against my better judgment," waffled Alvarado. "But go."

"Thank you for your gracious permission, Captain." Icy sarcasm edged Medina's voice. "José, come here," he called.

Alvarado folded his arms, unfolded them, then began stroking his beard with his right hand.

"You may go, but without horses," he said slowly.

Medina looked up toward the sky. Is it possible that what looks like a man is actually nothing more than the ass of a horse in disguise? He shook his head in disbelief.

"It would not have occurred to me to proceed otherwise," he then told Alvarado, not wishing to give the captain the satisfaction of hearing an objection. "Of course you will see to it that our horses are fed and tethered, won't you?" he added, addressing the captain as he would a stableboy.

Alvarado bristled.

"I will see to them," Sánchez intervened. Suddenly anxious to be under way, the priest moved toward the horses.

Mollified, Alvarado sought once again to have the transaction notarized so he could justify himself when reporting to Cortés. "Mark it clearly in your mind, Father. He acts on his own, against my counsel. *That* you must warrant."

"Yes, I warrant that," replied the priest as he mounted. "Come, Captain, let us return to the clearing. I wish to tend to the spiritual needs of the men." Then he turned in his saddle toward Medina.

"As for you, Don Marcos, enjoy your walk. It is a fascinating village. You will take to it, and learn much." He rubbed his tongue around his teeth as he smiled.

"I trust so," replied Medina curtly.

After mounting, Alvarado raised a gloved hand in a half-salute. "Fair warning. You are on your own. We intend to depart early morning. Please do not cause us an inconvenience."

He spurred his horse and, at full gallop, raced down the trail. Sánchez followed, more slowly, leading the two riderless horses.

Medina watched them go, and then turned and waded into the stream. José followed him across. In a few minutes they were several hundred yards along the trail into the forest. At that moment Medina heard a grunt behind him. Wheeling around, he saw a dark form on top of José, raising a club. As Medina reached for his sword, he saw the club descending onto José's neck. Medina heard a sickening slap, but that was all, for at that instant a thunderous weight hit him from behind. His mind entered a pitch-black tunnel.

When Medina came to, he had trouble focusing his eyes. He tried to prop himself up on his elbows, but found that his wrists were tied behind his back. What had happened? Where was he? He tried to clear his head. Helping hands assisted him to his feet. A gourd cup filled with water was being put to his lips. He swallowed deeply. His eyes started to clear. In front of him was a feathered warrior, his brown skin decorated with paint, holding a large wooden war club. There was no one else around. He smiled at Medina.

"My son," Atlacol said in Nahuatl, "we are going home."

CHAPTER

VI

Shortly after dawn Atlacol and his prisoner, Medina, reached the dry moat surrounding the village. Atlacol let out a high-pitched screech to alert the sentries, and wearily pulled on the rope to bring Medina into the broad ditch. He led his captive in a zigzag pattern along the bottom of the moat, knowing just where to turn to avoid the concealed pits of sharpened stakes.

"I come," Atlacol called up to the palisade. "I come with food for the gods."

Above him, unseen hands removed two upright timbers, and silently lowered a long log notched with steps. Atlacol shoved his prisoner ahead of him toward the ladder. Medina drew himself erect, and mounted the steps with dignity. Atlacol followed.

Within a few minutes they reached the center of the village where the small temple-pyramid rose above the bare plaza. Somehow word had already reached the priests, who were lined up in a row in front of the temple steps. One of them, dressed in a jaguar skin over his black-cowled cape and holding a staff in his right hand, stood in front of the rest. Atlacol led his prisoner forward to face the priest. Atlacol touched his right hand to the ground in front of the priest, raised it to his mouth and kissed it.

"I bring a deer-man as sustenance for our Lord Huitzilopochtli. I bring sustenance for the Lord of the Far and the Near, of the High and the Low. I bring sustenance for the gods, for the Powerful Ones," Atlacol said.

"I offer this, my son, to the war god, Lord Huitzilo-pochtli," he added, nodding toward the prisoner.

The priest bowed his head slightly. "Brother, the offer-ing is good, the offering is deserved, the offering shall be made. The gods will smile."

With this, the priest motioned, and two of the men behind him stepped forward to the sides of the captive. Cutting the prisoner's wrist-bindings, they marched him off between them to a long wooden cage at the side of the pyramid. The two priests removed several of the planks from the top of the cage. They climbed with the prisoner up the crossbars, and dropped him down into the en-closure. The priests replaced the planks and stepped up onto the rear of the cage roof where a large boulder sat. With some effort they managed to roll it into position over the planks, locking the prisoner in.

"Brother," the priest addressed Atlacol, "I will send word to your house when the time of the offering is set." He smiled. "You have done well, bringing us a deer-man. Did you do the deed alone? Or was there someone to help you?"

"No," replied Atlacol. "I had no help but that of the gods, they who are behind everything."

"Then, brother, in accordance with the holy rules you will receive three limbs. As you know, the fourth must go, smoked, to the capital, to the Lord Moctezuma. The hands and feet, and the inner part of the head, are the property of the temple."

"Yes, brother, I understand. I am thankful. My wife and daughters are thankful. I shall give a feast."

"It is good. Now go home and rest. I will send you word of the time of sacrifice."

Atlacol began walking toward his house. Around the plaza he saw his neighbors, all the villagers, gathered. He could see that they were watching the prisoner in the cage. As he passed from the plaza into a narrow street, the people bent down, touched the ground, bowing in his direction. Atlacol felt good.

"We will eat, brothers. We will eat, sisters. And the gods will eat," he said to them.

As he passed down the street of wattle-and-daub huts, his pace quickened. He wished that he could be giving the meat to his family right now. But they would have to wait until after the sacrifice. At least, he reassured himself, he had two lizards hanging at his belt. The traps had done their work and he was able to retrieve the lizards on his way back to the village with his prisoner. What a bountiful day! He turned into a doorway, pulling the homespun cotton curtain aside, and called into the room.

"I come," he announced.

"Sit down, husband," came the reply from a dark recess of the room. Atlacol sat on the wooden log lying by the door, and let his eyes adjust to the darkness of the smoky room.

He wanted to tell his wife of his great luck. But etiquette prescribed that he allow her to welcome him first with a gesture of homecoming.

She came from the darkness with a bowl. He nodded. She gave him the bowl, and then turned sideways so that he could drink in respected privacy. Atlacol poured a few drops of the bowl's contents onto the earth floor to thank the gods for his safe return. He drank heavily of the thin gruel of crushed maize and water. When he had drained the bowl, his wife disappeared back into the darkness with the vessel and soon returned with it refilled. Atlacol was pleased to see his wife smiling down at him. Although she was tired and weak from hunger, she was still young and beautiful, he thought, her long black hair hanging down below her shoulders. This time he drank more slowly.

"Enough, enough, wife," he said. She took the bowl and returned it to the far corner.

A small girl ran in through the doorway and embraced him around the neck. He sat her down on his knee.

"I have news, little one. I have brought a present for the gods. I have brought meat."

"Husband," his wife said from the corner of the room, "the gift for us is your safe arrival." Then she laughed. "And besides, I see you have two lizards for us. I would welcome a lame hunchback if he brought those!"

Atlacol roared with laughter. "You wretched woman! You love your husband only for his lizards." He pulled them from his belt and dropped them on the floor. She smiled, picked them up, and returned bearing a reed mat which she rolled out beside the small fire.

"Here, husband, rest. You will have food soon."

Atlacol laughed and patted his daughter on the head. He heard the baby babble from the corner. It was good, he thought, to have a family. The gods were truly favoring them.

In the morning Atlacol went to the plaza. He checked on Medina in his cage to see if he was well, bringing a large bowl of boiled hominy to fatten him. When Atlacol passed the bowl through the bars, the Spaniard looked up quietly into Atlacol's eyes without emotion. After Atlacol turned his back and went off toward the priests' house, Medina slowly reached into the bowl and began to eat.

Atlacol called into the door of the priests' building. In a few minutes the chief priest appeared. With him was a corpulent, middle-aged man, heavy-jowled, who walked, almost waddling, slowly toward Atlacol. He smiled and said, "Greetings, husband of my cousin."

"Greetings, *pochteca* Tezcatl. I hope you had a safe journey. I hope that you will honor our house with a visit."

"And your wife? My cousin?"

"She is well."

"Ho! Good. And how goes it for you in this new colony? Is life better for you down here in the eastern forest?"

"Trader, there is more game down here than in our old village in the high country. The Lord Moctezuma was wise to send us here, although our crops do not yet do well. And I have captured a deer-man. He is in that cage."

"The priest has just told me. Let me see."

Tezcatl, the priest, and Atlacol went over to the cage. Tezcatl studied the prisoner and turned to Atlacol. "You have here a great prize."

The announcement caused a ripple of murmurs among the villagers standing nearby. The village was small by Aztec standards, and important visitors like Tezcatl seldom came. But now they were doubly honored, for not only had Tezcatl graced them with his presence, but one of their own, Atlacol, had excelled. They all basked in his glory.

"Then it is fit you are here, trader," said Atlacol modestly. "The priests are even now preparing themselves.

I am privileged to be able to invite you to feast with me," he went on with deep formality. "You and also the other *pochtecas*," he added, referring to Tezcatl's traveling companions, who had stayed a small distance away in their overnight encampment. Tezcatl had ordered them to remain there with his prisoners, to avoid bringing all their treasures into the village. He wanted to keep the riches of his expedition away from the prying eyes of poor people.

He ran his hand along the edge of his tunic, as though to call attention to it. He knew the villagers rarely saw a fabric so rich.

"No, Atlacol," he said, "there shall be no feast." He enjoyed the finality of his words, and closed his eyes indolently, turning his face toward the sun.

"I do not grasp your meaning," said Atlacol, perplexed by Tezcatl's imperious statement.

Tezcatl did not answer at once, turning his cousin's husband's suddenly bright prospects over in his mind.

"Atlacol, listen to me," he said, rising from the log bench. "We shall take your prisoner to Tenochtitlan. There shall be no feast, at least not now, not here. Your captive is worth more to you there. You will be amply rewarded."

"You honor me, trader, to suggest these things."

"But," the priest interrupted, "the prisoner is consecrated for sacrifice. For tomorrow."

"Don't worry about that," said Tezcatl. "I have brought a cargo of fine dogs with me. You shall have six fat ones for a sacrifice. They are plump, hairless, and good. And besides, you would not want to offend our Great Lord Moctezuma by depriving him of this special sacrifice on the Great Pyramid of Tenochtitlan, would you?"

"Of course not, esteemed trader," the priest said hastily. "The arrangement would be a proper one."

"Then it is settled," said Tezcatl. "Atlacol and his prisoner can join me and my fellow *pochtecas* camped outside your village. They are holding other prisoners to go to the capital, too.

"And now," he said, turning to the priest, "I think that I'd best get on with my business here, buying children." He nodded toward Atlacol. "This is my way of helping, you see. Poor children will go to good homes in the city and then, when times are better, I will help their parents redeem them. This is my path of helping."

Atlacol did not answer, but he knew that parents rarely saw their children again once they had sold them to a passing *pochteca*. He was aware that many of the smallest ones, the three- and four-year-olds, would end up not in fine homes, but as offerings to Tlaloc, the rain god.

"Very good, my wife's cousin," Atlacol said, "I await your instructions for the departure. I will prepare myself."

Later in the day Tezcatl bought eight children from impoverished mothers and fathers. The peasants brought their children, one by one, in through the doorway into Tezcatl's chamber. There he had them sit and welcomed them with bowls of pulque. When the proper interval had passed of pulque-drinking and a small amount of idle conversation, Tezcatl declared, "Ah, what a nice child you have there. What a nice daughter! She would be most happy in a noble household in the capital city. At least for a little visit. She will eat well there. Allow me to borrow her."

"It would be an honor to lend our daughter to a family

of High Ones. But we will miss her help in the house and garden. She is a good worker. It will be hard to do without her help."

"Oh," Tezcatl replied, "that can be easily handled. Just loan her to me, and I will give you a large sack of maize, a sack of beans, and even some salt from the sea."

Then the father of the child slowly rose up and led her over to Tezcatl, who sent the child to the rear of the room. For the rest of the day Tezcatl's business proceeded similarly. The parents would leave silently without looking back, carrying the food over their shoulders. Once outside, sometimes the mothers would cry as they took the food home.

In the morning, Atlacol arose early. His wife had fixed him tortillas and hominy to take on his journey. At the plaza he met Tezcatl. Atlacol's prisoner was now let out of the cage, and four of Tezcatl's men-at-arms took him under their supervision. They placed a wooden yoke on his neck, and tied a rope to it. He walked erect, with dignity, as they led him away. Two more guards herded the eight children before them.

As they left the plaza, Atlacol looked back and saw his wife in a distant corner, holding their baby, and with their daughter by her side. She nodded, and he nodded back. He hated to leave her, but he knew that soon he would be back. As soon as his prisoner was sacrificed. His eyes flickered over the rest of the plaza. He noticed that at one end, beside the temple, the priest's assistants were beginning to build the fires on which the dogs would be cooked after they were killed on the altar.

Fringing the plaza he saw people watching his band depart. Among them he recognized some of the parents of the children who had been sold. They watched gravely in silence. Atlacol shrugged. There was nothing he could do about the will of the gods. He turned his head back to the path ahead. To the west he could see the mountains. The sun was climbing behind him. With luck, in a few days he would be in Tenochtitlan. He quickened his pace and caught up with his prisoner. He looked up at him sideways and smiled.

"Soon you will fly in the heavens with Lord Tonatiuh, my son," he said.

CHAPTER

VII

Medina's leg muscles were stiff from the two-day confinement in the cage. As he walked along the trail, he felt them protesting the rapid pace. The slight discomfort, however, was an insignificant price to pay for his liberation from what had looked like certain death on the sacrificial block. Now, as they walked away from the village, he had a new appreciation of the gift of life. The earth was still damp and cold from an early morning rain, and wisps of ground fog hugged the garden plots visible in the distance. The air was fresh and good. He inhaled deeply several times as he strode behind the children.

Beside him his captor smiled and chatted. Although Medina could not understand the words, it was clear that the man was happy and was attempting to communicate something of his pleasure to Medina. He wondered what it meant. Was it possible that they were going to take him to Vera Cruz? Possibly in hopes of receiving some of the green beads in return? He glanced at the sun. No, it was in the wrong place. They seemed to be headed west, farther inland. Were they taking him to a larger town? For a more elaborate sacrifice? But then why was his captor so jovial with him?

Just then Medina's thoughts were interrupted by the appearance of a group of men down the trail. There were fifty or more of them, and they seemed to have been waiting for the group to which he belonged. As he got closer, he could see that some of them were porters, standing by their burdens, others were warriors, and a few were dressed in white tunics like the leader of his own caravan, and some were prisoners roped together. As he scrutinized them, he gasped. In the middle of the captives, staring at the ground, was a disheveled, dirty Pérez!

"José!" he called.

The sailor jerked his head up and gaped. "My God!" he exclaimed. "You're alive!"

Medina rushed over and embraced him. His captor did not interfere.

"I thought they had killed you," said José.

"They almost did," replied Medina. "But they seem to have some new plans for me." He looked around at the Indians who stood watching them. "Plans for both of us, it appears."

The *pochteca* Tezcatl stepped over to them and uttered a sharp command. At once several Aztecs stepped forward and quickly bound the new prisoners, putting a wooden yoke like Medina's on José's neck. When they finished, they attached them to the other prisoners with a cord.

With a flourish of his cane, Tezcatl started along the trail, his body casting a long shadow in front of him. The entourage fell neatly in behind: four Aztecs dressed approximately as well as Tezcatl and also carrying identical polished black sticks; the porters, all leaning forward in the same attitude, tumplines across their foreheads; four powerfully built Aztecs carrying long stone-edged swords; the prisoners and the children, also in single file; and, bringing up the rear, another set of armed guards.

Tezcatl maintained a brisk pace, looking potent and robust. The light made his tunic blindingly white as he held the black staff in his hand. Behind him, in his entourage, at least twenty-five bearers carried loads on their backs. Probably provisions, thought Medina, scrutinizing the burdens. One of them bore a large basket filled with what sounded like live birds. Despite the loads, the porters walked crisply, without the tropical indolence he had noted in the Cempoalans, the Tabascans, and most of all in the Indians who served as slaves in Cuba. Instead, they moved like Europeans, like the Dutch—quickly and purposefully.

Beneath that outward display of energy, moreover, he detected a core of intelligence and cunning. Escape would not come easily, he thought glumly.

"How did you get here?" he asked José as they paced along together, linked by the rope.

"After they clubbed you . . . I thought you were dead, you know . . . they grabbed me and dragged me off to a village where these miserable slave-traders were. They sold me for several bags of God knows what. Then we left there and camped here last night. What is going to happen to us?"

"I don't know," Medina replied, not wanting to depress his companion with his real thoughts about their possible fate. "Perhaps they're taking us to some official who will trade us back to Cortés."

José looked skeptical, but said nothing.

After descending the edge of the plateau on which the village was located, they crossed a level, sparsely vegetated plain, plunged into a strip of forest, and by midafternoon began climbing a steep and narrow trail winding through the mountains.

"At least it's cooler up here," sighed José wearily.

Medina didn't answer but continued to trudge ahead,

his thoughts murky and out of focus. His boots had been stripped from him, and he had to force himself to withstand the pain of his raw, shredded feet.

Not long after, a switchback on the trail allowed them a view of the palisaded village, green, white, and gemlike below. Tezcatl called a halt, and he and the four other *pochtecas* promptly seated themselves on various boulders, engaging in conversation. Everyone else remained standing, shifting their weight like livestock.

Medina looked back. He could make out the river flowing past the plateau directly to the south of the village. He could see also the principal trails radiating from it. He strained his eyes.

"It's beautiful from up here, isn't it?" he commented remotely.

"Maybe. But I prefer Vera Cruz," said José without enthusiasm.

An eagle soared into view below them. Medina watched it for a moment, bemused by the sensation of looking down on a flying bird.

Shortly before nightfall, the company reached a meadow flanked on three sides by towering mountains. Wild flowers abounded, and a waterfall spilled down from a point halfway up one of the peaks, hurling itself into a stream that rushed tumultuously along the meadow's lower border. Close by the stream stood a pavilion, open on the sides but covered with numerous layers of branches supported by wooden posts and beams.

Almost immediately the *pochtecas* settled themselves within, their cushions and blankets neatly spread for them. Before reclining, they huddled for a moment near the center of the pavilion. When the *pochtecas* broke up,

Medina could see they had stacked their black sticks vertically, tied together at the top and splayed out at the bottom. Two of the guards, meanwhile, quickly kindled a fire outside as two others ran back and forth to the stream for water.

Ignored, the prisoners stood idly by as the Aztecs made preparations for the night. At length, Medina lay down. When none of the guards objected, José did likewise, heaving himself on the grass with a long sigh.

"Sit," José said to the other prisoners, trying to construct a gesture by tilting the yoke on his shoulders. They paid no attention. Finally a guard approached and told them they could rest.

After perhaps an hour, the *pochtecas* rose, entering immediately into animated conversation. Passing a jar among themselves, they splashed minute amounts of water on their faces.

"Not much of a bath," observed José dourly.

The prisoners all sat facing the pavilion, its interior still visible in the diminishing light.

The *pochtecas* now gathered in a group by the fire. Their conversation stopped. Drawing from their garments what appeared to be little flags, they cast them one by one into the fire as Tezcatl's voice rose in a slow chant.

Carrying a covered basket, one of the guards approached the fire. Without interrupting his chant, Tezcatl reached in and pulled out a fluttering bird.

"A quail, it looks like," whispered José.

Tezcatl raised the bird in front of him. With an obsidian blade, he cut off its head. He held the body like a vessel in both hands and, snapping it forward, sprinkled blood onto the fire. The drops sizzled on the glowing coals. Stepping back, he sprinkled more blood in front of him, and then three more times as he turned in a circle.

"Compass points," murmured Medina. He felt an odd curiosity.

Still chanting, Tezcatl walked slowly into the pavilion sprinkling blood here and there. When the bird had run dry, he ended the chant and returned to the fire, handing the quail to one of the guards. Beginning another chant, Tezcatl took a long thorn from the hand of one of the other *pochtecas*. He closed his eyes. Then, locating his left earlobe with his left hand, he brought the other hand up and plunged the thorn through the lobe. Blood began coursing down his cheek, first in intermittent drops, finally in a long, thin trickle. Once more he plunged, his chant subsiding. After returning the thorn to the *pochteca,* he leaned over the fire so that the blood would fall into it, kneading the lobe with his left hand to expel more blood.

"Please accept this atonement for my sins, Lord of the Traveling Merchants, Lord Yecatecuhtli," Tezcatl prayed in Nahuatl.

When he stepped back, the other *pochtecas* broke the silence with what sounded like a hymn. Tezcatl smiled.

Jovially, the *pochtecas* returned to the pavilion where an Aztec attendant had placed small baskets heaped with maize cakes and fruit obtained from the village. As they fell to, the guard outside put the skinned quail on a spit, and placed it over the fire. The smell of cooking meat soon filled the air.

The aroma was too much for José. He cursed loudly

when the guard removed the quail, and carried it to the pavilion.

"Rotten savages," he yelled at the *pochtecas*. "Feed me, too, for God's sake, you fat swine."

"José, be quiet," said Medina. "We're their prisoners."

"I don't care. I'm hungry," he said, glowering.

Tezcatl looked up from his bowl. Still chewing, he said something to his attendant who turned toward one of the guards and nodded. After taking a wooden club, the guard left the pavilion, and walked to where José sat, hovering over him.

"I'm hungry," moaned José, too angry to feel intimidated.

The blow landed straight across José's face, propelling him onto his back. Blood gushed from his nose.

"Crude bastard," growled Medina.

Without responding, the guard returned to the pavilion.

"Jesus and Mary, are you all right?" asked Medina, leaning toward José.

"I think," he replied feebly. "Though I've lost a nose. My face feels empty."

"Well, then your appearance may improve," said Medina lightly, relieved that the blow had not been very serious.

Medina looked back toward the pavilion. In addition to the fire outside, the Aztecs had lit several braziers within. Having finished their meal, the *pochtecas* smoked long cane tubes of tobacco. They sat in a loose, convivial circle, puffing and talking.

"Don Marcos," said José, almost inaudibly, "do you know where they're taking us?"

"I think to their city," came the reply. "To Tenochtitlan. I've heard them use the word several times."

"What will they do with us?"

"I don't know. But the leader seems to be some sort
of merchant or trader."

"A slave-trader?"

"It appears so."

"Maybe he works for the priests and collects people
for sacrifice."

"That may be the saving of us," said Medina.

"The saving of us for what?" replied José. "What a
pretty picture! Tell me, how do they sell in this country,
whole or piecemeal?"

"Go to sleep," said Medina, irritated. "That blow un-
balanced you."

But after a few minutes of silence, José spoke up again.

"How much does an ordinary human head weigh, Don
Marcos?"

He didn't answer, and at length he concluded that José
had given up waiting for a reply and dropped off to sleep.

Feeling grateful for the silence next to him, he looked
up at the night sky trying to sort the conflicting emotions
he felt toward José. One moment he liked him, the next
he found him stupid and insufferable.

Over to one side he could see the children huddled
together for warmth. He wondered why they were tied
together like prisoners. Were they to share some common
fate with him and José? He probably would learn soon
enough, he thought. He closed his eyes.

A commotion near the outside fire woke him. He
couldn't tell how long he'd been asleep. The air had

turned agonizingly cold, and the roar of the waterfall seemed deafening. A sliver of moon hung in the sky. Raising his head, he turned his body so he could see the fire.

His captor, Atlacol, stood before it, its embers casting lurid waves of orange across his face. With gestures and a chant nearly identical to those used earlier by Tezcatl, he began driving a thorn through an earlobe, letting the wound drain noiselessly into the fire. One of the guards attended him.

Medina watched sleepily, his eyelids slowly closing.

When he opened them again the man and the guard had disappeared. Someone had fed the fire. The sky, too, glinted with light, cooler and paler.

Twice more that night he woke, each time snatching segments of the same sight: a *pochteca* mutilating his ears, a guard standing nearby, a slice of moon somewhere else in the sky.

The second day a cloudburst forced the party off the trail. They sat huddled against the vertical face of a large granite outcrop to keep dry. The air had turned bitter cold, as though it were nighttime. The *pochtecas* covered themselves with blankets.

"I don't know what aches more, my feet or my stomach," moaned José. "Do you think they'll feed us at all?"

Medina didn't reply, for a movement in the brush at that moment caught his eye. Glistening in the rain, what seemed like the upper torso of a man—naked and emaciated—had suddenly appeared, and just as suddenly vanished.

"There's someone on the trail below us," he whispered.

"Where?" asked José, alarmed. "I don't see anything."

"He's gone, but I saw him. He looked like a skeleton."

"Mother of God, what now?"

The guards had seen the man, too. Tezcatl barked an order. The two guards hurried off down the trail as two other guards appeared. The *pochteca* issued a second order, then abruptly walked back toward the head of the train. The prisoners had scrambled to their feet and one of the guards pulled José up roughly. Within seconds they were moving up the trail at a pace twice as rapid as before, the guards prodding them to keep up with the prisoners ahead.

A half-hour later, the guards who had been sent to investigate returned, running up from behind. Evidently unsuccessful, they murmured breathlessly to the guards in the rear as they passed.

Medina did not understand the single word they used.

What had been an almost stately procession now turned into a forced march, furtive and desperate. Keeping their eyes on the brush and boulders at the sides of the trail, the guards now moved back and forth along the line of prisoners.

The rain increased as they groped blindly forward; the footing was slippery and treacherous. With night came exhaustion; still they kept climbing.

Near what he guessed was midnight, the rain finally tapered off. Stars began to appear through thinning night clouds, and the shapes and forms of the landscape became visible, black and gray masses pressing up against streaks of flecked sky.

The pace quickened, then slowed again as the trail became steep. They stopped altogether when they reached what appeared to be a sheer vertical wall rising in front of them. A huddled conference at the front of the column produced a delegation of guards with instructions to remove the yokes from the prisoners. Moments later they began to climb up a narrow cleft in the wall. When the trail leveled out again, the prisoners were not retrussed into the yokes, though they continued to carry them.

All night long they marched, Medina passing through periods of intense pain and near-unconsciousness, punctuated both by fleeting moments of lucidity, and by long stretches of euphoria when his mind seemed to float. He hadn't realized how mobile pain could be. Many times during that night a pain would invite itself down where—mysteriously, unaccountably—it would take up residence in a thigh or ankle bone.

At other times a deep calm settled over him. The air, the sky overhead, the vague shapes of trees and rocks along the trail, even the labored breathing of marching bodies and the rustle of their garments struck him as comforting and strangely beautiful. The past didn't matter, nor did the future. Only the things he saw now, felt in his body now.

Once, however, he stopped short. Braga! Grinning, the figure on horseback loomed out of the darkness. Medina recoiled for a moment, flustered, confused. The figure vanished, as though swallowed by night itself. The prisoner behind nudged him. Haltingly, he resumed the walk. An apparition, that is what it was, sent to remind him of this mission, sent by Fonseca. Braga. He had not thought of him since his capture. Why not? he asked himself accusingly. Why not? Why not? Because, he answered, struggling to understand, because . . . because this is a dream, not to be taken seriously. Yes, exactly. In dreams it is unnecessary to think, or plan, or harbor expectations. That is why I have not thought of you, Martim Braga, for I must wait until this dream is swept away. A bright, stiff morning wind will rise to dispel it. Then I will attend to you, Braga.

He stopped short again, and again the prisoner behind nudged him, this time grumbling as well. But now a new fear took hold of him as he moved forward—was it the other way around? Perhaps Spain, Italy, Fonseca, Cortés, even Braga— perhaps all *that* comprised the dream? This real, all that not. Yes, it could be so. No Fonseca, no Caterina. Grief started welling up in him, as though all his family and all his friends had just died. Or had he just died? No, no, he fought the fantastic notion, no one has died. No one. He forced himself to search his memory, wanting details to grasp. But they swam before him only in loose, nebulous eddies; disordered, indefinite, tumbling in a dizzy, inconclusive whirl.

José! Where is José? José is the test, the bridge.

"José!" he called out shrilly.

"Yes," came the reply from the figure walking ahead. "What is it?"

Thank Jesus, thank Jesus.

"Nothing. How are you?"

"Hungry. Tired."

A stab of pain shot through Medina's right knee. Relieved, his mind floated down to the knee, to live there awhile.

The attack came just as Medina thought he detected a subtle brightening of the sky, and when the caravan had settled into a steady, exhausted walk. The bandits struck first in the rear, leaping out from their concealed positions with fierce shouts, and assuming threatening postures. The children started screaming and huddling together.

The Aztec guards quickly formed up in front of the attackers and held firm, their stone-edged swords poised. Ragged and dirty in the dim light, thirty Indian brigands stood in an almost formal line, wielding stone knives and long wooden clubs. No blows were struck, nor did the *pochtecas'* men return the vociferous taunts hurled by the bandits as the two sides faced each other.

Suddenly, a few feet in front of Medina, a naked man emerged from the trailside, and hurled himself against one of the porters, knocking him down. The nude attacker wrenched the porter's basket from him and swiftly retreated. He had scarcely disappeared when another came on from the opposite side of the trail, and assaulted a second porter, but unsuccessfully, the porter stubbornly refusing to let go the tumpline despite the blows raining on him.

Racing back from the front of the caravan, a guard interrupted the tug of war with a stroke of his sword, the stone blade crashing through the naked man's collarbone and cleaving his shoulder. Shuddering, the man collapsed, his face twisted in speechless shock. Three more attempts at snatching cargo were repulsed by the caravan's guards who had quickly adjusted to the bandits' strategy by herding the porters and prisoners into a group and then surrounding it.

The final assault was launched not at the porters but at the prisoners. Five bandits, their clubs thrashing through the air, advanced first toward Medina, then, veering, toward a small boy close by. The boy attempted to run, but tripped, his momentum throwing him to the ground. Two of the attackers grabbed him, and started to drag the boy away as the others continued to wave their weapons in a defensive arc keeping the guards momentarily at bay.

Without thinking, Medina stepped forward, raised his yoke, and brought it down diagonally, catching one of the attackers across the back of his head. Instantly unconscious, he fell forward. Drawing a short, stone knife, the other bandit made a last lunge for the child. Taking him by an ear, he slashed deftly down, slicing it off. Then he ran, joined at once by two of his companions, another having fallen to a guard's sword. Medina looked from the man he had struck in time to see the fleeing attacker stuff the ear into his mouth.

It was suddenly still except for the moaning of the child who had lost an ear. Three of the ambushers lay nearby, dead or dying.

"You hit him hard," said José with a touch of admiration. "Is he dead?"

"No," replied Medina, transfixed and distant. The vibration that traveled through the blunt weapon when it struck still seemed to course up and down his arms, a palpable but disembodied force seeking somewhere to settle. He looked down at the prone figure, the blood trickling from the gash in his head. He could see traces of the scalp's fat tissue, an incongruous yellow glinting through the darkening blood and tangled black hair. The man looked frail and tiny, his skin taut and transparent.

"He should have died long before today," remarked Medina.

"Aye. Poor excuses for brigands," added José. "All of them."

Medina turned away, uncertain which sight—the dying, emaciated man before him or, still vivid in his mind, that of the naked man eating the ear—bothered him more. He saw the boy, crouched and crying. Medina squatted down, and put his arm around him.

Two of the warriors strode up, grasped Medina's victim by the ankles, and dragged him toward the front of the caravan. Another warrior took the boy away, apparently to tend to his wound. A moment later, Tezcatl and Atlacol approached Medina, stopping before him.

A gush of words streamed from Tezcatl's mouth. Though Medina understood none of them, he noticed that Tezcatl addressed him in a different tone than heretofore, almost respectfully. His face, too, had lost the characteristic haughtiness Medina had come to associate with high-ranking Aztecs. It had softened instead, the eyebrows and forehead less set in the formal Aztec frown, the jaws relaxed, the lips breaking open by tugs of smile. At length Tezcatl took Medina by the arm, and guided him away from the cluster of prisoners toward the head of the caravan, the other *pochtecas* following.

"What about me?" shouted José desperately as they left.

He received a cuff as an answer from a warrior standing nearby. When Medina glanced behind him, he could see the warrior tying José back into his yoke.

At the head of the caravan, the attendants had already started preparing a temporary camp. They spread blankets and cushions in a small clearing at one side of the trail, while, across the way, other attendants drilled a piece of

wood to kindle a fire. The sun hit the uppermost mountains near them with dazzling effect, gold-tipped peaks
thrusting into a milky blue sky. The Aztecs evidently did
not fear a further attack, thought Medina.

Tezcatl led him to a pile of cushions, and motioned him
to recline. Medina sank gratefully onto the mat, resting
his head on a small pillow. Shortly he fell sound asleep,
unaware that Tezcatl stood over him deep in thought.
Atlacol crept up, and covered the Spaniard with a blanket.

Tezcatl faced a dilemma. He didn't really plan to deliver the deer-men for sacrifice to Moctezuma, although
that was what he had told the village priest and Atlacol.
There would be no profit in that, he thought. Their skins
were pale, weren't they? Perhaps he could even color their
hair somehow, lighten it so that they resembled the rare
albinos that were brought from the far regions of the
empire. Albinos fetched high prices in the market, since
they were needed by the priests for their special sacrifices
during eclipses.

No, he could not take the chance. The eyes, dark and
flashing like his own, could never be disguised or painted.
It could spell humiliation. Possibly even worse. Ever
since Moctezuma had come to power and reemphasized
the stature, privileges, and inviolability of the higher
classes, it had gone badly with the *pochtecas*. The nobles
and priests now took every opportunity to obstruct and
harass the merchants, particularly the wealthier ones such
as himself, whose riches they envied. No, it was better not
to tempt the arrogant officials at the Emperor's court by
indulging in any questionable transaction.

Instead, he would enter the city under cover of night to

avoid any confiscation of his prizes by minor officials, and the next morning parade them to the market, as usual. Everything straightforward and above reproach. That way, even if government officials stepped in, and took the two prize slaves from him by declaring them political property, they would, being in the marketplace, be obliged to compensate him. And, of course, he would give a small portion of the payment to Atlacol.

That they might actually expropriate his prisoners seemed very possible, for the capital was filled with rumors of the strange deer-men who had landed on the morning-sun-coast. News of their coming had thrown the Emperor into dark, unpredictable moods. The priests and sooth-sayers, too, had begun issuing dire warnings, some going so far as to claim that the strangers were led by Quet-zalcoatl, the ancient Toltec god who had promised to re-turn from the eastern sea.

Nonsense. He looked down at the exhausted Medina and scoffed at the priests. "This is no god," he said out loud.

No god. But by clubbing the bandit, the stranger who now lay asleep at his feet had taken a prisoner. This meant that he could no longer be treated as a low person. The other *pochtecas* with him had witnessed the act, and would verify it. The bandit, moreover, was alive and would remain so, at least until they reached the city, living testament to the stranger's bravery.

"Make sure the wretch with the open head is treated and given food," he interrupted his thoughts, giving the order to an attendant working close by.

Sitting down next to Medina, he closed his eyes in pleasure, contemplating the successful conclusion of his journey. Ten adult slaves and nineteen children legally purchased, eight loads of cacao beans, four loads of jade, three of chalcedony, and one of gold; four remaining loads of high-quality fabric, the fifth having been seized by the bandits; and, best of all, the two strangers, one unquestionably salable as a low slave if he succeeded in getting him past the government and onto the market, the other now elevated and worth considerably more.

But take care, he cautioned himself, these hungry peasant scum may strike again. The strain of the all-night march and the warmth of the sun combined to make him sleepy. Stretching out near Medina, Tezcatl fell into a light sleep, lulled by the sound of a foraging bee.

When Medina opened his eyes, afternoon shadows knifed down into the little clearing where they camped. The Aztecs bustled about, packing up. His throat hurt and his eyes felt strained and sore. Atlacol, who woke him, knelt solicitously beside the mat. He offered a bowl of steaming broth to Medina.

The aroma of the broth under his nose burst through the haze of waking like a charging animal. He gulped it down, scarcely tasting at first the tomatoes and chili peppers blended into the meaty flavor—though the sharpness of the peppers quickly asserted itself. Smiling, his captor handed him in addition two small, breadlike cakes and a bowl containing a chocolate beverage laced with honey, all of which he consumed with unabashed relish. Overwhelmed, his stomach twisted and growled.

Atlacol laughed at the sound, and rubbed his own stomach sympathetically.

When Medina finished, he lay down again, contented,

waiting for the food to give him energy. He wondered idly why he had suddenly been fed such good soup.

At length Atlacol disappeared, and Medina realized he was no longer being closely watched. But where would he escape to anyway?

Then he saw standing next to a tree the attacker he thought he had killed. Curious, he went over and examined the back of his victim's head. Though the wound had been cleansed, it had begun to fester, a milky liquid oozing down through the matted hair. Yesterday's nausea started to build again at the sight of his handiwork. A fly settled on the wound.

The emaciated peasant stared vacantly at the ground, his wrists tied to the yoke on his shoulders. Medina recognized it as the yoke he himself formerly carried. He went to search for José. He found him sitting on the ground tied to three other prisoners.

"Good afternoon, José," Medina said.

No answer.

"Were you fed?"

Still no answer. Rigid and unresponsive, José scanned the peaks to the north.

"Are you angry because I'm loose?"

No answer, though the muscles in José's face tightened and served as one.

"I think it's because of him they let me go," said Medina, as he nodded toward the wounded captive.

At that moment the caravan began to move. José shuffled along with his fellow prisoners, leaving Medina standing at the side of the trail. He fell in casually beside the rear guards when they passed.

The next few days proved to be quiet ones, the bandits failing to reappear. After crossing several deep ravines over swaying suspension bridges, the trail leveled off somewhat, then gradually descended as they passed down into a vast, rather desolate valley. Far away on the horizon, to the south, an active volcano emitted a long plume of smoke.

During this part of the journey the *pochtecas* enjoyed prolonged, leisurely meals, smoking what seemed to Medina an inordinate amount afterward. On these occasions they seemed intoxicated. They became animated and garrulous. Some of them would attempt what sounded like weighty tirades, though these were frequently hooted down, while others told stories that resulted in long, sustained howls of laughter. More than once the *pochtecas* summoned a certain guard to perform for them. Dressing as an old woman and changing the pitch of his voice to a high, haglike squeal, he sang, danced, and recited an apparently ribald dramatic narrative in which he included various members of his audience as characters, scolding one, supplicating another, and—obvious to Medina—pretending to seduce a third. Even the prisoners, watching and listening at a distance, could not help but be amused by these performances, laughing among themselves, and nudging each other knowingly.

This was also a time when Tezcatl took to ordering the nightly halts earlier than before, a schedule the guards and porters apparently found to their liking, but one which imposed great tedium on the prisoners, including Medina, who began to yearn for a brisker pace. His feet, like those of José, had toughened considerably, and his freedom from the yoke made him restless.

Appealing by means of a few words in Mayan, which

Tezcatl seemed to understand, he had managed to have
José's yoke removed, too, though, far from being grateful,
José maintained his cool and sullen attitude, preferring to
walk near the wounded prisoner rather than Medina.

One evening the truth came out.

The *pochtecas* had just finished their customary ritual
of tongue- and ear-piercing which Medina concluded was
a kind of blood sacrifice for holy protection while traveling. Aguilar had told him of a similar practice in Yucatan.

"Would you like to know what the ear-piercing means?"
he asked José.

The Italian glowered, but for the first time since
Medina had been unyoked deigned to reply.

"I don't want to learn anything from you," he said
curtly.

"My friend, what is the matter?"

"I don't want to talk."

"José, there are only two of us."

"And one corrupted."

"Corrupted?"

"You know what they did with the attackers they
killed?"

"No. Left them to rot, I presume," said Medina, suddenly tense. "Or buried them."

"Butchered them. While you were asleep on the royal
cushions."

Medina said nothing.

"Then they prepared a little stew, and fed some of it to
a Spanish gentleman," José went on brutally.

Instantly the spicy taste of the broth flooded into
Medina's memory. So that's what it was, he thought, feeling oddly calm at the realization. Three times more he

had been offered the broth and, without questioning its origins, each time he had taken it gratefully.

"Have you had some?" he asked José.

"No."

He looked toward the group of *pochtecas* who at the moment sat savoring their bowls of chocolate. I don't feel any different, he thought.

"I didn't know, José," he said finally, his voice low, almost indistinct.

José remained silent for a moment, either satisfied with the explanation or unwilling to rub Medina's nose any more in what both of them considered the depth of barbarism: eating human flesh.

"They fooled you," he said at last, charitably.

"It was no great piece of cunning," replied Medina, skeptical. "I was served only a broth. There were no pieces of meat in what they gave me."

The next morning, as the *pochteca* caravan resumed its march, Medina found José trudging alongside him. The Italian seemed eager to talk.

"Don Marcos," he said, "last night I lay awake for an hour thinking about this matter of human flesh-eating."

Medina groaned. "My God, let us pick some other topic, José."

"But I have something new to say." José grinned up at his companion. "It is based on a dialogue I had last night with my stomach."

"All right. Let's get it over with."

"You see, hungry men aren't the most discriminating sort. Like the bastard who tore off the ear." He meant to be diplomatic but his words produced the opposite effect. Medina felt a surge of anger.

"I am not a cannibal, José," he announced flatly.

"That's not what I mean."

"What *do* you mean?" asked Medina.

"Merely that eating is better than starving to death, and that the highest born will eat the bark of trees if necessary to stay alive. And even one another."

"One another?"

"I think so, yes, Don Marcos."

"Not among civilized races or Christian ones."

"Maybe what you fancy-pants Spaniards call civilization is nothing but the absence of hunger. Let famine hit Spain. Let all the cattle, goats, and sheep fall to a plague and the crops fail. What then of those civilized, Christian Spaniards? The country will turn murderous."

"No, not that murderous, José. Christians and Spaniards would sooner die than knowingly nourish themselves on the flesh of others. They will kill for the last mutton chop, the last olive, but there it will stop."

"I am amused, Don Marcos."

"What a ghoulish thought. Amused by what?"

"The vision of the final days of this mighty famine. All the last mutton chops and all the last olives will end up at court, you can be sure. Treasure does have a way of ending up at court, doesn't it? By then food will be the greatest treasure of all. Think of it, Don Marcos, those chops and olives in the treasure chests of Castile."

"I don't see anything amusing about it."

"Nothing amusing about all the great lords and ladies vying and scheming for greasy chops and homely olives?"

"You are a pervert and an upstart. You hate the nobility. Moreover you are wrong."

"Look at the *pochtecas*," said José. "Are they well fed?"

Medina glanced back toward the spot where the *pochtecas* sat coddling their chocolate. Tezcatl, as a matter of fact, looked particularly porcine at that moment, decked luxuriously in a long, flowing robe.

"They're not nobles, they're merchants," said Medina. "And not Christians but Aztecs."

"Men of rank, nevertheless, and men of religion. Now take in the guards and porters. A bit thinner, no?"

It was true. The *pochtecas* seemed ponderous compared to the guards and porters, though these struck Medina as lean and muscular rather than thin.

"Now, by that tree. Your bandit, Don Marcos."

Till that moment José's argument seemed specious, but now it struck home. He didn't need to look. The man's abject, emaciated frame became vivid in his eyes, even closed. For the first time since he learned the contents of the soup, he felt queasy. It was one thing for a starving man to abandon all scruples in order to survive. That was the situation the bandits must have been in repeatedly. But it was quite another for the fat to feed, literally, on the wretched, as the *pochtecas* had done—and as he had done, although unknowingly.

He felt a sense of revulsion. Before, he had been intrigued with the Aztecs—their serious, cultivated demeanor, the intricacy of their costumes and goldwork, and their language, so foreign yet so strangely resonant. He had thought them civilized despite the rumored crudities of their religious practices, some of which he had himself witnessed. Odd how he had come nearly to accept human sacrifice, but balked at the other thing; now he felt genuinely perplexed. Why did the killing bother him less than what was done with the bodies afterward?

"I suppose there's only one question left," said José, "though you will find it a cruel one. But, forgive me, I want to know."

Medina looked at José and, in that moment, found himself admiring his partner in captivity, realizing with belated surprise that the tough, irascible Italian took life far more seriously than his antics, mischief, and bad manners suggested.

"Well, may I ask?"

"Yes, José."

"How did the soup taste?"

Medina closed his eyes. This troublemaker. This rude, ignoble troublemaker. Though he can pierce and injure with his cynicism, he is nevertheless honest and curious enough to ask a question the rest of the Christian world would regard as morbid and refrain from raising. No, he thought, the question isn't cruel. It is human—pitifully so.

"It filled my stomach, José. And it tasted good. Salty, but good."

CHAPTER

VIII

Their journey now took Medina and José through a more populous region, with villages no more than one or two hours apart. They were composed of single-storied red-and-white adobe houses, separated into blocks by narrow streets, and the buildings were almost invariably decorated with flowers growing not only at the base of the dwellings but also from window boxes and roof gardens.

Medina had first noticed the Aztec love of flowers when the delegation from Moctezuma visited the Spaniards at their beach encampment bearing extravagant bouquets. The *pochtecas,* too, always saw to it that flowers graced their encampments as well as their persons, wearing them on their ears or simply carrying them in their hands as they walked. But the villages fairly burst with blossoms. A blind man, thought Medina, would know at once that he was walking in the streets of an Aztec settlement. However, he wouldn't be able to see other things, whose presence—for Medina—cast a deep pall over the otherwise pleasant, colorful villages: the bloodstained pyramid-temples, the skullracks, the human bone piles, and, at several villages, the stout wooden cages containing prisoners, forlorn creatures languishing in close confinement.

Most of all, Medina was struck by the contrast between his fat, well-fed *pochteca* companions and the undernourished, obviously hungry commoners of the villages. They watched the passing caravan with hollow, lifeless eyes.

Their emaciated, wasted bodies reminded Medina of the bandits.

The caravan now barely arrived in a village before the inhabitants brought out their starving children for Tezcatl's inspection, hoping to sell them into slavery in exchange for food. But Tezcatl by now had more than 120 boys and girls linked together with ropes in his caravan. He was not sure he could even sell all of these in the capital city, so he was stoically refusing to purchase any more. He urged his men through the settlements as fast as possible.

At one village Medina watched, appalled, as a crippled man covered with rags limped forward, and tried to sell the *pochtecas* a sack full of crawling lice. Tezcatl snarled negatively, then returned to his nose the bouquet of flowers he carried.

By the time they reached and began to cross a second, more altitudinous mountain range, the wretched condition of the Aztec peasantry made Medina more aware than ever of the gluttony and self-indulgence of the *pochtecas*. With this awareness came a growing apprehension over his own and José's fate, and even, paternalistically, over his bandit's, as it became obvious they were nearing the capital. The guards became jocular, and even the children seemed to be more cheerful. The *pochtecas* examined and reexamined the cargo during each stop, appearing to be haggling over percentages.

Then, suddenly, crossing the summit of the mountain range, Medina saw what was like an inland sea below him. The lake was truly vast, and its size surprised him. A white island-city, resplendent with alabaster temple-pyramids, rose from the blue water like some childhood fantasy. Medina told himself that the strands connecting it with the mainland were illusory, some trick played by distance on fatigued eyes. He looked again. Bridges? Causeways? Was it possible? Could the Aztecs have built this fantastic dream city, which rose magically from the waters? It was far more spectacular than Venice. Around the lake Medina could see an almost unbroken chain of smaller cities and towns. He guessed that more than a million persons resided on the edges of the lake and in the main island-city. Nowhere in Europe had he seen such a concentration of people in one place.

More towns nestled on the hills and at the foot of the mountains that stretched behind the lake's east coast, as well as lush, green fields of young maize reaching like a blanket through the valleys. And on the lake itself, toward the shore, he saw another blanket, bright algal green, undulating in the small colliding swells of the water. Medina held his breath, awed by the size and beauty of the spectacle below. Somewhere in the back of his mind the Biblical story of the Canaanites buzzed: "And they reached a fertile valley alive with milk and honey."

Before descending toward the lake, Tezcatl and the other *pochtecas* proceeded to dress themselves in rags, so that they looked more like beggars than men of wealth. Under Tezcatl's supervision, the guards thoroughly daubed a muddy solution over Medina and Pérez' bodies and hair until any suggestion of their whiteness had disappeared. Tezcatl made it clear to Medina, with gestures and words, that he and José were not to talk.

Throughout the rest of the day they hiked down toward the lake, appearing to avoid the main roads and the larger towns, which were now becoming very numerous. The roads were filled with commoners, most of them dressed in tattered clothing and staggering under huge burdens on their backs. Odd, thought Medina—he saw no beasts of burden, no horses, donkeys, or any other animals for transport. All the commerce of the Aztecs seemed to depend upon human bearers, tired-looking thin men who often stopped to rest by the road.

Once they encountered a caravan of four canopied litters surrounded by warriors coming up from the direction of the lake. Medina guessed that the litters, festooned with feathers and bright textiles, bore persons of high rank. Tezcatl waved his men off to the side of the road to a group of trees, and had everyone sit down, as though resting. Medina could not help but feel that Tezcatl was avoiding a direct meeting with the litter caravan, which passed them at a stone's throw. As soon as it moved past, Tezcatl ordered them all up and on their journey once more.

In spite of what he already knew about the Aztecs, their dark rites and sanguine appetites, their city filled Medina with admiration, even at this distance. His spirits rose with each step now, for he felt he was approaching a center of civilization, and therein lay the promise of rationality. There, he convinced himself, he would be able to communicate, perhaps also negotiate their release. Who knew, he thought, he might even be able to get help to find Braga and complete his mission.

By nightfall they reached the edge of the lake, a secluded point far away from any of the causeways and lakeshore towns. Here a flotilla of dugout canoes and paddlers waited in the darkness. The guards removed the yokes from the prisoners, and bound their hands with cord. Medina and José were seated together in the bottom of a canoe, along with the wounded bandit, and the guards got in with them. The paddlers, wading alongside, guided the dugouts through the lakeshore reeds. When the water reached their waists, they pulled themselves into the canoes, and started paddling from a standing position.

Lights began to appear around the lake, and looking over the bow of the canoe toward the west, Medina knew that Tenochtitlan lay directly ahead where, coming on almost one by one as he watched, a thousand flickering lights flared, their reflections dancing and flitting on the water like luminescent butterflies. He sat up. As the canoe approached, the floating city rose before him out of the shimmering, fiery lake as though it were an invention, a conjuration, a dream city of the orient, some brilliant fabled citadel of Cathay where god-kings must surely choose to assemble.

Torches and the faint afterglow of sunset illuminated its temples and towers. He could see ramps and steps, and human figures moving slowly about. At the city's edge he could make out what looked like rows of barges berthed side by side and covered, incredibly, by a thick growth of vegetation. And, to his right, he saw a long, straight bridge or causeway linking the city with a point of land to the north. He noticed, too, on the causeway, an endless procession of Indians. Then, from the city, he began to hear a sound like that of a trumpet—low, wailing, and, to his ears, forbidding. He looked back over the stern in awe and almost tumbled out of the canoe. For a moon, nearly full, glided into view over the shoulder of the mountain range. But it was so close and vast, he did not know whether—in some unfathomable concatenation—he, the canoe, and the lake had been freed from earth and were coursing toward this awesome, mottled planet, or, an even deeper fear, it was a different moon from the one he knew, a moon the Aztecs had made in one of their temples and had just released.

Medina felt a great exultation. He and Pérez would soon be the first Europeans ever to set foot in the fabled city of gold. His uncertain future seemed somehow irrelevant.

The flotilla arrived at a quay crowded with canoes and illuminated by smoking torches. Disembarked, Medina and José were led through a series of narrow dark streets, torches flickering up the facades of imposing buildings. Suddenly the guards shoved them into a dark alleyway. From there they were led through a doorway into a vast room lighted by several torches projecting from the walls. The room was empty of people. Tezcatl removed his ragged coat. Beneath it he wore his most ornate tunic, gold threads running geometrically up his shoulders and across his chest. His face took on its familiar smugness and arrogance, the brows arching in their creased, postured lines as though painted on.

The room soon began to fill with Aztecs, all of them *pochtecas,* all greeting Tezcatl effusively on entering. Then they approached the two Europeans, and stripped them of their clothing.

The *pochtecas* inspected the captives very closely. They ran fingers through their hair, tugged at their beards, and examined their eyes, staring at them for long moments. Medina kept calm, but felt like a horse at auction or, worse, a pig. Behind him, he heard José cursing. Shortly after, they were given back their tunics, and were led outside again, this time by one of the guards, and placed in a small, empty room. Three partially unraveled fiber mats lay strewn across the floor. A narrow window slit was cut high up on one wall.

When the guard left, Medina tested the door and found it firmly barred from the outside. A torch flickered on the wall.

"The place is locked, José."

"We are done this time, Don Marcos, truly done."

Medina kept quiet, and thought over their situation. That they had been brought in under cover of night, and been led skulking through the streets worried him. A more public arrival would have guaranteed intervention by some official or other, with the possible result that word of their presence in the capital would reach Moctezuma. But if Tezcatl was going to deal with them on strictly a covert basis, then they might well be lost indeed. It was one thing to be a prisoner in a foreign land, even a hostage, but quite another to be human contraband.

"It is a true city," said José, seating himself cross-legged on one of the mats. His voice carried the flatness of defeat. The comment was an idle one, to cover the void within him.

"So it is," replied Medina, also seating himself. "I expected a large town, nothing more. It's bigger than Rome, and in some ways more beautiful."

"And Rome has no lake."

"But it has the Vatican."

"And this city the sacrificial temples. I saw several," said José. He crossed his arms and hugged himself, as though he were chilled.

"Yes," replied Medina. "Some of them look to be even higher than the cathedral."

"I should hate to have my steps take their measure." José coughed. "That damnable torch is smoking. Shall we douse it? What good does light do us?"

"None," replied Medina, acceding. He picked the torch off the wall, and crushed it in a corner, plunging them into darkness. A sliver of light from another torch outside spilled faintly through the window slit.

"We should sleep, José, so we can exert ourselves tomorrow if we have the chance." José, already stretched out, didn't answer. He was contemplating the confines of the room, and a deep, visceral fear settled over him. He felt alone and bereft, faced with an ultimate horror: to be given over to pagan gods. By comparison, Christian Hell loomed as a heaven and Satan a friend.

He looked toward Medina, trying to make him out in the dark. Even Medina, he realized, was lost and powerless in so gigantic and otherworldly a city. No bows and scrapes would be tendered to his protector, Don Marcos de Medina, distinguished nobleman and knight. The omnipotence of the Spanish gentility amounted to nothing here. Nothing. Though he despised that gentility, in a way he had trusted in it.

José's thoughts turned back to the city. He loved cities, large, sprawling Mediterranean ports in which it was possible to wander, poke, and explore the crowded avenues and intriguing back alleys where pleasure and sin flourished in mocking contrast to the dicta of church and state. Please God, let me wander forever in the dark, luring alleys filled with enticing whispers and probing female hands. Hot-blooded gypsy women and their pounding, sensual music. He remembered one from the night before he sailed from Seville. My God in Heaven, he said to himself, let me then take the gypsy woman. . . .

When day broke they were ushered out into the street by the *pochteca* guards. The city lay open and revealed in a burst of sun. Chalky walls reflected tinted morning light, and the flowers cascading down them every few feet sparkled with moisture. Clean and unlittered, the pavement shone, still slightly wet from a washing. The Aztecs hurrying by avoided small, evaporating puddles. Rarely did one of them look up and take any notice of the two Europeans and their guards walking up the street.

Despite a chronic lack of sleep and the uncertain prospects facing them, Medina felt alert and energetic. José, too, had put aside his customary sullen humor. He had stretched gymnastically on waking, run his fingers through his hair, and discovered no lice. On stepping out in the street, he indulged in the fanciful conceit that it was Sunday and he was on his way to church.

"An excellent day for a stroll. Which way to the cathedral, my friend?" José asked one of the four Indians escorting them.

The guard grunted, but not unpleasantly, as they turned off the narrow street onto a broad, teeming avenue. Their banter quickly faded as they found themselves carried along by a steady stream of Indians.

The city rose on either side of them, two- and three-story buildings set back from the avenue and fronted by open courtyards ringed with low, sometimes crenellated walls. Through irregular spaces between the buildings they could glimpse taller structures beyond, some of them clearly pyramids with colorful temples perched on their summits. Though still detectable, the sounds of the drums and the strange trumpetlike wail that had accompanied them throughout the night were muted by the hubbub of the crowd.

At length, the avenue gave out onto a vast, paved plaza rapidly filling with Aztecs. Bypassing the empty area in the center, where only a few unfinished booths stood, the guards led them along the plaza's edge. There, booths and stalls had already opened for business, their keepers displaying wares beneath makeshift roofs and stretched awnings.

If any doubt remained in the mind of either Medina or José that they were in a major city, it was quickly dispelled by the size of the market, the variety of goods offered, and by the swelling number of people spilling into the plaza from several broad avenues opening on to it.

The market was arranged in sections, each one containing a specific class of products or industry. On their right they passed, successively, sections offering fruits, vegetables, flowers, earthenware pottery, jewelry (the gold- and silversmiths distinctly separated by an intervening no-man's-land), and fabrics, this last covering the largest portion of space they had yet seen, and in which was sold every conceivable form of Aztec apparel, from crude blankets to exquisite feather capes. The guards dawdled near the cape stands and conversed briefly with a woman who was tying feathers together next to her stall. They moved on, their prisoners in tow, when a group of seemingly prosperous Aztecs converged on the woman to examine her work. She appeared to take them more seriously than she had the guards, her face breaking into a large, bright smile as they approached.

Next came a series of little eating houses which, despite the early hour, were already crowded with patrons, most of them well-to-do according to Medina's quick guess. Stools and low tables stood arranged in front, while cooking fires sputtered within these establishments, the smoke curling up from roof holes and the enticing odors of food wafting out. A few hungry-looking peasants lingered outside.

The guards must have breakfasted well, thought Medina, since they walked past this section without either pause or comment. The smell of food still turned his head and made his nose itch. José looked similarly discomfited by the nearness of food.

Around them the crowd continued to swirl. The people struck Medina as mainly poor and probably hungry, but a sizable portion were obviously members of an aristocracy, well fed, gay, and lighthearted. Still, he wondered about the blankness that occasionally crept into an aristocrat's unguarded face, as though the person were momentarily communing with some inner fear.

After skirting a set of stalls where various building materials were sold—white piles of lime and neat stacks of wood, stones, and sun-dried bricks lay inertly at the feet of bored-looking merchants—they came upon a group of herb sellers. Bunches of dried plants and leaves hung pinned around the outside of their stalls while an array of bowls and jars lined makeshift counters spanning the fronts of them. Here the sellers behaved more aggressively, accosting potential customers with long, animated tirades. Though he understood only isolated fragments, Medina concluded they were essentially testimonials of the efficacy of assorted herbs and medicines. Some things don't change in the world, he remarked to himself, vividly recalling both Spanish and Italian hawkers of the same ilk.

It was near this point that the atmosphere—until then increasingly reminiscent of the market in Florence or of almost any large European fair—began subtly to change. For one thing, the crowd immediately about them became thicker and perceptibly less festive, as though they had left regions of impulse, with their baubles and amusements, and now faced those demanding more deliberate reactions. Possibly, thought Medina, they were taking the herbalists quite seriously. For another thing, they could all hear now the high-pitched yelping of dogs, and smell their urine, an ammoniacal knife piercing the delicate aromas of the medicinal herbs and curative potions surrounding them.

Then he saw the first of the cages directly beyond the last herb stall. It contained a group of small, hairless dogs running frantically back and forth, and leaping wildly up the sides of the cage. Their eyes bulged dangerously, as though swelling from rampant internal pressure, and nearing the point of rupture. The first stall sold only live dogs, the second only dead ones, blooded and dressed, their legs tied around short poles for easy carrying. Abruptly the dog cages gave way to larger and stouter ones. The guards, eager to see as much of the market as they could while still conveying their wards with dispatch, paused momentarily, and then edged up closer to this new set of cages.

Medina suddenly halted.

Two boys, chubby and naked, sat indolently on the floor of a small cage. They looked to be five or six years old. One of them stared out at the ogling crowd with mild curiosity, the other toyed with a tiny stick.

Or were they girls? They must be, thought Medina, finally noticing that they lacked male genitals. But something still wasn't right. He forced himself to look again at the one staring out. Now he could see a jagged scar in the shape of a half-moon running transversely across the pubic region. As the likelihood of castration began horribly to dawn, a guard nudged him to move on. My God, he thought, with a sickening realization. Were they castrated to hasten the fattening process? Already injured by the dogs, his earlier sense of well-being now vanished completely. He glanced at José and saw that his eyes had retracted into their usual hostile defensiveness.

The next set of cages held adults, two and three to a cage, all young men, all gazing calmly about. Past these stood a raised wooden platform, still empty. Behind it, however, a line of slaves had started to form, with *pochtecas* bustling among them, shouting to one another as well as to an occasional slave. The line contained as many women as men.

Suddenly a familiar voice rang out, beckoning the guards. Tezcatl came forging through the crowd, his face flushed with excitement. Another *pochteca* unknown to

Medina followed in his wake. When he reached them he spoke gruffly to the guards. The guards cowered, their leader struggling to explain their delay.

Cutting him short, Tezcatl brought the other *pochteca* face to face with Medina, showing off his prize prisoner. His voice boomed out over the crowd as he pointed first to Medina and then to himself, at the same time relating the story of the capture of the bandit.

"Never," Tezcatl announced loudly, "a prisoner so valuable!"

The other *pochtecas* gave no hint of being impressed, only grunting tactfully now and then when Tezcatl paused. The crowd continued to stream past, though the island created by Tezcatl's impromptu performance grew larger as passersby stopped and listened in, captivated by his dramatic description, and seeking a glimpse of the extraordinary prisoner.

The collision between this stationary island and another that had been moving rapidly across the plaza toward it was audible when it occurred. Bodies thudded against each other, and some of them were hurled to the ground on impact. Tezcatl wheeled about, livid at the interruption. His jaw dropped.

"These slaves are declared the property of the Emperor," asserted a ranking warrior slowly to Tezcatl. It was a formal pronouncement, rehearsed and perfect, and he pointed to Medina and José as he delivered it, claiming them by gesture as well as word. A host of warriors stood rigidly behind him, one of them holding aloft a banner signifying that the contingent was properly commissioned and embarked on official empire business.

Tezcatl was indignant. These are my prisoners! Compensation! I must insist on compensation, he thought desperately. Didn't they know he was an important *pochteca*, perhaps *the* most important in all of Mexico?

He realized that he had misstepped by not registering his prisoners promptly. He knew by the presence of the priest and the stony face of the head warrior. They weren't searching him out to negotiate compensation. That would have been done politely. The delegation exhibited all the bad manners reserved for criminals. He? His mind ran through options. Very well, they had him. Yes, he was delinquent, but that would only mean they intended to bring him before the tribunal, the body of elder *pochtecas* which regulated the empire's commerce. He had many loyal friends on the tribunal. Still, his mouth dried as though swabbed with cotton.

"For concealing the prisoners from the Great Speaker, Moctezuma, the Lord, you are hereby arrested," the spokesman went on, "to be encaged until judgment is rendered."

The proclamation completed, an officer emerged from the group of warriors, and took Tezcatl lightly by the arm. Four warriors accompanied Tezcatl and the officer into a side street. The others surrounded Medina, José, and the spokesman. The crowd melted before them as they herded the two Europeans across the plaza.

CHAPTER

IX

In the distance, at the end of the avenue that ran from the plaza, the blue lake of Mexico sparkled in the sunshine. Hundreds of canoes plied back and forth though not a single one seemed powered by sail. It was a warm, clear day and the streamers hanging from poles near the palace snapped in the breeze. The sky looked less blue than the lake.

Walking fast, the warriors, Atlacol, and the two prisoners reached the outer walls of the sacred precinct and turned right, climbing diagonally the few long, wide stairs that ran along the side of a very long low-slung building, as they made their way toward a rear entrance. Neither Medina nor José had yet said anything, each still shocked at the swiftness with which they had been seized, and the *pochteca* taken away.

Entering the building, they were greeted by an aged priest whose eyes had milked over. A smoking censer dangled from a golden chain the priest held in his gnarled hand. Stepping forward, he waved the censer back and forth in front of Medina and José, as though fumigating them. The scent, thick and like cedar, clung to their bodies.

The ranking warrior exchanged a few words with one of the civilian Aztecs, then departed briskly with his men back through the portico. His little ceremony concluded, the priest disappeared into an antechamber near the entrance. The remaining two Aztecs, neither of them particularly burly or wearing any visible weapons, motioned the Europeans and Medina's captor to follow.

José looked expectantly at Medina, sensing an opportunity to overpower the Indians and escape.

Medina shook his head. "No, this is not the time," he cautioned.

The corridor was long and immaculate, potted shrubbery placed every few feet in small alcoves on either side. They passed several doorways, most of them closed off by hanging fabrics. But one stood open. Looking in, they met the equally curious gazes of five or six male albino Indians sitting comfortably in a small chamber. A titter of excitement ran through the room as they passed, but then rapidly subsided.

Once again José and Medina exchanged glances.

Twenty feet farther along, the escorts stopped. One of them reached over and parted a thick white curtain while the other turned and gestured them into the doorway.

"Mother of God, what is this?" José blurted out on peering into the vast chamber.

Medina, when he saw, was also astonished.

Within, four young girls, each perhaps thirteen or fourteen years old, sat in a tight little circle whispering. As soon as the curtain parted they rose and faced the doorway. Embroidered in gold and scarlet, white mantles covered their shoulders, and fell almost to the floor. These were not fastened in front nor did the girls wear any garments beneath. The black hair, the tan skin, and the white edges of the mantles running down across small tight breasts with uniformly large dark areolas made José feel weak.

Expecting death, he had been led to an earthly paradise instead.

The interior of the room itself also added to the total effect. Sunken in its center were two large pools, one of them steaming with heat. Shining blue and red tile covered the floor, and cushions and mats lay neatly stacked off to one side. Near them in a corner stood two featherwork screens, each six feet high and almost as wide. On the opposite side of the room a stream of water ran out of the nub of a large clay pipe emerging from a spot halfway up the wall. The water fell into a shallow basin recessed in the floor. Visible even from the doorway, the garden off the far side of the room formed a quadrangle sequestered by high, impenetrable-looking cactus shrubbery.

"It's a pleasure chamber," José stammered.

Off to one side stood another girl, slightly older. A young woman. Like the others, she wore a lavishly ornamented white tunic. But what startled Medina immediately was her jewelry. Those were Spanish beads. Cheap cut green glass. Part of the collection of gifts given by Cortés in Vera Cruz! He was sure of it.

Scrutinizing her, he wondered how she had come by them. From some high-placed admirer? If so, he could understand why. She carried herself like a noblewoman, he thought; the way Marina carried herself. Taller than the others, she also wore her hair differently, swept back from her forehead rather than tumbling over it. Her face was moonlike, reminding him of the Tabascan women they had taken on shipboard. As he stared at her, she looked back at him unflinchingly, almost aggressively. He felt at once that he faced no ordinary woman. Woman?

Girl, he corrected. Nevertheless, a self-possessed, confident one. He saw intelligence, too. A person's face revealed it, particularly the eyes. Hers flashed, but in a cool, detached way.

He suddenly realized how long it had been since he regarded a woman so directly. No. How long it had been since one looked so hard and intensely at him. Certainly she took her time appraising him, and communicated little in return. Only that she was strong, unimpressed— even by someone as foreign as himself—and perfectly in control of her circumstances. He became aware of her breathing, and watched her chest heave evenly up and down.

She uttered a single word too low for him to hear. At once the girls fell to their knees, touched their right hands to the floor and kissed their fingers.

One of the escorts gently pushed Medina forward.

Charily, Medina and José stepped in.

Medina looked behind him. The curtain had fallen closed, the escorts and his captor remaining outside in the corridor. He and José were alone with the girls who, regaining their feet, walked toward them. Something unseeing, even otherworldly, resided in their eyes.

The girls took them by the hand, and with a coaxing tug pulled them toward the pools.

Turning away, the older girl walked unobtrusively to the garden.

"They're just children," complained Medina.

"Virgins, maybe, but not children," replied José.

Medina didn't answer, for two pairs of skilled hands began to remove his garments. Stark naked, he was guided into the steaming pool where he willingly surrendered

himself to the attentions of the two girls. Solemnly they
bathed him with a fondling intimacy that made him
oblivious to their lack of years. He felt emotions that he
almost had forgotten existed. The other two girls bathed
José at the same time, in the same pool.

After the baths, the girls dried them, covering them in
thick, comfortable robes. Then they served the strangers
food, none of which contained suspect meat; only fish
fillets, white and tender, slices of avocado and tomato; a
variety of unleavened bread, shaped in rounds; and two
beverages, one a froth-topped chocolate drink clearly
sweetened with honey, the other a whitish liquid, uniden-
tifiable but mildly fermented and, despite its strangeness,
surprisingly refreshing.

For the most part, the meal passed silently. José ner-
vously watched the curtain covering the doorway as he
ate. Medina, without appetite, picked at his food. He
felt warm and drowsy. Still unable to comprehend the
reason behind their royal treatment, he gradually left off
his questioning, turning his thoughts instead to the older
girl, her of the green beads. As yet, she had not reappeared, and he discovered himself annoyed by her absence.
He thought of her slender neck and of her breathing.

Following the meal, the girls took their guests to the
cushions, gesturing them to recline.

"Oh, Mother of God, what next?" sighed José, finally
letting his defenses flag. "Maybe I can sleep."

Medina merely shrugged as he lowered himself onto a
bank of cushions.

Within a few seconds the older girl reappeared in the
chamber. Without seeming to notice Medina, she pulled
one of the screens between the two men, giving them, in

effect, the privacy of two rooms. She did not look in on Medina, as he hoped she might. He tried to dismiss her from his thoughts.

The other girls divided up once more, now kneeling beside their respective charges and, taking hot, aromatic oils from heated earthenware jars, began rubbing the men's bodies.

The oil made Medina's skin supple. He lay back, relaxed and sleepy. When one of the girls bent over him, strands of her hair brushed against his face. He glimpsed her breasts and closed his eyes, feeling the beginnings of arousal, but wishing it were not so. They are only girls, he reminded himself. But the flutter in his loins resisted the urging of his conscience, stirring him into wakefulness. Responding to their deft touches and languorous massage, he decided he liked the way these two girls felt to him. Even if it was the roundish face of the older girl that crowded more insistently into his mind. Why didn't she minister to him in this way?

One of the girls glided her hands—smooth, warm, and glistening with oil—across his stomach. Lower and lower the hands moved, as though drawn to his manhood. As they caressed him, his own hands reached out, and began stroking one of the girls. Barely conscious of which one he held, he pulled her closer, nuzzling his face into the base of her neck and then between her breasts as his lips sought rosebuds. The tempo slowly mounted. Arms, fingers, legs, hands, breasts, and mouths mingled anonymously; probing, discovering, tasting. New smells rose, folding into the botanic oil. Their three bodies wound themselves into a rhythmic, moistening, voluptuous tangle. Yes, yes, thought Medina as a tide of want swept him ever closer, ever inward, ever deeper. Now, from somewhere in that dense throbbing tangle, a set of delicate hips and their downy fulcrum slid noiselessly, warmly across his thighs. The recess—open, dark, succulent—aligned itself, as though in a dance, and hovered, with exquisite patience, before slowly engulfing him below. He arched his back, delirious. He found the hips with his hands and pressed them close to him, pressed harder and harder as his tongue, in unison, thrust itself into the damp suction of a girlish Indian mouth. Teetering at some edge, a single being—girl/man/girl—shuddered, gasped, quaked, and clutched. Glassy, his eyes widened, amazed at the hurtling approaching lightstorm. Then it struck, its power surging through him, peaking, and finally exploding in a blinding, white, ecstatic flash. Convulsing in fulfillment, his calves cramped as he emptied himself into the high recesses of a flooding womb; his groan, long, full, and shameless, reverberated through the chamber, like the growl of a jaguar.

Disengaged, he lay back, his head, chest, and wrists still thumping. Wet all over, a liquor of oil, semen, and perspiration covered him. In a moment the girls returned with lengths of thick cotton, and began swabbing him dry. As his heartbeat slowed to normal, his mind cleared. He entertained, for him, a novel, almost revolutionary notion. It would not go away, and associated itself partly with the recent trek through the valleys and mountains of Mexico but also, irresistibly, with the girl of the green beads. He allowed himself—a sacrilege, he knew, but why stop?—to wish he were an Aztec. Could it be mostly because of her? No, what does a woman have to do with my destiny, he argued. Nothing. Particularly not one as haughty and distant as she.

The girls sprinkled scented powder over him, making him think vaguely of Alvarado. The village where José and he were captured had turned out to be less peaceful than he had been led to believe, he thought to himself, admitting for the first time that he had been duped by Alvarado and Sánchez. But he decided not to waste time resenting their duplicity or plotting. That matter would have to wait. Indeed, perhaps wait forever if some resolution here in Tenochtitlan weren't forthcoming.

Sleep, postponed once, crept back. Closing his eyes, he grew inexplicably wistful, images of his dead father merging with the landscape of Spain. Fonseca's room materialized, and then Martim Braga, astride his horse, seemed to ride by in the background. "But besides Braga," Fonseca was saying, "it would be most useful to learn everything about those people in that strange land: their language, what they eat, what they believe, even, my dear Medina, if you get close enough to them, how they procreate."

A twinge of guilt snapped him back awake. Dear Jesus, he thought with a shiver. I have discharged my seed into an unbaptized Indian, a pagan. But then, with a slight shake of the head, he smiled. May God forgive me, he told himself, but nothing has ever been so sweet. And, dear Bishop, they procreate as we do.

Turning over on his side, he reached out to touch the two girls. They had covered him with a blanket. Each smiled, and one of them patted his hand in return. No, neither revealed anything of pain or remorse, he noted gratefully. To the contrary, each looked content, even radiant. Freeing his arms from the blanket, he pulled both

the girls to him, relishing the simple warmth of what he
had come to regard as a deliciously compound body. He
paid no attention when he heard José moan on the other
side of the screen. Nor did he feel disloyal to his girls
when he allowed his thoughts once again to focus on the
girl of the green beads. Her presence seemed to assert
itself in the cooling air of the chamber as he drifted off.

He awoke at dawn, a question banging in his mind.
The girls slept peacefully on either side of him. Without
disturbing them, he arose and walked quietly to the outside doorway of the chamber. Yes, the escorts—guards, he
corrected himself—were still there. His captor, too. Atlacol
smiled cheerfully at Medina when he poked his head
through the curtain. The guards remained alert, well
armed, and vigilant, he noted, storing the fact. Withdrawing, he moved back into the chamber, looking for
the girl with the Spanish beads. He found her near the entrance to the garden, asleep on a reed mat. Seating himself beside her, he laid his hand gently on her shoulder.
She awoke at once, regarding him, as before, fearlessly.
There was only one language he could try: the ele-
mentary Mayan he had learned from Melchorejo and
Aguilar.
"Hello," he said.
The woman's mouth opened in astonishment. She
burst into a throaty laugh.
"You speak like a human. Are you a real human?" she
asked.
"Yes."
"You have so much hair, I thought you were a monkey
god," she said.

Medina laughed. A great sense of relief swept over him. He suddenly felt some hope for the first time since he and José were captured.

"What is your name, sister?" he asked.

"Nacha. And yours?"

"Marcos."

"Marcos. Marcos-tzin," she said, interjecting the Aztec title of respect into her Mayan.

"Are you from Tabasco?"

"From near Tabasco. My name, too, comes from that land," she replied. "And you? You are a son of Kulkul-kan," she lowered her voice, "whom these Aztecatl call Quetzalcoatl?"

"Who is Kulkulkan?"

"He who came from the East, and who returned to the East on the great serpent raft," she said.

"I do not know him. But you, how did you come here?"

"When I was small, my brother and I were captured in war. Later we were sold to a trader," she said. "A trader, a *pochteca*, of the Mexica. He brought us here to Tenochtitlan. I was raised here in a noble house."

"And your brother, where is he?"

She looked at him pensively, and said simply, "He went to the mansions of the sun, my Lord."

Medina did not know what to say. He laid his hand on her shoulder. She seemed to quiver under his touch. Or was it his imagination?

"And these girls," Medina asked, nodding in the direction of the room to which they had gone with José, "who are they?"

"They are Untouched Ones, Marcos-tzin. Reserved

Ones. They are for the gods. They are for the sons of Quetzalcoatl-Kulkulkan to enjoy. As am I. Come with me, my Lord."

Nacha took his hand, and led him to a room adjacent to the one into which José had disappeared with the girls. It was a cozy chamber with a copal torch illuminating beautiful textiles hanging on the wall. Woven into their fabrics were strange-looking beasts and gods. On the floor was a reed mat with a cushion. Beside it sat a brazier in which aromatic charcoal burned.

Medina lay down on the mat, the cushion under his head. He lay back luxuriously and closed his eyes.

When Medina awoke, a black-cowled Indian was standing looking down at him. He had a narrow, ugly face and scorching eyes. His feet were dirty, and a vile smell surrounded him. Medina had seen men like him before: the butcher-priests of the Indian temples near Vera Cruz.

What was this unpleasant man saying to him? The words merged into an alien jumble.

Nacha suddenly appeared at the side of the priest and, whispering something in his ear, guided him away from Medina. Gratefully, he sank back.

Medina wanted to fall asleep again, but he could not. The beautiful, airy chamber now seemed unbearably close and musty. Traces of the evil-smelling priest lingered until Nacha returned and relit the brazier.

"Who was that man?" he asked. There was no reply, and he slowly opened his eyes. She was standing beside him, looking down.

"That was Molotl, my Lord Marcos-tzin. A high priest, a *tlamacazqui*."

"What was he doing here?"

She did not reply. Instead, she knelt down beside him, and opened his tunic. From a small jar on the floor, she took an ointment and began to massage his shoulders.

Medina's mind was still on the priest. There was a question he had to ask.

"Nacha, am I to be sacrificed?" he asked.

She raised herself to a sitting position, and paused before answering. "Yes. There will be a feast. You and your friend are the gods of the feast. It is a great honor."

"But they will sacrifice us," he said.

"Yes. And me, as well."

"You?"

"Yes, and the girls, too."

"We will all be sacrificed?"

"Yes, we have been chosen."

The words did not shock him, he had lived with the expectation so long.

"Nacha, it must not take place."

"Why not, my Lord?"

"Why not?" he repeated. "Because we should not die." He thought rapidly. "I can help the Lord Moctezuma."

She furrowed her brows, struggling to understand him, but plainly not succeeding. The distance between them seemed suddenly unbridgeable. It occurred to him that they did not even have the fear of death in common. Too Indian, he concluded reluctantly. But the beads. Perhaps the green beads meant she enjoyed access to the ruler.

"The necklace. How did you come by the necklace?" he asked.

"A gift," she answered, her hands automatically reaching to her neck to feel the beads. He wondered if she had slept with them on.

"From Moctezuma?"

"No, my Lord."

"Then who?"

"Molotl," she said, turning her face as before.

So, she was, or had been, Molotl's concubine, he thought with disgust.

"I should have known," he said in Spanish as he lurched to his feet and stalked off. Bending over, he thrust his head in the stream of cool water tumbling out of the wall fountain.

Cooling off, he turned to Nacha. "Tell Molotl I must see Moctezuma. Tell him I have important information for the Emperor."

That afternoon Molotl paid them another visit, strolling imperiously about the chamber, his hair reeking as always. Ignoring Medina, he paused for a moment in front of José, mumbled something to himself, then abruptly left.

"Goodbye, you hateful bag of piss," muttered José after him.

Medina noticed that Nacha slipped out to the garden and followed Molotl.

When she returned, she brought grim news. "Priest Molotl says it is too late. You are now reserved for the gods alone."

José reacted bitterly when Medina told of their fate.

"It's as though they've been feeding us a prolonged last supper, girls and all," wailed José, almost regretting the thoughtless enthusiasm with which he had accepted this most recent brand of Aztec hospitality.

"We've got to try to escape . . . tonight," Medina said.

"Yes. It is that or the pyramid."

"It's too thick to get through," José said. They stood in the moonlight next to the thick wall of tall spiny cactus that enclosed the garden. The girls and Nacha had long since retired.

Medina stole back into the chamber and returned a minute later with two of the small eating tables. Placing one on top of the other, José grasped them as Medina clambered up and tried to peer over the hedge, leaning perilously forward. "Hold the tables steady," he ordered.

The warning came too late. The bottom table suddenly buckled backwards, tumbling Medina headlong into the hedge. He bit his lip from the pain, his body scored and punctured by the sharp needles of the cactus. He jerked back, bleeding.

Rummaging in an adjacent storage room for cloth to wipe the blood off himself, Medina found several chests containing ceremonial costumes. Among the beautiful textiles, feather capes, and ornaments, he saw two black-cowled robes of the type worn by Molotl. My God, was this the answer? It was worth trying! If he and José could somehow get past the guards at the doorway, they might walk out of Tenochtitlan disguised as priests.

Returning to his chamber, he stole a look at Nacha, and decided it would be unwise to share his plans with her. All he could hope for was that if the so-called gods fled, a sacrifice of the girls would be meaningless.

* * *

"But there's no route out," whispered José. "Those guards are changed all the time and they never sleep."

"The hedge," said Medina.

"But we tried that. We'll never make it through that tangle alive."

"It's the only way."

"Jesus Christ!" said José. "We have no idea what's on the other side either. It could be crawling with snakes and tigers for all we know."

"Believe me, José, it's the only way."

José gave in. "Will the cowls cover our heads?" he asked.

"And most of our faces if pulled forward. There's also something else we must do to enhance the disguise."

"What?"

"Shave."

Shaving proved less difficult than they expected. The stubby, squarish obsidian knives that accompanied their meals proved remarkably sharp. Having slipped silently into the warm pool and lathered their faces with the excellent Aztec soap, each became the other's barber for want of a mirror. They used a small copal torch for light.

After drying themselves, they slipped into their cowled robes. Medina cast a last, parting glance at the slumbering Nacha. Odd how he regretted leaving her. He realized, too late now, that something unexplored and incomplete existed between them. Forcing it from his mind, he shook his head, lifted a wicker screen from the floor, and carried it out to the garden.

José stood waiting with another screen. They leaned one of them against the cactus hedge at a sharp angle. Medina climbed to the top.

"Quick, hand me the other one," he said, keeping his voice low.

José passed the screen upward. Medina took it and lowered it to the other side. Then he slid down.

"It's safe, not even a scratch. Come over," he whispered through the cactus. A moment later, José came sliding down the screen. When he landed he looked warily about.

"See anything?"

"No. Let's go," Medina ordered.

They moved stealthily along the inner wall. The sky was lit with a full moon. Across this new section of courtyard they could make out the shape of more hedge. Above it, in the distance, they saw illuminated second-story windows. They passed close to a row of darkened windows, ducking low as they went by.

"Those must belong to the albino room," whispered José.

The shadow of a doorway loomed ahead. Just as they reached it, José stumbled over something. A shrill cry went up as a dark living form mustered itself in a flurry, and rose ten feet in the air.

They froze.

Squawking, the thing fluttered across the expanse of garden, and disappeared over the hedge opposite. Then silence.

José waited a long time before daring to speak.

"Some kind of bird," he exclaimed under his breath.

Waiting a few more minutes, and hearing nothing except the by now familiar throb of drums and accompanying flutes beyond the palace, Medina led José past the doorway. Ten feet farther along they came to another hedge, higher and more impenetrable than the first.

"Damn," swore Medina. "We'll have to go through the door."

Doubling back, they pushed through the heavy fabric covering the albinos' quarters, and stepped cautiously in. The sounds of sleep suffused the dark room: breathing, wheezing, even a restless stirring.

Midway through the room, Medina suddenly stopped. What if guards were posted at the corridor entrance? The albino room had been unguarded when he and José had been led past it their first day in the palace, but that didn't necessarily mean it was always unwatched. They would have to risk it. There was a good chance there would be no guards. The only thing more conspicuous than a European in this city would be an albino. It might even be that the albinos were not prisoners at all, but residents, though for what purpose he could not begin to guess.

Another stirring in the room prompted him to continue toward the corridor. José followed closely. Parting the curtain, Medina sighed in relief. No sentries.

They turned quickly down the corridor, found the same porticoed door through which they had originally entered, and, hearts pounding, walked bravely out of the building. Expecting a deserted city this time of night, they discovered the opposite. The streets buzzed.

"Where to now?" asked José, awed once again by the level of activity on the street.

"Toward the east," replied Medina. "Follow me."

Affecting a leisurely pace, Medina led José along the edge of the avenue in a bank of almost continuous shadow, broken only intermittently by the light of flaring torches.

Festive and animated, the Aztecs on the street seemed absorbed in badinage: laughing, whispering, gesturing, their faces bright with anticipation. It vaguely reminded Medina of the Saturday night promenades in Valencia—the high spirits, gaiety, the strutting.

As they crossed a bridge over a canal, Medina stopped short.

"Those priests," he murmured, indicating with his eyes the center of the streaming flow of people.

José looked, instinctively pulling the cowl more tightly around his face. A group of Aztec priests wearing robes and cowls identical to their own moved slowly toward them.

"Oh, Mary, Mother of God," uttered José. His knees felt weak.

One of the Aztec priests saw them and waved, at the same time obviously alerting the others to their presence. As the priest began to thread his way through the crowd toward them, Medina decided to act. He returned the wave as though he had been looking for the priests all along, and, nudging José to follow, charged toward the group of priests, but at an angle that would bring them to the tail end of the group. Medina and José were abruptly heading back in the direction from which they had come, though now members of an official party. Following the priests—one of whom appeared mysteriously at the elbows of the Europeans like a sergeant-at-arms—

they recrossed the bridge, and approached a high wall from which merlons of carved stone snake heads jutted. The procession passed through an open but heavily fortified gate.

CHAPTER

Inside the gate, the spectacle of the sacred precinct jolted them all at once, like an unexpected blow. The main plaza stretched before them, a vast expanse of smooth flagstone dotted with thousands of milling Aztecs underneath the full moon. Lavishly decorated buildings rose on either side, some high and monolithic, others low and sprawling, their facades and cornices painted gaudy colors. Tall poles festooned with trailing red ribbons and net bags stuffed with green and white feathers were planted here and there. Hundreds of torches turned the night into a flickering twilight. Monumental statuary, most of it grotesque—serpents, jaguars, and stylized human figures—flanked the buildings like guard animals or footmen.

As they moved toward the center of the plaza behind the priests, they saw to their left a group of low platforms. A stone disc more than a foot thick and at least six in diameter lay flat on one. On another, a gigantic, coiled snake rested, its stone body painted green, its red mouth agape, its yellow fangs gleaming malevolently in the torchlight. Farther to their left the skull-rack appeared. Though each had seen similar racks in the smaller Aztec towns, neither had seen one that approached this in size or in the quantity of skulls it held.

Medina quickly estimated a hundred thousand, at least. With rods driven through their craniums, they hung like tiers of ghostly spectators in a flat, vertical gallery waiting for their numbers to swell. While José envisioned his own skull adorning the rack, Medina turned to stare at the temple opposite. It was a small building and, compared with the others, quite ordinary. Except for its entrance, which had been carved and painted to resemble the gaping jaws of a gigantic serpent. Anyone going into that building, he thought, would be swallowed.

Their entourage finally stopped in the center of the plaza. Dwarfing them and the throngs of Aztecs in front of it, the Great Temple-Pyramid loomed up like a stark, angular volcano. Some three hundred feet wide at its base, it rose more than a hundred feet in four colossal slabs, each six feet smaller around than the one below. Large braziers burned at each corner of each slab, sparks flying into the air amid the curling gray smoke. On the stucco surfaces of the Pyramid's sides, carved snake heads jutted out in neat repetitive ranks, their mouths uniformly open in a frozen, reptilian snarl. Twin staircases, with balustrades running between them and down either side, climbed steeply up the front of the Pyramid, and led to its spacious summit. There, toward the rear and not completely visible to the people below, sat two tall temples with identical pitched roofs covered with cement and lime. The temple on the left was painted white and blue, and a frieze of seashells ran playfully around its roof. The other, though ornamented with drawings of butterflies and hummingbirds, wore a more menacing aspect, for carved white skulls had been affixed to its blazing red exterior. In front of the temples, within a foot or two of the top of the stairs, sat a curiously shaped block of stone. It was two feet wide, perhaps four feet long, and nearly three feet high, reaching to about the level of a human waist. Its top surface, however, was convex, as though the stone bore a humped back.

Medina and José did not at this moment concern themselves with the constructions on the summit. Rather, they focused on the stairs, for it had become apparent to both of them that the dark, brownish residue covering the steps was dried blood. It gave off a strong, fetid odor which the incense in the air barely concealed. No wonder so many of the Aztecs walked about holding flowers to their noses. Strange, too, thought Medina, that this stinking river should just be left there to rot while everything else he had seen in the capital was kept scrupulously clean. They even washed the streets, he had noticed.

"No better than the slaughterhouses in Spain," José whispered, wrinkling his nose in disgust.

"Just be grateful you can still smell," replied Medina.

Like blackbirds picking their way through a flock of brightly plumed parrots, the Aztec priests moved again, the two Europeans and their sergeant-at-arms in tow. The group seated itself on a row of stools facing the plaza at one corner of the Pyramid. Nearby lay a cloth sack and, next to it, a large reed basket. Medina and José looked out at the crowd. The din had increased. The undertone of male conversation, spiked now and then by rollicking laughter, grew to a roar. The children still screamed and shouted as they raced through the crowd, but now it seemed their cries became hysterical and abrasive. One boy collapsed altogether, tears streaming down his face. His warrior-father spoke to him harshly.

In a corner of the plaza a troupe of musicians struck up an odd, dissonant medley on clay pipes of different sizes. Closer by, surrounded by a ring of Aztecs and giving off what sounded to José like a comic harangue, a juggler lay on his back spinning a log in the air with his feet. Women strolled back and forth vending lush, purple garlands in singsong voices. Others, in raspier tones, sold yellow cookies in human form with short, stubby arms and legs, sharp pine-nut eyes, noses, and mouths. Even the burning copal and pine pitch torches lent a hiss and crackle to the air, as though a holocaust were imminent, or just ending.

Atop the Pyramid, the curtains of the red temple suddenly parted, and five priests emerged one by one, their nearly naked bodies smeared with black. Attired in a red mantle fringed in green and resembling a dalmatic, Molotl emerged behind them and strode about the summit like an ornate prince. The green and yellow feathers of his headdress fluttered across his shoulders and down his back. His ears glinted with golden earplugs inlaid with jade, and a labret of blue stone swung from below his pierced lower lip. In his hand, he wielded a stone knife, sharp and wide.

The lesser priests, garbed in white dalmatics embroidered in black, carried tiny paper shields dyed in different colors. Their hair was tightly curled and tied with leather thongs that went all the way around their foreheads. One of them held a wooden yoke carved in the form of a snake. The priests huddled momentarily and then, one by one, advanced to the stone with the convex top where they looked out over the plaza, visible to all those below. A broad, white circular band had been painted around the mouth of each priest, and the bands now stood out garishly against their blackened faces. When the conch shells blared abruptly from behind them, they started chanting and dancing. The sound of rattles accompanied them.

Below, an old man next to Medina and José stood up as the shells sounded. He walked to the reed basket and extracted a pottery bowl and several cups. Filling each with liquid from the bowl, he handed them to the other priests, who passed them among themselves. After a small sip, the priest beside Medina offered him a cup. Accepting it, Medina studied its contents, trying to find something familiar in appearance or smell. Finding neither, he took a brief, tentative taste before handing it to José.

Strange, very strange, Medina thought, as the elusive, faintly piquant flavor quickly vanished from his tongue. He had expected something crude and less subtle. Three more cups came to him, and from each he took successively bolder sips, endeavoring with each one to penetrate with his teeth what he now envisioned as a solid kernel flitting teasingly over his tongue, and somehow, causing tiny clusters of sensation to explode around the roof of his mouth and in his ears.

A half hour, or was it an hour, passed quickly. He looked at José and flashed a large, ludicrous, affectionate smile, careless about his cowl. José smiled back, shrugging at the same time. Medina's eyes were shining. He leaned luxuriously against the Pyramid, folding his arms, and crossed his legs. A few moments later, accompanying the strident conch shells, a drum on the Pyramid's summit began rolling like thunder.

The crowd fell silent and turned to face the Pyramid. The juggler scrambled to his feet and perched on his log. The vendors disappeared and the musicians stowed their clay pipes in their belts. The priests and, lagging a few seconds behind, the two impostors rose from their stools. But instead of facing the Pyramid, they converged in a circle around the cloth sack. One of the priests reached down, and began pulling out short obsidian knives, which he distributed to the others, including Medina and José, who hardly noticed. Their heads swam. Despite their priestly impersonation, their fugitive status, and the hush in the plaza, they had lost their self-control. Medina found himself unabashedly grinning at the old man whom they regarded as their sergeant-at-arms. He, in turn, grinned back, his eyes equally glazed. It occurred to Medina that this old man, this sergeant-priest, must surely know that he, Medina, was a Spaniard; moreover, he must know that he, Medina, knew that he, the priest, knew. As Medina struggled with the next generation of reciprocal awareness, José entered a fantasy involving the cloth sack, which he believed was twitching. Surreptitiously, he placed his foot at its edge to hold it down.

From the western gateway, the prisoners entered the plaza walking three abreast. Led by a contingent of Aztec generals, the file wound around the temples and past the stone disc platform, coming to a halt in front of the Pyramid. Covered with green and blue feathers, the generals wore broad gold bands on their wrists and ankles. Small gold bells sewn to their tunics jingled when they walked. They carried feathered, ceremonial shields and their long obsidian-edged war clubs. The prisoners were naked.

After the file stopped, a swarm of Aztec warriors moved rapidly up and down the line of prisoners to locate those they had captured personally, in this way apprising themselves of the approximate order of sacrifice. The procedures were rigid, and it was their responsibility to know when to step forward to claim the portions due them. On finding their prisoners, the warriors spoke kindly to them, the relationship between captors and captives like that between fathers and sons. Meanwhile, bands of old men assembled at the base of the Pyramid, joking among themselves with lewd gestures and toothless mutterings.

The conch shells and the drums suddenly became quiet. His headdress disarrayed from his long dance, Molotl moved again to the edge of the Pyramid stairs where all could behold him. He spoke, his mouth moving within the borders of the painted white circle like a pink animal.

"O Master Huitzilopochtli, O our Lord, O Lord of the Near, of the Nigh, O night, O wind," he began, "remember how thy hasty wrath killed thy sister Coyolxauhqui, the Moon, whose head now hangs in the sky. Let not thy wrath again kill those who are thy people. We make this gift in the presence of Coyolxauhqui, the Moon, so that thou may remember.

"Let me not meet thy annoyance, thy wrath. And do thou dispose as thou wilt dispose. And it was ordained above us, it was arranged in the land of the dead, in the heavens, that we have been forsaken. In truth now thy annoyance, thy anger, descends; it gathers, thou who art the Lord of the Nigh. Castigation, pestilence grow; they increase. For the plague is reaching the earth."

Waving his knife, he paced back and forth, gazing fiercely at those below or alternately, at the full moon overhead.

"May this be all; cease amusing thyself, O Master, O Lord. May the smoke, the cloud of thy ire, cease; may the fire, the blaze of thy rage, be extinguished. May the earth be at rest. May the spoonbills sing, may they preen themselves. May the people call to thee, supplicate thee, know thee."

He paused, closing his eyes, and bringing the knife up flat against his chest, as though to embrace it.

"This is all. Thus I fall before thee, I throw myself before thee; I cast myself into the place whence none rise, whence none leave, the place of terror, of fear. May I not have aroused thy annoyance; may I not have walked upon thy fury. O, Master, O our Lord, I perform thy office, do thy work."

On a signal from a general, a single column of prisoners began mounting the stairs. They went up slowly, up the left-hand staircase; they did not look about them. When the lead prisoner reached the top of the stairs, he looked directly at Molotl. "My son, my son," said the Sacrificial Priest, returning his gaze. "You are the food of Huitzilopochtli; your heart will be in heaven to give him strength."

After that brief benediction, which Molotl would repeat to each of the prisoners, the man was seized by four of the lesser priests, who placed him on his back over the stone. Each priest held an arm or a leg, and the fifth placed the yoke around his neck. His chest was arched upward, the convex surface of the stone block pressing into his back. Molotl approached and, without hesitating, sank his knife into the man's chest, which opened like a ripe pomegranate. When the knife went in, the prisoner gasped; his body convulsed, though the priests had it firmly pinned. The high priest immediately reached into the open chest and, with a twist, wrenched out the heart. He held it aloft, steam rising from it. Still palpitating, it pumped out a small amount of blood, which ran down the Sacrificial Priest's arm. Uttering a scream he dropped the heart into a fire burning in the center cavity of a huge wheellike horizontal stone. The other priests meanwhile rolled the corpse off the block and, with their feet, sent it tumbling down the stairs. Several ushers, stationed at various steps, made certain it reached bottom. Even as its downward journey began, Molotl addressed the next victim. "My son, my son," he said, looking into the doomed man's eyes.

After the first body reached the base of the Pyramid, it was dragged by a group of the old men across the courtyard, and out through the narrow courtyard gate, escorted by the captor-owner. Medina focused on the fresh coating of blood on the stairs. His ears throbbed from the strange brew, and his forehead dripped with perspiration. The red-brown river, he thought, cascading down; down, down, down, through the courtyard, down the avenue, past the palace, into the canal, into the lake. The red-brown lake, the lake that smelled. The red-brown ships, the red-brown sails, the red ice, the red-brown ships skidding over the red-brown ice. He stared at the trail of blood and the old men dragging the body. Old men, new men, no men, all men, amen. Amen, body, Christ, red, blood. This is his body, his blood, my body, my blood, whose body? his, his, his, forgive me, Lord, for I have sunk, sunk, sinned to the river sliding in the blood of the lamb, on the lamb. As the second body came down, an usher slipped momentarily in trying to right it. See! Sliding slipping. Oh, wonderful, José, wonderful. Look, look, look. He turned to José, and opened his mouth, but nothing came out. As his body began rocking back and forth, the old sergeant-priest took his arm, and with José on the other side, led them out of the courtyard along the trail of blood toward the skull-rack.

Relays of old men were now hard at work, dragging body after body to the rack, dropping them in front of it in orderly rows. The captors crowded around a low table at which a government official sat, reconfirming their claims, and recording them. "How many captives?" the official asked.

"That is the first of two," answered a warrior. "The second has not yet arrived."

"Please wait then until it does. Mark the first with your token. Next?"

The warrior pulled a ribbon bearing the insignia of his family from his sash and, walking over to his prisoner, tied it around his ankle. He expected to come away with an arm and leg at least, resigned to the likelihood the priests would press their claim to all of the second captive. This one was by far the better of the two, he reflected, knowing it had been fattened at least a month longer than the second.

"José, where is he taking us?" asked Medina aloud in Spanish as the three skirted a pile of firewood.

"To Hell," replied José amiably, pushing his cowl off his head. He too had been unable to keep up the shallow pretense afforded them by their robes. But while Medina had simply left off playacting, José had entered it more deeply. Under the influence of the drug, he regarded himself as a fully ordained Aztec priest. That he happened to be Catholic struck him as insignificant. Hardly worth concealing, he told himself unctuously, considering the extent of the holy power bestowed on him by the dancing god on the Pyramid, he in the red vestments with the white circle around his mouth.

"Hell?" repeated Medina. "Hell?"

He looked at his friend. José was walking with a strange stateliness, holding his bare head high, and nodding condescendingly to a group of Aztec warriors.

"Good evening, my friends," said José, addressing them in perfect Italian, and raising his hand in a blessing.

"No, no," cried Medina, certain not only that Hell was about to engulf him, and that he was destined to be sacrificed, but also that—worse in a way—he had lost his friend. He spun on his heel, to escape, to run, to save himself. All he succeeded in doing, however, was falling down, his knife clattering to the flagstones. Taking hold of him more firmly, the old sergeant-priest reached down and lifted him to his feet. Then he guided Medina to the temple facing the skull-rack. As they entered the yawning serpent mouth that was the doorway, Medina shuddered. He felt his soul being devoured, felt the serpent greedily chewing on it, felt it die, felt it slithering, broken, down the monster's gullet. An acute pain seized him.

"My soul, it's gone," he wailed drunkenly, tears gushing from his eyes.

"Nonsense, my friend," said José, his face suffused with calm. "I have it here in my pocket, and I will make sure it is returned to you, perhaps even somewhat improved."

Instead of following Medina and the sergeant-priest into the temple, José headed toward the other priests. They were already at work on the prisoners and José wanted to see exactly how they were proceeding and whether he might assist. They were priests of his own order, after all.

Inside, the walls and ceiling of the temple were black with soot. Large pots filled with water stood at one side. In the center of the floor, a fire blazed beneath a pot of boiling water. The old sergeant-priest led Medina, still weeping disconsolately, to a stool and made him sit. He handed him a cup. Medina drank. The mysterious liquid! Delighted, he took another sip, and as his tongue sought out the familiar, evanescent kernel, his grief for his recently departed soul vanished as quickly as it had come. He watched the steam rising from the pot. The sergeant-priest, who had also taken a sip from the cup, returned Medina's knife to him almost gently. He liked the deer-men. It was good they were priests.

José leaned over and studied the actions of the priest's hands. The priest had made an incision around the base of the prisoner's neck, and up the back of the neck and head. Without removing the ears, he pulled the skin neatly over the skull and laid it aside. Then leaning heavily on the knife, he sawed through the neck, forcing the blade through with a straight downward stroke. The head came off. He quickly severed the hands and feet, placing them near the head and the skin. These belonged to the priests.

No sooner had he finished than the warrior who was watching took what remained of the corpse, and dragged it to one of the several wooden blocks standing off to one side of the temple. There, he began removing the limbs with a much larger knife. Several members of his family joined him, as did a government official, who soon departed with Moctezuma's portion, the left thigh. The entire plaza between the skull-rack and the temple had by now taken on the aspect of a vast butchering area. The old men kept bringing bodies, the priests exacted their toll, the government its, and the warriors theirs, the remaining torsos destined for the carnivorous animals in the royal zoo. The stench became so powerful that no one breathed through his nose. Everyone had something to do, and they worked with industrious efficiency.

Confident he could perform the priestly function as expertly as the priest he had watched, José knelt beside an unattended corpse, and made a neat incision around the base of its neck. As he struggled to pull the skin off the head intact, a newly radiant Medina suddenly appeared beside him. Medina watched for a moment, fascinated.

When José pulled the skin off, Medina moved closer, peering into the eye sockets of the skull. Then, in a slow, deliberate gesture, he reached down, and thrust his hand into the prisoner's chest. It was still warm inside. He withdrew his hand and stared at it, first one side, then the other. There was a small amount of blood on it. He wiped the blood on his face, his hand passing over his forehead, his eyes, his nose, his mouth. His tongue tentatively tasted it. He shifted his body toward the prisoner's midsection, pulling his knife from his belt, his eyes traveling over the smooth skin. He inserted the knife into the thigh, and carefully carved out a small section. When he finished, he raised the flesh over his head for an instant to look at it in the light, then lowered it into his mouth. He tore a piece off with his teeth and began to chew, handing what was left of the morsel to his friend.

"Here, José, share with me," he said.

"That should be cooked," came an Aztec voice from behind them.

Medina knew the voice and did not want to hear it. He kept chewing, his eyes clinging to José. It will go away, like everything goes away, he thought magically.

But it was José who went away, for the voice had cut through the insanity of the night. Though he could not understand the words, he knew the voice. That was enough. His shoulders sagged as he let the knife drop from his hand. Sorrowfully, he turned his face upward.

His red ceremonial robe tinkling as he moved his arm, Molotl pointed to the Europeans.

"Remove their garments," he commanded.

The sergeant-priest stood alongside him, and watched as three of Molotl's assistants approached and began to peel off the cowls, first José's, then Medina's. At the same time, one of the priests slipped a short cord around each of their necks. It was an act more symbolic than essential, for the cords were light and flimsy.

On their feet and naked, Medina and José looked at the high priest, Medina dully, José with hatred.

"What imperfections are these?" asked Molotl, examining the scars remaining from Medina's encounter with the cactus hedge. An expression of revulsion crossed his face. "No, he is not fit. Gods are immaculate. Like you, Lord," he trailed off as he turned toward José. He let his hand slide down José's thigh.

"You see, he is perfect," said Molotl to the other priests, who murmured assent. Then to José, "Come, my Lord, let us prepare ourselves in private." He took the end of the cord holding José from the hand of the same priest who had slipped it around their necks, and led José away. "Keep the other here," he ordered over his shoulder to the old sergeant-priest.

"José! Stay here," cried Medina. Something was dreadfully wrong. He lunged blindly forward, grasping for José. But arms came from nowhere and enclosed him.

Medina struggled a moment longer, before collapsing. José had neither fought nor looked back.

For two hours, Medina sat dumbly on a stool not far from the serpent-mouth temple. The sergeant-priest, sitting next to him, had covered Medina with a large maguey-fiber cape. No longer reeling, his mind nevertheless refused to anchor itself, flitting capriciously from one surface to another, whether thought or object, like a fickle yellow insect. When he saw José come out of the building beside the main Pyramid, part of his mind reached out in recognition. José! José! My friend! it cried. The rest of it, however, danced and gyrated, pushing diversions between him and José and casting doubt that it was José at all. So downcast and ashen-faced? José? Never! Do you hear? José, listen to me! Please turn around and listen to me. I have something important to tell you.

It was a mute, unheard speech. José did not look back as he was led up the Pyramid. Medina could not move except to look away.

A few minutes later a conch shell trumpet sounded from the top of the Pyramid. Medina forced himself to turn and look up. José's naked body, splashed with blood, tumbled slowly down the steep stone stairway below the sacrificial platform. Suddenly it stopped, legs splayed upward, one arm bent beneath the back, the other arm and the head dangling down over a step. Two black-robed acolytes followed the body down, and gave it a kick in unison. The corpse resumed its twisted roll a few feet farther and halted again. The two men climbed down the steps once more, one of them almost slipping on the bloody stones, and kicked again. After perhaps two dozen repetitions, José's lifeless form finally hit the flagstones at the base of the Pyramid.

Medina stood paralyzed. José was dead. There was nothing he could do. Yet he wanted to scream, to kill. That viper Molotl! A taste of Toledo steel would straighten him out. If he only had his sword. He would show them how a Spaniard dies.

The old sergeant-priest gently touched Medina's arm, softly muttering a few unintelligible words. Medina paused, and brought himself under control. He could accomplish nothing now. But later!

Four elderly attendants approached José's body and dragged it in the direction of the great skull-rack. Medina could watch no longer. He let the old man take him away.

CHAPTER

XI

Medina was returned to his chambers in the palace almost immediately. There he found Nacha waiting. She was alone. When he told her what had happened, that José was dead, she did not seem disturbed.

"Do not mourn for your friend," she told him. "He has gone to the mansions of Lord Tonatiuh, the sun. There is no greater reward than to die on the stone of sacrifice. From that stone one rises again."

"Jesus Christ rose from the dead," he told her in a monotone, "to help the living reach the kingdom of Heaven." Grief seemed to bury Medina.

She cuddled close to him on the mat in his chamber. Medina could sense that she was trying to share the burden of his sorrow, trying to comfort him. He put his arms around her shoulders, drew her close, and fell asleep, exhausted.

As the days passed, Medina gradually recovered from the shock of José's death. He and Nacha spent almost all their hours together alone, passing the time in simple pleasures and long conversations. The other girls were gone, and Molotl made no more appearances. Medina gave up guessing what the next day might bring. There were, he noticed, more guards posted around the chambers than before. Escape no longer seemed a possibility.

Tonatiuh, the sun, was dominant, a looming presence who bored deeper and deeper into Medina's consciousness. Part of it was because of his isolation, but another part was Nacha's teachings. Gradually, Medina spoke less of Christianity, and found himself more and more entwined in the theology of the Indians as she told him what she could of the Aztecs, and introduced him to the pantheon of their gods.

Sometimes Medina would stretch out, rest his head in Nacha's lap and let her relate the histories of her people near Tabasco or of the Aztecs. He was always curious about the origin of the great civilization in which he found himself.

"The Mexica, the Aztecs, came down from the north a long time ago," she told him, "at first living in the swamps like animals, despised by the other tribes then in control of the valley. But gradually the Mexica became strong and excelled in war. I do not know when, but a long time ago they started building Tenochtitlan. First, it was nothing but reed huts, some of them floating on the lake itself, for, according to the stories, there was so little space. The good lands were the property of their enemies. But you see what they have done. Now it is the greatest city of all."

"It is very large and very beautiful," said Medina, saying it in such a way as to compliment Nacha rather than the Aztecs. She was pleased.

"I have told you of Tonatiuh," she went on, "but there are many lesser gods, too.

"Quetzalcoatl, God of the Star in the East, was once a strong god. It is said he left Mexico many years ago, on a serpent-raft sailing from the morning sun-coast, as I have told you. The priests say he had light skin—like yours—

and that he promised to return one day. There is talk
that among your people Quetzalcoatl may dwell. The Emperor sometimes fears that it is so."

"No, there is no such god among us, Nacha. Only that
One we carry in our hearts and minds. He of whom I
have already spoken."

"Then there is Tlaloc," she continued, unable to recon-
cile what Medina said with the palace rumors of Quetzalcoatl's imminent return. "He is the God of Rain and almost as powerful as Huitzilopochtli, the God of War."

"Does Tlaloc also demand human sacrifice?" Medina
asked.

"Yes. But not war captives, like Huitzilopochtli."

"Who then?"

"Children."

"Aztec children?"

"Yes. Often. But children of Enemies-of-the-House,
too."

"It is a terrible thing."

"It is our way, Lord. My own people have the same
customs in Yucatan." She slipped back into the usage for
which he had once chastised her.

"Do not call me 'Lord,' " he said firmly.

"But it is a true thing," she replied, "for now that your
scars have healed, Molotl has decreed that you are the
Lord Tezcatlipoca."

"Never mind what Molotl decrees," he answered. But
he said it unconvincingly. To be addressed as a god, even
an Aztec god slated for sacrifice, no longer disturbed him.
Nor did the irony of his position escape him. I was sent
to kill a man for claiming to be a Christian prince, he

thought, and I end up no less than a pagan god.

When Nacha called him "Lord" again, he made no attempt to correct her.

That night, Medina had a vivid dream. In it, he had the sensation of being awakened by someone talking beyond the curtained door to the corridor. He got off the bed, walked to the doorway, and pushed the curtains aside.

An Aztec officer stood in the dim torchlight of the hall conversing in a low voice with the two guards. On seeing Medina, he nodded as though he had been expecting him. The officer said a few more words to the guards, then beckoned to Medina, and set off down the corridor. It seemed completely natural for Medina to follow him.

After they emerged from the building, the two of them were joined by an escort of four warriors who followed them discreetly across a plaza illumined by the light of a crescent moon. Without uttering a word, the officer turned off the plaza into a dark side street. After a few minutes they reached another plaza, in the center of which stood a low rectangular building with an open door which emitted a faint light. The officer led Medina to the door, then stood outside as Medina stepped on through. Medina felt completely calm, like a disinterested spectator. He was detached, without emotion. Even his body seemed to be flowing along more than walking. An incredibly realistic dream, Medina realized somewhere in his mind.

The inside of the building was a single room, perhaps two hundred feet long, and empty except at the far end where a wooden cross stood on an altar on a raised dais under the glaring light of two large torches. Medina saw a man kneeling in front of the altar, his head bowed before the crucifix. Then the man slowly stood up, raising a chalice toward the cross. Medina could see the white surplice hanging from the man's shoulders.

My God, my God, he thought. A fellow Christian, a priest and here in Tenochtitlan! Medina wanted to call out, to run up to him, to embrace him. But as a Christian he refrained from interrupting the Mass. Instead, he quietly moved forward until he was about twenty feet behind the priest. Then he knelt, unbelieving, listening to the almost inaudible words in Latin. Medina crossed himself, and made his own silent prayer of thanksgiving. He felt part of a miracle.

Finally the priest set the chalice on the altar and covered it. He stepped backward three paces and knelt again. Finally he rose, genuflected, and turned around from the altar. The priest had no clothes on under the surplice except for a loincloth. For the first time Medina saw his face. A chill went up his spine. It was the face of no ordinary priest, no paunchy, tonsured Franciscan, no serious, paternal Dominican. The bearded face was the same one Medina had seen in the battle at Tabasco, the tattooed forehead, and ornaments stuck through the ears and the nose. The face above the beard was hideously painted with white circles around the eyes. The mouth grinned broadly at Medina.

"Yes, my son?" said Martim Braga.

Medina was speechless. He just stared at the macabre figure before him.

"Ah, I perceive the question." Braga smiled. "Yes, my

son, it was here in His travels that He learned of the Holy
Eucharist, before He sailed back to the East on the serpent-
raft."

Braga slowly walked back toward the altar. Then he
turned, facing Medina again.

"My son," he said, "I will ask the Emperor to send you
to your Spaniards with the message that no new priests
are needed here. If the Spaniards wish to come, tell them
to throw away their weapons, to approach on bended knee,
as did their Saviour before them."

The last thing Medina remembered was a smiling Braga
making the sign of the cross.

In the morning, when Medina awoke, he was half-
startled to find himself on the bed in his room. Then
he had to smile inwardly. A Knight of the Golden Fleece
confusing a vivid nightmare with reality, like a small boy.
He shook his head in mock self-chastisement. He did not
mention his experience to Nacha.

Each dawn brought with it the throbbing of a giant
signal drum and the wails of conch shell trumpets from
the tops of the city's many pyramids. Although Medina
could not see the pyramids from the enclosed patio, he
knew that the trumpets signaled another day of sacrifices.
He knew, too, that when they sounded again at noon,
when the sun was in the zenith, somewhere in the city
human chests were being torn open with gray flint knives,
and hearts were being offered to the burning orb above.

On one level of his consciousness he was aware that it
was only a matter of time until guards would enter their
chamber and take him or Nacha, or both, to meet the
sacrificial knife. Another level of his mind, however, re-

fused to accept the possibility, and told him that when the heavy curtains of the corridor doorway opened, and the guards entered, it would be to take him to Moctezuma, that the Emperor would seek his counsel in the matter of the deer-men, and that then he, accompanied by Nacha, would be sent as an emissary of peace to Cortés. Several times each day, the curtains did open, but only to admit attendants bearing exquisite dishes of food, replacements of clothing, or new charcoal and incense for the braziers.

One evening, as Medina and Nacha sat in the garden beneath the canopy of emerging stars, he felt that the woman beside him was somehow his connection to the bright, sparkling mysteries in the sky above. Through her, because of her, the power of the universe flowed from him and to him. Because he was in an alien land, because he was merging his life substance with an ancient, distant race, he was all the more awed by the discovery of his connectedness. The woman beside him was not a Spaniard, not a European, not a Catholic, but simply Woman. And he, Man. Their sharing, their unity, reached deeper than if they merely came from the same historical stream, the same religious heritage. The oneness he felt with her and, through her, with the starry universe above them, was primeval, incredibly ancient, almost from before there was time.

He reached out and touched her arm, feeling suddenly as though he was touching all life, all living things. Lost in her own thoughts, she murmured softly, then turned to him. She reached out and grasped his arm. They looked at one another in the darkness, sensing that they had reached some new level with each other, an intimacy that transcended self, that transcended hurt, and that transcended expectation. The exchange of touch meant everything, for by it they had blessed each other. They marveled silently at their unity. At length, he drew the cotton blanket over her shoulders to protect her from the chill of the night air. Later, much later, they walked back to the chamber, walked as though they were helping each other.

It was still dark when she awakened him by breathing into his ear.

"Nacha, Nacha," he murmured, opening the covers to let her in. He realized he had been waiting for her; not for hours, days, or weeks, but for his entire life. Her small, vigorous body bestowed on him early that morning a complete healing. And he—broad, powerful, and passionate—taught her that the Lord Tezcatlipoca, at least this Lord Tezcatlipoca, was a lord of tenderness.

Afterward, floating in a luminous peace, they held each other in their arms. In his mind's eye, a beautiful city of curious architecture magically appeared, gleaming in a sunlit jungle. Then it was gone.

To pass the time, Nacha taught him to play *patolli*, a board game at which they spent long hours in the patio beside the whispering fountain. The center of the board was a Greek cross around which they moved colored stone "men" according to the toss of bean dice. He always played with green stones, Nacha always with the red. When the red and green occupied the same space on the board, it meant that the color that first occupied the space was "killed." The roll of the dice determined whether a man was "killed." On one occasion, he pointed out to Nacha

that each day for them was like the roll of the dice; that
he never knew whether a new dawn would bring death or
another day of pleasure in her company.

Nacha smiled at him and gave a small, tinkling laugh.
"My Lord, there is nothing uncertain about your fate. It
is all ordained. Ordained by your *tonalli*."

"What do you mean?"

"Your day-sign, your day of birth. That is your *tonalli*,
your destiny in this world."

"You mean my fate is determined in advance?"

"Yes, my Lord. Even the day of your death. All this is
known to the gods. Even to the *tonalpouhqui*."

"*Tonalpouhqui?*"

"The soothsayers. They study the books of days, the
tonalamatl. From these they can tell you your fate."

"Have they told you yours?"

"Yes, my Lord."

"What did they say?"

"I am not allowed to tell, my Lord. It would not be
respectful to the gods."

Medina shifted his position on the mat in front of the
patolli board. He looked down at the board, and picked
up one of his green pieces, and set it in a space occupied
by one of her red men. He looked up at her.

"There. Your man is dead. Was that determined by
your *tonalli* or by my *tonalli?*"

She smiled and reached out her hand, gently resting it
on his arm. "Marcos-tzin, the *tonalli* determines one's
overall destiny. Within that destiny the gods determine
our successes and failures."

"Why do the gods bother?"

"They put humans on the earth to serve the gods. We

are their servants. If we serve them well, they are happy and smile on us. If we serve them poorly, they are angry."

"So that is what the sacrifices are for?"

"Yes, my Lord. When the gods have smiled, we give them offerings of thanks. When the gods are angry, we give them offerings so they will no longer hurt us."

"But why do the priests kill humans as offerings?"

"Not only people are offerings, Marcos-tzin. When I burn incense at dawn, noon, and sunset, it is an offering. They enjoy its odor."

"But," Medina persisted, "why cannot they be satisfied with incense alone? Why do they have to be offered humans?"

"My Lord, the gods have no way of being fed except by us, whom they put on earth to be their servants. If we do not feed them, they will punish us. Just like you, they could not live on the odor of incense."

"But why human flesh? Why not other creatures?"

"We do give them other creatures, dogs, birds, and other things. But when there is drought, when there is hunger, we know that those offerings have not been enough. We have to give them the best food we know."

"But why must so many die?"

"If drought, famine, or pestilence persists, we know the gods are not satisfied. We have no better food for them, so we simply must give them more of it."

Medina thought he perceived a hole in her logic. "If the people are hungry, why shouldn't they just feed themselves rather than the gods?"

She smiled at him, as though she were answering a small child's questions. "They do, my Lord, they do. The gods only want the heart and the blood. That's what they live on. The rest of the body, the meat, is left over. But it feeds the people, and the gods are happy for them to have it."

That evening, when the torches had been lit in their chamber, and after their supper, Medina found himself looking at the walls, wishing he could take Nacha by the hand and fly through them, over the city, over the lake, over the smoking mountain to the east. But to what? To Cortés and his band of gold-hungry pirates? Would he take her to them? To Seville? He thought of the naked Indian slaves he had seen there. To his family's castle in Castile? To Florence? A cannibal in the court of the Medicis? He smiled inwardly at the thought. But deeper inside he felt pain, the hurt of hopelessness. It must have shown on his face.

"Marcos-tzin, are you sad?" The concerned eyes of Nacha confronted him. "What is the matter?"

"Nacha, I don't want us to die, to be sacrificed."

"But it is an honor, my Lord."

"I don't need that honor; I would rather have you, and life."

"You do have me, Marcos-tzin, and it is a sweet joy for me, too. But those who die on the stone of sacrifice are reborn in the mansions of Tonatiuh, the sun."

"The mansions of the sun? Where are they?"

"Only the dying know that, my Lord. The wise men say that we, the living, only need to know that the joys of life are but brief, empty dreams. That we are blind except when the gods let us see."

"We are blind now?"

"Yes, my Lord."

Medina got up and paced the room. Across his mind

flitted his strange sensations and experiences with José during that night of sacrifices in the sacred precinct. He *had* felt that he was seeing things with an extraordinary clarity at the time.

He turned to Nacha. "Even if this is a dream, aren't you afraid to die?"

"Yes, my Lord." Nacha nodded. "I am afraid. But that is because right now I am blind, and don't want to leave you. So I forget, and think that this," she waved her hand around the chamber, "that this is a place of reality."

Medina came to where she was kneeling and touched her shoulder. "Nacha, this *is* real," he said. He bent over and kissed her on the lips. "And this, too."

Nacha's lips quivered, and Medina thought he saw a tear in one eye. She threw her arms around his legs and pressed her cheek against his knee. After a moment she jumped up, wiped at her eyes and did her best to smile.

"Marcos-tzin," she said, "I will dance for you."

She put some cushions behind his head and went into the patio, and then into the adjoining room. When she returned, she was wearing a fresh, elaborately ornamented and fringed white dress. Two garlands of blossoms encircled her head, and in each hand she carried a bouquet of flowers. From her hair hung tassels of gold and feathers. Around her wrists were bracelets of turquoise beads, and bound on her ankles were strings of gold bells that tinkled as she walked. She knelt before him, bowed her head and rose. She took the top garland off her head and laid it on his.

"Thanks to the Lord God Tezcatlipoca, who brought music to us from the Lord God Tonatiuh, the sun," she said formally. Nacha turned and dropped a pinch of incense in a brazier.

She began to move her feet to the left and right, the bells lightly jingling in time to her steps. She faced Medina as she moved to one side and then the other, her arms outstretched, gently waving the bundles of flowers. She smiled as she kept her eyes fixed upon him, and began to sing in a light, happy voice. Medina could not understand the words, but he could tell they were a message to him. Occasionally she would twirl and start what seemed to be a new verse. After about fifteen minutes, she knelt, then rose, and came over to sit beside him. He kissed her, touched by her beauty and grace.

"What were you saying?" he asked.

"Many things, my Lord."

"Tell me one of them."

She paused, and then recited gently:

O my friend and beloved,
Enjoy the sweet flowers I bring.
Although these pleasures will leave us,
So will the pains of life.

Be happy while spring is with you,
Rejoice in the beautiful garden,
And wearing a garland of flowers,
Enjoy my steps and my song.

Truly the joys and pleasures of life
Are but a bouquet of flowers
That, passed from hand to hand,
Fades, withers, and is dead.

I remember that we must leave flowers
   and songs.
Let us enjoy ourselves now,
Let us sing now!
For we go,
We disappear.
I shall have to leave the precious
   flowers.

"*You* are my precious flower," he said.
"And you mine, Marcos-tzin."
He reached up and pulled her to him. She responded by
caressing his face and kissing him. She pulled aside his
tunic and her own. Whispering to him, she turned onto
her back, and pulled him onto her. Minutes later, spent,
he felt himself melting into a distant past. His eyes closed,
his head resting on Nacha's breast, he saw her again, walking away across a field of wild flowers. She looked back
over her shoulder at him and smiled.

CHAPTER

XII

The two men walked purposefully through the immense gardens of the Emperor's palace. One of them was an Indian, dressed in the garb of a *pochteca* and carrying a black staff. The other, Martim Braga, was taller, tan, with a trimmed black beard and a tattooed forehead. Dressed in a white tunic, he carried a bouquet of flowers in his right hand, in the style of a noble. Occasionally he lifted the flowers to his nose as he walked past the fishponds, the fountains, the rare shrubs, and trees. Ahead of him was a massive alabaster building surrounded by colonnades of red jasper, each column carved out of a single block of stone. Braga was impressed, but not as impressed as he had been by some of the ruins he had seen during his years in Yucatan.

"The House of the Animal Gods," his companion explained to him in Mayan.

As they approached the building, Braga could hear the screams and roars of the big cats waiting to be fed. There was a wild smell, too. Shortly he and the interpreter entered a very large open court paved with mosaics of different-colored stones. Low walls divided the open area into three sections. The larger wild animals, including jaguars, ocelots, cougars, and coyotes, were kept in low cages made of thick wooden beams.

Attendants, unmindful of their presence, engaged in their feeding chores. Several approached the cages with baskets and then, setting them down, began tossing pieces of meat between the bars to the screaming jaguars.

The two men fell silent and watched the keepers move over to the ocelot cage with their baskets. Then Braga touched the *pochteca*'s arm. "We must get on for our meeting with the Lord Moctezuma," he said.

They walked toward a large doorway at the end of the zoo's court. On their right were deep square pits, some twenty feet across, in which Braga could see eagles and other birds of prey. Half of each pit was covered with a wickerwork mesh and half with stone slabs. Under the stone slabs he saw wooden perches jutting from the walls.

On the far side of the court they passed walled ponds in which alligators floated. Beside the ponds were rows of huge pottery jars, some half the height of a man. The *pochteca* stopped, turned to Braga with a half-smile, and motioned for him to look down into one of the jars. Braga leaned over, peered in, and saw rattlesnakes coiled on the bottom. They seemed to be resting on a bed of feathers.

Braga nodded. "Truly this is a temple of living gods."

They passed from the court through a small antechamber, and suddenly found themselves in a large hall whose beauty almost made Braga gasp. There was nothing like it in Yucatan. Slabs of gold and silver completely covered the walls and ceilings, reflecting light from three side doors. The slabs appeared to be almost a finger in thickness.

What the Spaniards would do for this! thought Braga.

"This is the Great Speaker's private chapel, his most holy place," whispered the *pochteca*.

At the opposite end of the hall sat the god-king on a raised dais, surrounded by a cluster of noblemen and priests, including Molotl, sitting on mats on the floor.

Looking down on them from the center of each of the three main walls were mosaics representing an eagle, a serpent, and a jaguar. The mosaics were constructed of red stones, turquoise, jade, and pearls. Mosaic constructions also outlined the tops and bottoms of the walls.

The interpreter, seeing one of Moctezuma's aides nod toward them, said, "We should go to the Emperor now, my Lord."

They went forward and knelt before the Emperor, touching their hands to the floor and kissing them. Then, keeping their eyes averted, they joined the group sitting below Moctezuma.

The Emperor turned to the *pochteca*. "Please communicate these words to my son, Martim-tzin, from the south." He nodded toward Braga.

"I want to know what you have to say about these deer-men coming from the east."

The *pochteca* translated Moctezuma's question from Nahuatl into Mayan.

"Great Speaker," Braga answered, "these men are mere mortals. They kill for gold." He pointed to the precious metals paneling the room about them. "They will want all this to take away with them on their floating pyramids. They are destroyers."

"But my son," said Moctezuma, "they send me rare gifts of green obsidian." The Emperor touched the necklace of glass beads that adorned his neck.

"Great Lord, those are but worthless trinkets in the land from which they come. They only wish to deceive you," said Braga.

"Then what do you propose that I should do?" asked the Emperor.

"It is simple, my Lord," said Braga. "I have come to you because I have a plan. I know their ways of battle. As you have heard, I have fought them successfully in the Yucatan."

"My emissaries say the deer-men have strange ways of battle," said Moctezuma. "They do not seek prisoners for sacrifice to their gods."

"Exactly," replied Braga. "They are killers, not capturers. Whereas your warriors fight alone, each trying to capture a prisoner for himself, those of the deer-men work together as one creature to kill as many of the enemy as possible."

"But then how do they get prisoners to sacrifice to their gods?" asked Moctezuma.

"They believe in the one great sacrifice, my Lord. The sacrifice that was made for them by the Son of God, Jesus Christ, long, long ago in a distant land."

"You mean one sacrifice long ago was enough to satisfy their gods?" The Emperor was astonished.

"Their God, my Lord. They have only one."

"Only one? This woman-idol they put in our temples on the coast?"

"No, Great Speaker. She is not their God."

"But I have reports that they worship her," said Moctezuma.

Braga did not know how to proceed. He decided to return to the subject he had come to discuss. "My Lord," he said, "I wish to help you. As you know, these deer-men are Enemies-of-the-House. I know how to defeat them in battle."

"Speak."

"I can train your officers in how to fight them, how to win in battle against them. There are secrets."

"What are these secrets?"

"First, your soldiers must be taught not to try to capture these deer-men. Instead they must do only one thing: kill."

"The gods will be angry if we ignore their need for offerings."

"Some will surrender, and some will be wounded. You can offer those."

"Wounded captives are too imperfect for the gods," replied the Emperor. "But what are the other secrets?"

"There are special ways of fighting, ways that I can show your generals."

"What of the thundersticks that kill many each time with their lightning?" asked Moctezuma.

"There are ways of dealing with these. One way is to wait for rain before attacking them. Rain makes it hard for them to make fire in their thundersticks."

"But thunder and lightning are the companions of rain." The Emperor sounded skeptical. "And what of the giant deer that they ride? They are the most dangerous of all. Even now I hear that the brave Enemies-of-the-House, the Tlaxcalans, run from these creatures."

"There are ways to deal with the giant deer, too," replied Braga. "I can tell your generals."

The Sacrificial Priest Molotl bent his face down so that his irritation would not be apparent. "My Lord," he said, "these are just words. And they may be lies. Whether the deer-men are gods, sons of the Lord Quetzalcoatl, or whether they are ordinary mortals makes no difference.

Let them be welcomed to our city here. They are few in number, and here they would be surrounded by the millions of our people in the center of our land. If they should prove to be less than the sons of Quetzalcoatl, we can easily capture them, as in a giant trap."

Braga could not understand the interchange between Moctezuma and his high priest, but the *pochteca* gave him a summary translation. He realized that he must speak up.

"My Great Lord, to have these deer-men, these Castilians, in your midst would be like having poisonous snakes slip into your bed."

Moctezuma waved his hand. "I must think on all this. Let us stop this conversation now. It is almost dining time. We shall leave now and return to the palace." He got up, and they all followed him out into the courtyard.

As the entourage passed the jaguar cages, the Emperor paused. He turned to Braga and asked, through the interpreter, "What animals are worshiped by these deer-men, these *castlitans*?" The strange word came with difficulty to his lips.

Braga hesitated. He thought, then said, "None, my Lord."

Moctezuma looked astonished. "How strange!" he exclaimed.

Braga thought. "But there is one kind of godlike animal that all in their country fear," he said. "It is the enemy of their God, and is a kind of man-serpent with wings, called the Devil."

Molotl looked at Moctezuma. "How can these be the sons of Quetzalcoatl when they fear Quetzalcoatl himself?" he said. The Emperor shook his head incredulously.

As the entourage started up again, Braga happened to glance into a basket of food a zoo attendant had left beside the jaguars' cage. Inside was part of a human torso.

The next day, Braga was called into Moctezuma's presence again, this time in the Emperor's chambers. Molotl and a one-eyed general were there, but not the rest of the group that had been present the previous day.

"Martim-tzin, my son," the Emperor said, "the Sacrificial Priest here and others say that your way of fighting the deer-men would be offensive to the gods. If we killed in battle instead of capturing prisoners for sacrifice, the gods would be angry. War is a holy activity. If we failed the gods, we, their servants, would be destroyed by them."

Braga started to speak.

The Emperor raised his hand to silence him. "My generals are, however, interested in learning how to fight the giant deer."

"My Lord, I can tell them all."

"Words are not enough, they say, Martim-tzin. They wish a demonstration."

"I do not understand, my Lord."

"The priests hold a deer-man here in Tenochtitlan. We will arm him in the manner of a warrior, and put him on the giant deer you brought. You, on foot, will show us how it is done."

Braga felt a surge of anger. The fools didn't believe him. And this was his only horse! He was going to have to kill it, or the man on it, in order to prove himself. He held his breath until he could calm down.

"Very well, my Lord. So be it. When shall we do this?"

"In ten days. As the sun approaches the ninth heaven."
The Emperor pointed toward the zenith.

When Braga and the *pochteca* withdrew, the Sacrificial
Priest turned to Moctezuma. "My Lord Great Speaker,"
he said, "the deer-man for some days now has been in the
role of the Lord God Tezcatlipoca. To put him onto the
back of a deer may offend the gods."

Moctezuma nodded. "Well spoken, *tlamacazqui* Molotl.
There must be an offering, a high offering, to atone for
this departure from holy ritual. What do you suggest?"

"There is a woman, my Lord," said Molotl, "who is his
god-bride and dwells with him. That would be atonement
for his act."

After the Sacrificial Priest left him, the Emperor rose
and left the chamber. He crossed a garden in which a silver
fountain played, and sat down on an alabaster bench in
his aviary. A quetzal, bronze-green and rose-breasted,
perched on a pine bough not far above him, preening
itself. Its long tail plumes waved lightly in the breeze like
fern fronds.

When he closed his eyes and pressed the palms of his
hands to his temples, the god-king thought he could see
the dark on the other side of the sun.

CHAPTER

XIII

One morning, a large collection of elegant Aztec clothing, carefully folded and packed in three ample baskets, arrived in the chamber.

"They are for you, my Lord, so that you may walk about and be known," Nacha told Medina.

"Walk about from the chamber to the garden?" he laughed.

"No," she smiled. "You must walk in the streets so that the people can see you and admire you. Tezcatlipoca is a handsome, unblemished god. Like you, my Lord."

"Nacha, you are equal to me."

"No, Lord, I am your servant."

That afternoon, in an entourage that included several priests as well as a pair of discreet guards, Medina was led through a residential section of Tenochtitlan, away from the sacred precinct. As Medina and the group walked, the people stepped reverently aside to let them pass, at the same time making what Medina took to be gestures of obeisance. Their fawning reminded him of the behavior of Moctezuma's emissaries on board Cortés' flagship. That incident seemed to Medina to be years in the past. For weeks now he had not let himself think of the Spanish army even though he heard through Nacha that Moctezuma had not as yet been able to discourage Cortés from setting out toward Tenochtitlan.

On the third day of afternoon walks, as they skirted

the sacred precinct once again, Medina suddenly stopped short. He could see in the distance, heading toward the precinct and surrounded by a throng, the long, gray neck of Montejo's riderless charger. The incongruous sight of a Spanish horse in the capital, and what it signified, shook him violently out of his godlike bearing.

He began to stride toward the horse; after momentary confusion, his retinue fell in behind him. They, too, were curious about the strange apparition ahead of them. It was one of the giant deer all Mexico had heard about.

As Medina came closer he could see that he was correct. Without question it was Montejo's horse, a Spanish saddle cinched around its belly. Yet nowhere could he make out the tattooed face he had glimpsed at the battle of Tabasco.

The crowd stood well back from the horse, fascinated but apprehensive at the same time. A single Indian, clearly not an Aztec, held the horse by its bridle, and was leading it slowly across the plaza. The Indian must have had lessons, thought Medina, noticing the correctness and confidence with which he handled the animal. Also, the Indian appeared to enjoy the attention lavished on him and his charge. He walked with his shoulders back, a look of superiority on his face, obviously mimicking the traditional haughtiness of the Aztecs. A contingent of Aztec warriors cleared the way ahead.

"Halt," demanded Medina. In spite of the authoritativeness of his command, the procession continued on.

"What do you wish, my Lord?" asked Nacha, appearing at Medina's elbow. She discreetly accompanied him as his interpreter.

"To know how this . . . " There was no word in Mayan for horse. Medina fumbled for a moment, at length finding the substitute. "To know how this deer came to Tenochtitlan. Who brought it here?"

"I will ask, my Lord," replied Nacha. She questioned the warriors walking near the horse. Smiling, she returned to Medina's entourage, which had fallen in behind the horse and slowly followed it.

"It comes from my land, Tabasco, my Lord," Nacha reported, "where it was captured in a war with the white ones. Your people. He who captured it is a great warrior and is now in the palace. The Emperor has asked that he be brought before him."

"What is the name of the warrior?" asked Medina, his heart starting to race.

"The Aztec warriors do not know."

"I wish to learn it."

"Yes, my Lord. It will be known in the palace."

Just then the warriors and the horse entered one of the numerous enclosed courtyards. The gate closed behind them, shutting out the crowd that followed.

Medina swore to himself, then ordered that he be taken back to his chamber. The sooner he got back to their house the sooner he would hear of the circumstances surrounding the arrival of the horse.

"Yes, my Lord," responded Nacha, turning at once, and setting out in the direction of the chamber, followed by an intent Medina, the priests, and his guards.

Yet for two days afterward not a shred of information reached Medina's ears. Nacha could learn little.

"No one will talk of this in the palace, my Lord," she told him.

"Leave me then with my thoughts awhile, Nacha," he replied, resigning himself to more long hours of ignorance. He walked out to the garden by himself, sitting down on one of the low stone benches. The guard, one of several stationed near the hedge since Medina's aborted escape attempt with José, ambled off toward a distant corner. Though he had been instructed to keep a watchful eye on Medina, he had also been told to be solicitous toward the living god, and to allow him as much privacy as possible.

Medina had barely seated himself when he heard a commotion coming from inside. When he looked toward the chamber he beheld the dark visage of Molotl. The Sacrificial Priest stopped at the garden door, and looked contemptuously at Medina.

"My Lord Tezcatlipoca," Molotl said by way of greeting, an unmistakable tone of derision in his voice.

Medina could not bring himself to nod, though he kept his eyes fastened hard on the black-garbed priest.

Suddenly Nacha stepped out of the entranceway of the chamber, stopping next to the high priest.

"Tell him," Molotl ordered Nacha.

Murmuring assent, Nacha obediently approached Medina. The usual liveliness in her face had vanished, thought Medina. Nacha looked pained.

"I am once again honored to address you, my Lord," Nacha began formally, her voice loud enough for Molotl to hear. "Molotl, the great high priest of the Aztecs, speaks for the Lord God Huitzilopochtli."

"He speaks for himself," growled Medina irreverently.

"It is the Lord Huitzilopochtli's desire," Nacha went on, "that the Lord Tezcatlipoca demonstrate his strength and godliness in combat."

The words shot through Medina. When Nacha had

begun her speech, he suspected that the time had arrived when he would be led up the Pyramid to the killing block. But to have to fight was a completely unexpected decree. In all his talks with Nacha, ritual combat had never been mentioned in terms of the duties or tasks of Tezcatlipoca.

He knew what such combat entailed. A prisoner was placed on the stone disc with a leg tethered to a short, restraining cord. The prisoner was handed a sham sword, a club with feathers attached, and told to defend himself. His opponent, an Aztec warrior, stepped onto the disc armed, not with a feathered club, but with his very real obsidian-edged war sword.

To Spanish eyes, the ensuing combat lacked completely the sense of fairness inherent in the code of European chivalry. The one occasion during his first days as Tezcatlipoca that he had watched a disc combat, the warrior had made mercifully short work of his tethered opponent, slashing his sword through the club, as though it were a blade of grass, before decapitating the helpless prisoner.

Medina's first impulse was to insist that such combat was not suited to a god as lofty as he, Tezcatlipoca. He realized at once, however, that Molotl could change the rules governing the behavior of mortal gods almost at will.

"When?" he asked Nacha.

"Now, my Lord," she replied in a hushed, agonized voice.

Molotl's priests entered, and began to dress him for combat. Assisting them, Medina noticed, was his captor. The priests fastened a feathered cape over Medina's shoulders. Then Atlacol, smiling, presented him with a basketry shield adorned with feathers.

Nacha watched with a horrified expression. Medina could see tears running down her cheeks. He wanted to embrace her, but the priests stopped him. He searched for words that might comfort her.

"We'll be together soon in the mansions of the sun," he called to her. "Soon." He tried to smile.

When the next piece of equipment was handed Medina he was not surprised. They gave him a wooden club edged with tufts of green and yellow feathers. So, he thought, I am to die fighting a man with an obsidian sword. He was led outside the building.

Medina was completely unprepared for what he saw. There standing in the bright sunlight was Montejo's gray, saddled and ready to be mounted, with the strange-looking Indian holding the bridle. He was still absorbing the situation when Molotl motioned him toward the horse.

"Tezcatlipoca will fight from on top of the deer," he declared.

Medina glanced back at Nacha, and saw that she was leaning against the doorway, crying. He forced himself to walk to the horse. He checked the cinch, tightened it, and patted the animal's neck.

As he led the horse toward the sacred precinct, he found himself thinking not of the coming combat, but of Nacha. What would become of her if he was killed? Even if he lived, would he ever see her again? He buried the pain he felt in his chest. He struggled not to look back, and started preparing himself mentally for battle.

The familiar smell of a horse and the creaking of its empty saddle gave Medina a sense of comfort. An expert horseman, he felt confident he could control the powerful animal whose hooves now clanked dully on the flagstones underfoot. As he looked about, he could see signs of festivity, the same festooned poles and burning braziers that had decorated the plaza when he and José had first entered it. A feeling of repulsion echoed through him as he recalled the night of sacrifice, the long lines of doomed prisoners, and the death of José.

As they approached the plaza surrounding the main temple, he saw the architectural features that gave it its monumental, grisly character: the little wooden temples atop the Pyramid, the skull-rack, the stone disc on which he had seen the defenseless prisoner lose his head.

The crowds had already started to stream into the precinct, word having been passed that a special entertainment was in the offing. Spectators were filling the plaza, even sitting on the lower tiers of the pyramids to get a view of the central section.

Medina and his attendants stopped a short way in, and the priests brought him alongside the horse, indicating that it was time to mount. One of them took his shield and club to permit him to swing up unencumbered. The horse felt unfamiliar to him. As he found the right stirrup, his sword and shield were handed him. The non-Aztec Indian grasped the lower part of the bridle. The image of the familiar figure astride this same horse in Tabasco crossed his mind as well as associated images of that battle.

He took the club in his right hand, and felt the power of the beast on which he sat. He thought of the panic that it could induce in a people ignorant of horses. The idea occurred to him to dig his heels into the horse, and wrench it free from the Indian holding the bridle. Then ride back and forth swinging the club they had given him. That would surprise them. And the fact that they had designated him an Aztec god might heighten the effect. He knew he could terrorize the courtyard, at least for a time. Ultimately, they would stop him, however. That he recognized, too. Thousands of Aztecs thronged the courtyard. How many could he attack before he exhausted himself? One thing, Molotl would be the first target. Perhaps the spectacle of his death would be seen as a supernatural event, a signal from the gods that all Aztecs should fall to the ground in awe of the terrible Tezcatlipoca. It was his only hope.

The Sacrificial Priest stood a few feet off. It would take but a moment. As Medina readied himself to strike, he looked again around the courtyard, trying to absorb its shape and the height of the wall enclosing it. But now a parting of the crowd in the courtyard caught his attention. He paused.

Abruptly a flash of color made him start. Among a distinct cluster of Aztec warriors coming through the crowd was a tall figure, taller than the others. The man's face was light with a black beard. On his forehead were tattooed designs. Medina struggled to believe what he saw. The strange horseman of Tabasco. It had to be Braga. But why was he, Medina, on horseback this time and Braga now on foot? The horse was definitely Montejo's gray, and Braga must have brought it with him.

Medina's thoughts were interrupted by the dull throb of a signal drum atop the Great Pyramid. The crowd became silent, and fell back from the center of the plaza as Aztec warriors motioned them away. As the center of the plaza cleared, he found himself and Braga almost alone, facing each other at a distance of about one hundred yards. Between them stood a thin line of armed Aztec sentinels.

Out of the corner of his eye he could see a dozen figures moving up one of the side pyramids. Was it a sacrifice?

Suddenly from the opposite side of the plaza a single line of about one hundred Tabascans trotted through the crowd toward Braga. Each of them carried an upright lance about six feet in length with a hooked crosspiece just below its obsidian point. Halberds! Braga had taught his men to make and use halberds, the European infantry-man's primary weapon against cavalry. Medina's mind sped. So that was it. Braga was using him for a demonstration. To show the Aztecs how to combat the Spanish horses. And he and the horse beneath him were to be the victims.

The line of halberdiers now reached Braga and, without visible command, formed serried ranks on all four sides of him. The outermost rank knelt, their halberds pointing outward. The rank behind them stood upright, with theirs at a forty-five-degree angle. The third and last rank stood at attention, their halberds pointing vertically toward the sky. Hidden in their center, Medina knew, was Braga commanding the unit. My God, he thought, they've formed the Spanish Square. Was he supposed to single-handedly fight a battle formation that had stood up successfully to some of the best cavalry in Europe?

The thin row of Aztec sentinels withdrew into the crowd on the sidelines. In the bright sunlight of noon, Don Marcos de Medina, Knight of the Golden Fleece, Lord Tezcatlipoca of the Aztecs, or whoever he was, certainly had his work cut out for him. This would have made a hell of a spectacle in Florence, he irreverently thought, as he raised himself in his stirrups, tightened the reins with his left hand, and gently urged the horse for-

ward to check the Square. The warriors looked disciplined
—but *were* they?

The Tabascans, he observed, held their halberds in
their right hands like European infantry. That meant
that their best blows to unhorse him would be to their
left side. Accordingly, their right flank, the one to his own
left, was their weak side. Touching his heels to the horse's
flanks, he guided it to the left, keeping about fifty yards
away from the Square. Then he had the gray break into
a trot, raised his club so that the halberdiers might think
he was about to attack, and started circling clockwise
around the Square, moving closer and closer. He wanted
to see if the men turned to the right to cover their weak
side as he went past them. If they did, it would be a sign
of vulnerability, an indication of a lack of training and discipline, for such movement created openings in the ranks
to the left. First-rate infantry would not move a hair's-
width to the right. The warriors showed no movement.
Damn, Medina thought. He rode the horse in an even
tighter circle, getting to within thirty yards. Still no
movement.

He remembered what Cortés had told him, that the
Indians usually fled the field of battle if one could kill
or capture their head chief. And wasn't that his assignment, anyway, to get Braga? But how to do it?

By now he had completely circled the Square. He put
the horse into its fastest trot. Perhaps if he got in closer,
some of the halberdiers would break ranks to try to get
to him. Thirty yards, twenty-five yards, twenty. He could
see the eyes of the Indians following him, but the only
movement in the Square was Braga himself turning to
watch him. Medina was impressed. The Portuguese had

done a first-rate job of training his men. As he completed his second circle, he decided to return to the opposite end of the plaza, where he had started from, in order to evaluate the situation.

There he wheeled about and looked at the Square. He could wait them out, he thought. Sooner or later they would have to come after him. How they did it would be the critical matter. If they opened ranks as skirmishers he would stand a fair chance of riding through them to Braga. But if they kept the Square formation as they moved, they could simply pin him in his end of the plaza. The advantage he had of the horse's speed and weight would be lost without running room.

Almost as if in answer to his thoughts, the Square started inching forward. The men who had been kneeling remained low, but now waddled slowly toward him in an almost squatting position, the points of their halberds held low. The Square, like some single living creature, moved slowly and silently across the plaza toward Medina. He held his breath, fascinated at the Square's approach, feeling like some small insect prey in a web awaiting an advancing spider. Abruptly he roused himself from the sight. What should he do? He could gallop around them, and force the Square to move in a new direction. He could do that again and again. But sooner or later his horse would tire, or worse, slip on the flagstones, and it would be all over. Besides, he had no patience for a waiting game.

Medina looked hard at the advancing Square. He decided what he had to do. He estimated the distance. About fifty yards. Too close. He turned the horse, and trotted it back to the edge of the crowd of spectators. He wheeled the animal and estimated the space again. About seventy yards. Good, he thought, enough distance to build up near-maximum momentum with the half-ton of horse-flesh beneath him. He crossed himself, kicked the horse full-force in the ribs, and yelled, as much for the benefit of the animal as himself. The horse bolted forward toward the Square.

As the horse picked up momentum, Medina could see the first rank of halberdiers dropping to one knee. Time almost seemed frozen. He would never have used up a horse this way in a regular battle, he thought. Under normal conditions it would be suicidal. But this was his only chance, to hope that the sheer, accelerating mass of the horse would smash through all three ranks, and carry him to Braga before it collapsed. He saw Braga frantically shouting to the side ranks of the Square to turn and join the ranks facing the oncoming horse and rider. But it was too late.

Medina and the horse went catapulting over the first rank of halberdiers. He pulled his feet from the stirrups, clenching his feathered club tightly in his right hand as the horse smashed through the second rank and skidded, on its knees now, through the third. The jolt threw him over the horse's head and directly against Braga. They hit the pavement together, Medina tumbling over Braga and spinning around. Braga came up fast, obsidian-edged sword in hand. But not fast enough. In that instant, Medina swung his club hard against the side of Braga's head. Braga crumpled onto the flagstones, his obsidian sword dropping from his hand.

A conch shell trumpet immediately sounded, and the Tabascan warriors backed away, leaving Medina, Braga, and the crippled horse alone on the pavement. Medina felt disembodied, a spectator in some silent dream. The Portuguese lay before him as though asleep, his eyes closed, sprawled out on his side. Medina slowly bent over, and carefully laid his club down, picking up Braga's sharp sword. He flexed his arm, testing the weight of the weapon, contemplating the distance to Braga's neck. He vaguely remembered there was something he was supposed to do about the head.

Braga stirred slightly. His eyes opened. He blinked, and stared up at Medina, up at the raised obsidian sword. Medina hesitated.

Braga grinned. "Yes, my son?" he said.

Medina shivered. The voice, the words, were the same as in his dream. Or was it a dream, or was this a dream? Or. . . .

At that moment Medina thought he heard a woman's voice calling his name . . . Marcos-tzin . . . and then he heard a distant scream, as from the top of a pyramid somewhere in the sacred precinct. He did not know why, but the cry tore at his insides, hurt him. It was followed by the wail of conch shells, and then there was silence, except for the groans of the wounded horse on the pavement behind him.

Medina slowly turned his back on Braga, his weapon still upraised. He went over to the horse, splayed on the flagstones. It panted in agony, two of its legs broken, three halberd points broken off in its flanks and belly. Somehow, a shipboard incident distant in a haze of memory came back to Medina's mind.

"Farewell, horse," he said. He raised his sword once again, brought it down, and put the animal out of its agony. Then he threw the weapon, clattering, onto the pavement. He walked slowly, tiredly, across the plaza back toward the building from which he had come. The crowd parted; he did not look back.

High above the plaza, Moctezuma, the Great Speaker, watched from behind a gold mesh screen on a raised gallery.

"We have been wrong," he said. "We have sinned in not welcoming the deer-men, the sons of Quetzalcoatl."

"Yes, my Lord, the gods are angry," agreed a seer standing at his side.

"We must make a sacrifice of penance," said Moctezuma, "of our most valuable prisoner. Prepare him."

When Medina returned to his chamber, Nacha was not there. A chill of premonition seized him. He called her name as he hurriedly looked in the adjoining rooms, in the garden, and then, again, in their sleeping room. He called again. There was only the sound of the fountain in the patio. Then he saw that a bouquet of flowers and the *patolli* board lay on their bed. The board was vacant except for one red man and one green man occupying the same square together. One of them was dead. One dead! He ran to the hallway door. There were no guards. Down the corridor he saw his captor sitting by the wall.

"Nacha?" Medina called.

Atlacol did not know how to explain, since he could not speak his son's language. But he had to tell his son somehow. Atlacol got up and walked to him. He grasped at his heart and jerked his hand upward. The meaning was unmistakable.

Medina went back into the chamber, back to the bed she

and he had shared. He picked up the bouquet. Inside, his brain was screaming. He could see her smiling face, hear her singing. *I shall have to leave the precious flowers.* He threw himself on the bed. He wept silently.

When Medina roused himself, the last reddish glow of the sun reflected through the patio doorway onto the limestone walls. Medina went to the doorway, and gazed at the sunset. A gentle breeze seemed to beckon him outside. He turned, walked through the chamber and out the door. There were no guards.

By the time it was twilight Medina had reached the sacred enclosure surrounding the great plaza. He found a stone bench not far from the western gate, and sat there as a full moon rose in the east. As he watched the rising moon reflect on the white facades of the pyramids, a figure came up to him.

"My son," said the figure, "I come to join you." It was Atlacol.

CHAPTER

XIV

In the darkness Atlacol led Medina to the rear of the serpent-mouth temple, behind the piles of wood. He motioned Medina to sit against a stone wall near the pool that was the source of water for boiling the priests' portions of the sacrificial victims. Medina could make out the silhouettes of the pyramids in all directions, their white-washed surfaces faintly reflecting the lunar glow. Atop the Great Pyramid at the east end of the plaza he thought he could see the pale mosaics of human skulls on the crest of the right-hand temple.

The Indian squatted down beside Medina and spoke softly to him. Medina could make out only a few words, something about meat of God or the gods, eat, good. Meat, he thought, Jesus Christ, all these heathens care about is meat. What or whom do they want to eat now?

Atlacol pulled a small pottery jar from his shoulder bag and showed it to Medina. In the dim light he could not make out its contents. The Indian nodded to him, turned around, and placed the vessel on the flagstones. He knelt before the jar, and began to whistle softly a strange, quavering tune. Over and over he repeated it for what seemed half an hour. Medina kept thinking of Nacha, visions of her coming to his mind's eye. He felt like a hollow man. Tears trickled down his cheeks. A cool breeze wafted through the city from the north, and Medina pulled his cotton cape around his shoulders.

Finally, Atlacol reached into the jar, took two small

objects out, and chewed them slowly. He reached in a number of times, repeating the process. Now he withdrew two of the things and offered them to Medina. Fully expecting the worst, roasted fingers or God knew what, Medina was surprised to find himself holding only a pair of mushrooms. They had longer stems and smaller heads than mushrooms he had seen before. His first thought was that they might be poisonous. But then he realized he did not really care. Medina chewed them. They had a mild, raw but not unpleasant taste. He swallowed. Again and again, Medina accepted more from the Indian, perhaps two or three dozen in all. Slowly the old man began the strange tune once more, this time singing words instead of whistling. The song had a kind of off-key, almost ominous character, Medina felt. Perhaps the man was a witch. *Christ! Killers, cannibals, witches! What would it matter if the mushrooms are poisonous. Hell couldn't be much different.* Yet this Aztec had been kind to him on the journey from the coast. He would sit with him, but pray to the true God. Quietly Medina began to recite the rosary. Holy Mary, Mother of God . . . Atlacol turned his head to him and nodded apparent approval.

It seemed as though an hour passed in this manner. Medina sensed an increasing change within himself. Almost simultaneously he and the Aztec stopped chanting, and fell into silence. Medina could feel energy flowing into his body. The full moon seemed to shine with incredible gentleness, connected somehow to the wind that caressed his face and almost whispered in his ears. He felt that again Nacha was in his presence, at his side.

From far off in the city he could hear the dull beat of a drum, and sometimes the sound of flutes. It was good that the people were celebrating, he thought. Medina felt content with being just where he was, on the solid earth, beneath the moon and stars. There was no place to go, no need to escape; it was all here. His senses seemed extraordinarily sharp. Every sound was magnified. The drumming had stopped, but somewhere there was laughter, and he could hear the beautiful sound of falling water. He slowly looked behind him. In the moonlight he could see the silvery water pouring forth from the mouth of a small stone aqueduct that projected over the edge of the pool. The sound of the water called him, told him to come.

Medina walked slowly to the edge of the pool, stood a few minutes, then removed his cape and loincloth. He dove in. The water was cool and gentle, like the moon, like the wind, like the earth. He swam back and forth under the cascade. Again he submerged, delighting in the sound and feel of the water as it fell onto the surface above him. Then he swam back to the edge of the pool, hoisted himself up, and sat quietly watching the falling water. Slowly the rippling pool became transformed into an ancient lagoon of moving creatures, shifting darkly. Their forms became more strongly defined. He began to see serpents, water animals, mysterious birds, something like a dragon. Their eyes were always upon him. No matter how they moved, their gaze was fixed. They were talking to him, addressing him; but without words. *We make the lightning, we make the thunder, the earthquakes. We are the ancient ones. Gods of Nature, all that lives.*

Then urgently: *Get out of here if you are just playing in the water. Get out of here, go away. We will forgive your ignorance. This is not that kind of place. This is a place to teach people serious lessons.*

Then a second message: *If you want to learn that kind of lesson, then take another dive; but this time it's going to be another kind of swim.*

Medina sat there for perhaps a quarter of an hour trying to make up his mind. He sensed that he could, from this point, go in two fundamentally different directions. Finally, he realized with clarity that he was risking his life. But the lesson seemed somehow worth it. *I'll have to die sooner or later anyway. At least here I have the choice to do it on my own terms. I can do it now rather than waiting for it to come to me in the future, when I don't expect it.*

Medina had faced death before, but this time it was different, the whole feeling now, the whole flavor of his encounter with death here was special. Finally he made his decision. Medina dove into the water again.

The pool was teeming with the demons, with very peculiar energies. They sardonically played with him, buffeted him. The intelligent entities were putting him through a trial of strength, of worthiness. They were benevolent, but they were very powerful, difficult, painful teachers. He became caught in a great whirlpool, roaring down into eternity, faster and faster. Again and again he died, was torn to pieces, was destroyed, was scared *to death, and to death, and to death.* Still the beings, the deities were benevolent.

Finally the lesson came to an end. The whirlpool had lost its force. Medina found himself, at least temporarily, alive.

When he emerged from the water he staggered around the pool until he found his cape and loincloth. He put them on with difficulty, all the time feeling a new pull reaching from the dark water. They were pulling him back, perhaps to drown him. The water would wash, dissolve his soul, his very existence, below the cascade. He realized he was again faced with a choice. Medina felt an urge to make a gift of his being to the water deities, to lose himself completely to them; but another part of his being was warning him to save what he believed to be himself.

He decided to try to get away from the pool. He could tell that it would rise up, flood, gush, up and over the plaza, coming to follow and engulf him, to drag him back, to drown him into eternal life-death oneness. Medina turned away and began to walk. He must get to high ground. He saw a small mountain ahead, a mountain-pyramid. There was safety from the Flood. Beside him, he became aware, was a man. He looked familiar. Of course, Noah! *Vámonos, pues! Adelante para Santiago y España! Adelante para Santiago, Cuba!* My mother, I want to come home! Medina tripped and sprawled on the flagstones. The earth was his mother. He lay on her breast. Honey and milk flowed up from below. He felt great strength pour into him. *Again, forward!* He pulled himself up and ran toward the Pyramid. Grinning dragon heads loomed out of the darkness. *Ah, the Devil! I will climb above him, above the Flood, to Heaven.* Heaven. He would reach it even if he died. He put his left foot on the first step. The step was high, the stone was slippery. Was it rain or blood? The wetness was purple, then red, then lavender, shimmering with an ethereal iridescence. Now there was lightning above, thunder from the east. Tears dropped down onto Medina.

He could see the steep steps above him disappearing

into the darkness, slippery with water and blood, a new ordeal. He felt vulnerable. Yet he had to climb. With great effort he made it up on all fours to a narrow terrace. He could hear the rushing flood rising fast behind him. No time to rest. Up the new steps, steep and narrow, dangerous, nothing to hang on to. He was slipping, falling. A wave of visions, of feelings, flowed into and out of him. His skull was shattering on the plaza below. Thousands were cheering, waving banners. The pain was excruciating. He was slipping, falling again. Sharp steps, broken limbs, skull smashing again, and again. A hundred times he died. Each time was different. Each time was the same. Over and over. With each step upward a slip, with each slip all the falls, all the smashings, all the drownings that had ever been and ever would be. With each step he also lost fear. Dying became almost routine. He had already done it. He began to experience a religious union, an ecstasy, in letting his death happen. A lesson: *personal destruction is freeing.* A lesson: *personal destruction is a return to the source.* Centuries passed, centuries of dying in thousands of forms, thousands of ways. His body did not seem to exist anymore, but he was pushing something upward. Somehow, incredibly it seemed, he reached the terrace on top of the Pyramid and collapsed forward. Before him in the darkness loomed a horizontal jade-green stone. The sacrificial block, its convex surface toward the knife, toward the sun, toward the sun-knife that came crashing down from Heaven.

Beyond the stone of sacrifice rose a temple, its dark door a cavernous opening to the underworld of the gods. From the door they came, flowing, smiling, baring their fangs. Other creatures poured their forms up the steps behind him, swirling about the sacrificial stone, inundating Medina. God-animals, he realized. They were silent, shifting their shapes at will. The spirits of the water, of the Flood, had joined him. A buzzing, flapping sound came from above. Broad wings, a great beak, gigantic claws clutched the sacred stone. Tremendous grinning, sardonic rattlesnake-dragons twisted, twined, and untwined over the stone, the terrace, the temple, around his body. They whispered silently into his brain. He became a lame deer, sick and old, tired. *Food!* Jaguars caressed his body, licked his face. A pair of glowing cougars tumbled, fighting each other for the food, the meat. *I am at the end place. Nowhere to climb, no place to escape to. This is the place where you lie down.* He lay back onto the sacred stone, face upward into the darkness. Giant claws tore a piece of flesh out of his body. He became the claws, the devouring beak, the lump of his own meat as it was swallowed. He became the great bird devouring him.

As the great bird he stretched his wings. He rose, rose. His outstretched wings became hands, arms. He was the crucified Christ, spread-eagled, accompanied by eagles, soaring in ever higher orbits, playing around the sun, the warm Source, offering himself. *Accípite, et manducáte ex hoc omnes. HOC EST ENIM CORPUS MEUM. Take ye and eat of this: FOR THIS IS MY BODY!*

My body, my body. Where did I leave it? *Ah, there, down below.* Lying on the Pyramid terrace, on the stone, blood flowing downward from the opened chest cavity. *Yes, the pure Victim, the holy Victim, the all-perfect Victim: the holy Bread of life eternal and the Chalice of unending salvation. Accípite, et bíbite ex eo omnes. Take ye all, and drink of this. FOR THIS IS THE CHALICE*

*OF MY BLOOD OF THE NEW AND ETERNAL
COVENANT: THE MYSTERY OF FAITH, WHICH
SHALL BE SHED FOR YOU AND FOR MANY. . . .*
He became his blood flowing down the Pyramid steps
into the flood, into the rivers, into the ocean, into the
mists of eternal time. *Orate, fratres: ut meum ac vestrum
sacrificium acceptábile fiat apud Deum Patrem omnipo-
téntem. Pray, brethren, that my sacrifice and yours may
become acceptable to God the Father almighty.* He was
happy. He no longer needed his body. He had surrendered,
and become all life, all existence. And now, silently, the
animals were telling him the lesson: *Your body is only
flesh, food for others. Accept this fully. Be prepared to
offer your body to us as food. With acceptance you join
the eternal brotherhood.* He accepted. *Yes, we are eating
each other. Life is feeding on itself.* He had a deep sense,
a sacred sense, of communion with the other animals.
*We beseech Thee, therefore, help Thy servants, whom
Thou hast redeemed with Thy Precious Blood.* He felt
their power. *Give me energy now. One day I'll return it
to you.* The animals seemed pleased. *Good, you have given
yourself to us. Enter the brotherhood now. Here is our
energy, our power. One day it will come back to us.*
Medina felt the energy surge into his system.

Dawn was creeping into the eastern sky. Medina felt
incredibly strong, elated. He rose up and spread his arms
in the cool breeze. Joining him on the crest of the Pyramid was his captor, his brother. Behind the temple the
horizon gradually crinkled with pink fluorescences. The
world became brighter. The edge of an ancient red sun
floated up behind the eastern mountain rim. Medina
felt that he was seeing the sun for the first time. He

watched, transfixed, as it brought its healing heat to his face, to all living things. He remembered this sun. He remembered it well. Many times it had warmed him anciently, as a fern, as a tree, as a crocodile on the shore of the swamps of time. He fell on his knees in silent awe. He now understood: *behind the brotherhood, behind the exchange of life, was the Sun, giving power to all. To all forms of life, the mansions of the Sun. GOD, THE FATHER ALMIGHTY. GOD, THE FATHER, THE SUN!*

From another pyramid came the trumpeting of a conch shell. Soon the morning sacrifice to the Sun. Medina smiled.

The next day Atlacol left for home. As he trotted along the causeway out of the city, he thought proudly of the feast the night before. He had received much honor for giving up his light-skinned son. And he knew his family would appreciate the sacred gift in his shoulder bag.

On the causeways there were other men trotting, too, runners to the eastern garrisons bearing orders for them not to resist the deer-men. In their pouches they bore protective talismans, small balls of maize dough soaked in blood, soaked in the blood of the god who had died for their sins.

EPILOGUE

On November 8, 1519, Cortés and his men finally entered
Tenochtitlan (now Mexico City) as guests of Moctezuma.
By the time they reached the capital city, many of them
had been wounded and killed in battles with Tlaxcalans
and other hostile Indians as they fought their way up from
Vera Cruz. They now numbered fewer than four hundred,
but they had been aided in their battles by their disciplined European concentration on killing enemies rather
than capturing them, by their "cavalry" of slightly more
than a dozen horses, and by a small army of Indian allies,
including the Tlaxcalans, who joined forces with the
Spaniards after being defeated by them.

No trace of any captured Europeans was found in
Tenochtitlan by Cortés and his men, nor are there reliable
reports of any arriving prior to the entrance of Cortés into
the city. Yet the events described in this book are entirely
within the realm of historical possibility, and many of
them are based on known historical fact. To take one
character as an example, the Portuguese Martim Braga
is modeled on a real person, the Spaniard Gonzalo Guerrero, who was a survivor of the same shipwreck as Jerónimo de Aguilar, and who is known to have taught
European battle techniques and tactics to the Indians

of Yucatan to help them defend themselves against the Spaniards. He was held responsible for the success of the Indian warriors in battle against the soldiers of the Córdoba expedition at Champotón, close to Tabasco. Given Guerrero's prestige among the natives and the widespread recruitment of warriors by the Tabascans to repel Cortés, it is very possible that he had a hand in that battle as well; and the fact remains that during the battle a mysterious horseman is claimed to have appeared riding back and forth among the Indians, one that the Spaniards could not identify. The solution they suggested was a supernatural one, that the horseman was Santiago, or Saint James.

The major historical figures, such as Moctezuma (anthropologists generally have given up the *Montezuma* spelling), Cortés, Alvarado, Marina, are based on fact, of course. Medina, José, and Nacha *could* have existed.

Famines and food shortages were indeed frequent in Central Mexico among the Aztecs and their neighbors, and had very important effects on Aztec life and culture. To emphasize this point in the novel, the conditions of the famine of 1505 and of the serious food shortages of 1501, 1507, and 1515 were transposed to 1519 to suggest the nutritional problems frequently faced by the population, especially the common people. Speaking of problems, bandits are reported to have existed in Mexico even before the arrival of the Spaniards.

The remarkable resemblances between aspects of pre-Conquest Aztec religion and Christianity, especially as regards the eating of the body and blood of one who has atoned for the sins of others, have been noted by many scholars, especially Father Diego Durán in the sixteenth century. The concept of sin was well developed among the Aztecs, as was the idea of confession.

The similarities between the two religions helped the Christians considerably in the "conversion" of the "heathen." However, it was probably the introduction of the pig and other European domesticated animals that was really critical, along with Spanish laws, in eliminating the human flesh eucharist of the Aztecs. In fact, the Indians were particularly enthusiastic about pork, telling the Spaniards that it tasted like human meat. Even today if you ask a peasant in Central Mexico whether it's proper to make *pozole,* a festive meat stew, with pork, there's a good chance that he will respond with a knowing laugh. If pressed, and if your rapport is good, he may explain to you what kind of meat really should be used in *pozole.*

Which brings us to the subject of cannibalism. It was, in fact, the strange juxtaposition of a high civilization and cannibalism that provoked this novel. We wondered what it felt like to live in such a civilization and what it might have looked like to a European visitor at the time.

The reader may be curious why cannibalism was practiced routinely in a major civilization. An answer was proposed in "The Ecological Basis for Aztec Sacrifice," published recently by Harner in the *American Ethnologist,* a journal of the American Anthropological Association.[1] The explanation seems to us to be a theory far

[1] The specific sources for the data may be found by the interested reader in the *American Ethnologist,* February 1977.

more consistent with the facts than that of the French anthropologist Claude Lévi-Strauss, who suggested that the extensive human sacrifice of the Aztecs was due to their suffering from a "maniacal obsession with blood and torture." In contrast to such a view, we firmly believe the Aztecs behaved quite rationally, considering their ecological circumstances. What follows is distilled from Harner's article.

Anthropologists have long pointed to human sacrifice in pre-Conquest Mexico as representing an extreme in known cultural behavior. Among state societies in the ethnological record, the Aztecs sacrificed unparalleled numbers of human victims, 20,000 a year being a commonly cited figure.

Yet cultural evolutionists have been silent when it comes to explaining this remarkable and central aspect of Aztec civilization. The nonevolutionists have not done much better, typically attempting to explain the human sacrificial complex on the basis of Aztec religion without suggesting why this particular form of religion demanding large-scale human sacrifice should have evolved when and where it did.

Recent research suggests that population pressure was a major force behind the huge human sacrifices. Before discussing further this Aztec enigma, it may be useful to review some of the basic ecological assumptions that are involved in the population pressure theory of cultural evolution.

Human population growth is as much an unmistakable prehistoric and historic trend as the evolution of technology. The long-term increase of human population led gradually to increasing degradation of wild flora and fauna used for food. The extinction of many big-game mammals by the end of the European Paleolithic and by Paleo-Indians in the New World is the first outstanding evidence of this human-caused environmental depletion. The later evolution into the Old World Mesolithic with its shift to marine resources and small-game hunting, and the development of a New World cultural analogue, can be seen as continuing and necessary responses to such environmental depletion. The increasing scarcity of wild game and food plants soon made the innovation of plant and animal domestication desirable and competitively efficient in several regions of the planet. With the passage of time and the further growth of human population on the Earth, more areas became similarly depleted, and plant and animal domestication necessarily became ever more widely adopted, providing an increasing proportion of the diet.

The need for intensified domesticated food production was especially felt early in such fertile, but environmentally circumscribed, localities as temperate and tropical riverine valleys surrounded by less desirable terrain. Under such circumstances, climate and environment permitting, plants always were domesticated; but herbivorous mammals apparently could not be unless appropriate species existed.

In the Old World the domestication of herbivorous mammals proceeded apace with the domestication of food plants. In the New World, however, the ancient hunters completely eliminated potential herbivorous mammalian domesticates from the Mesoamerican area. It was only in the Andean region and in southern South America that some cameloid species, especially the llama and alpaca, managed to survive the ancient onslaught, and thus were available in later times for domestication along with another important herbivore, the guinea pig (*Cavia porcellus*). In the Mesoamerican area the cameloid species became extinct at least several thousand years before domesticated food production had to be undertaken seriously. Nor was the guinea pig available. In Mesoamerica, emphasis was on the domestication of wild fowl, such as the turkey, as well as of the dog, for food. The Mexican hairless, or chihuahua, is generally assumed to be the outgrowth of breeding for such a purpose. The dog, however, was not an efficient converter, competing with its owners for essentially the same kinds of food, animal or vegetal.

As population pressure increased in the Valley of Mexico, wild game supplies were decreasingly available to provide protein for the diet. In his book *The Aztecs of Mexico,* George C. Vaillant noted that "the deer were nearly all killed off" before the Aztec period. The seriousness of population pressure in general in the Valley during the time of the Aztecs has been discussed by many researchers. In terms of carbohydrate production, this challenge was usually met by soil reclamation of marshlands (the so-called floating gardens) and other forms of agricultural intensification; but domesticated animal production was limited by the lack of a suitable herbivore. This made the ecological situation of the Aztecs and their neighbors unique among the world's major civilizations. It appears that large-scale cannibalism, disguised as sacrifice, was the natural consequence of this situation.

The contrast between Mesoamerica and the Andes in terms of the existence of domesticated herbivores was matched by the contrast between the Inca and Aztec emphasis on human sacrifice. In the Inca Empire, the other political entity in the New World at the time of the Spanish Conquest, annual human sacrifices could, at most, apparently be measured only in the hundreds. Among the Aztecs, the figures were incomparably greater. However, the annual figure of "20,000" so commonly mentioned is of uncertain significance.

A thorough analysis of the early reports on numbers of Aztec sacrificial victims is provided by Sherburne Cook in his 1946 paper, in which he estimates an overall annual mean of 15,000 victims in a Central Mexican population estimated at 2 million. However, the conservatism inherent in his paper is made evident by his later revision, in collaboration with Woodrow Borah, of the estimate of the Central Mexican population on the eve of the Spanish Conquest upwards, from his 2 million figure to 25 million.

Furthermore, Borah, who is a leading authority on the demography of Central Mexico at the time of the Conquest, has given me permission to cite his new unpublished estimate of the number of persons sacrificed in Central Mexico shortly before the arrival of the Spaniards: *250,000 per year,* or equivalent to 1 percent of the total population.

Beyond those numbers is the question of what was done with the bodies after the sacrifices. The evidence of Aztec cannibalism has largely been ignored and consciously or unconsciously covered up. One must go back to Conquest and immediately post-Conquest sources to gain an awareness of its importance in Aztec life. Bernal Díaz and other conquistadores such as Hernán Cortés and Bernardino de Sahagún are among the most reliable. Less reliable but basically in accord with the others is Diego Durán.

While some sacrificial victims, such as children sacrificed to the rain god Tlaloc by drowning, or persons suffering skin diseases, were not eaten, the overwhelming majority of the sacrificed captives appear to have been consumed. A major objective, and sometimes the only objective, of Aztec war expeditions was to capture prisoners for sacrifice. While some might be sacrificed and eaten on the field of battle, most were taken to home communities or to the capital, where they were kept in wooden cages until they were sacrificed by the priests at the temple-pyramids. Most of the sacrifices involved tearing out the heart, offering it to the sun, and, with some blood, also to the idols. The corpse then was tumbled down the steps of the pyramid, and elderly attendants cut off the arms, legs, and head. While the head went onto the local skull-rack, at least three of the limbs were normally property of the captor, who formally retained ownership of the victim. He then hosted at his quarters a feast at which the central dish was a stew of tomatoes, peppers, and the limbs of the victim. The torso of the victim, in Tenochtitlan (Mexico City), at least, went to the royal zoo to feed carnivorous mammals, birds, and snakes. Where towns lacked zoos, the fate of the torsos is not certain.

As the practice of cannibalism by the Aztecs and their neighbors was essentially terminated with the Spanish Conquest, some of the best evidence for its existence and extent is provided by the letters of Hernán Cortés addressed to Charles V of Spain; the account of the Conquest by Bernal Díaz del Castillo, a firsthand participant and its most thorough chronicler; the chronicle of Andrés de Tapia, one of Cortés' captains; and the memoir of Fray Francisco de Aguilar, who participated in the Conquest. The accounts are in the approximate chronological order of the expedition's history, beginning with its landings on the east coast of Mexico in 1519 and following through to the fall of Tenochtitlan in 1521.

Upon landing on the coast of Tabasco, Cortés and his men engaged in battle with Indians and took prisoners. Tapia states, "At camp these Indians told us how they were gathering to give us battle and fight with all their might to kill and then eat us." Cortés sent the prisoners back as messengers to demand the surrender of the Indians. Tapia goes on to relate: "The messengers did not return with an answer, but some warriors moving about in the canals and estuaries were saying to our men that in three days all the warriors in the land would be gathered and would eat us."

After additional fighting Cortés' forces reembarked in the ships, and sailed along the coast to what is now Vera Cruz. There founding a town, Cortés sent one of his captains, Pedro de Alvarado, with a force inland to reconnoiter and obtain provisions. Alvarado first entered some villages that were under Aztec rule. Bernal Díaz reports:

When Alvarado came to these villages he found that they had been deserted on that very day, and he saw in the *cues* [temples or temple-pyramids] the bodies of men and boys who had been sacrificed, the walls and altars all splashed with blood, and the victims' hearts laid out before the idols. He also found the stones on which their breasts had been opened to tear out their hearts.

Alvarado told us that most of the bodies were without arms and legs, and that some Indians had told him that these had been carried off to be eaten. Our soldiers were greatly shocked at such cruelty. I will say no more about these sacrifices, since we found them in every town we came to.

The Spaniards eventually reached Tlaxcala, the stronghold of the archenemies of the Aztecs. Díaz reports:

I must now tell how in this town of Tlascala [Tlaxcala] we found wooden cages made of lattice-work in which men and women were imprisoned and fed until they were fat enough to be sacrificed and eaten. We broke open and destroyed these prisons, and set free the Indians who were in them. But the poor creatures did not dare to run away. However, they kept close to us and so escaped with their lives. From now on, whenever we entered a town our captain's first order was to break down the cages and release the prisoners, for these prison cages existed throughout the country.

Cortés and his men then marched on to Cholula, a city hostile to the Tlaxcalans and under Aztec control. There Cortés made a speech to the Cholulans, accusing them of planning treachery, and said to them, according to Díaz, that "we had done them no harm but had merely warned them against certain things as we had warned every town through which we had passed: against wickedness and human sacrifice, and the worship of idols, and eating their neighbor's flesh, and sodomy." Cortés further told the Cholulans:

> So in return for our coming to treat them like brothers, and tell them the commands of our lord God and the King, they were planning to kill us and eat our flesh, and had already prepared the pots with salt and peppers and tomatoes.

The lecture ended with Cortés and his men making a surprise attack, and massacring a significant proportion of his audience.

Before ending his description of Cholula, Díaz says:

> I think that my readers must have heard enough of this tale of Cholula, and I wish that I were finished with it. But I cannot omit to mention the cages of stout wooden bars that we found in the city, full of men and boys who were being fattened for the sacrifice at which their flesh would be eaten. We destroyed these cages, and Cortés ordered the prisoners who were confined in them to return to their native districts. Then, with threats, he ordered the *Caciques* and captains and *papas* [priests] of the city to imprison no more Indians in that way and to eat no more human flesh. They promised to obey him. But since they were not kept, of what use were their promises?

The Spaniards soon reached the Aztec capital city, Tenochtitlan, where they initially were guests of Moctezuma. Later the Spaniards had to flee Tenochtitlan. Aguilar puts it, "The city was teeming with such masses of people that there was hardly room for them inside or out, and they were all hungering for the flesh of the miserable Spaniards." In the famous retreat of the Noche Triste, many of Cortés' men were lost to the Aztecs. Aguilar observes, "As we were fleeing it was heartbreaking to see our companions dying, and to see how the Indians carried them off to tear them to pieces."

After many months of recuperation and prolonged preparation, Cortés' forces finally returned, and commenced to make attacks along the causeways to reenter Tenochtitlan. Eventually, the Spaniards conquered the entire city, and the war in the Valley of Mexico was over. Spanish rule essentially marked the end of native warfare and cannibalism, and it seems likely that the new sources of meat, in the form of Old World domesticates, which the Spanish introduced, helped reinforce obedience to the new laws.

Besides the firsthand accounts from the Conquest, the works of Father Bernardino de Sahagún are probably the single most thorough and reliable source on the subject under consideration. Arriving in Mexico less than a decade after the Conquest, and using Aztec nobles as informants, he transcribed their written or dictated information in Nahuatl as a series of books. These volumes have the strength of presenting the upper-class insiders' view of Aztec culture; but this is also a limitation. For example, certain aspects of their behavior which might seem remarkable and significant to a European or to an anthropologist, such as cannibalism, probably were too routine an aftermath of sacrifice normally to deserve comment. Nevertheless, some very interesting details on such practices are provided. For example, Sahagún, in describing the ceremonies of the month of Tlacaxipeualiztli, states:

And so they [the war captives] were brought up [the

pyramid temple steps] before [the sanctuary of] Uitzilo-
pochtli.

Thereupon they stretched them, one at a time, down
on the sacrificial stone; then they delivered them into
the hands of six priests, who threw them upon their
backs, and cut open their breasts with a wide-bladed
flint knife.

And they named the hearts of the captives "precious
eagle-cactus fruit." They lifted them up to the sun, the
turquoise prince, the soaring eagle. They offered it to
him; they nourished him with it. . . .

Afterwards they rolled them over, they bounced
them down; they came tumbling down head over heels,
and end over end, rolling over and over; thus they
reached the terrace at the base of the pyramid.

And here they took them up. . . .

There they took [the slain captive] up, in order to
carry him to the house [of the captor], so that they
might eat him. There they portioned him out, cutting
him to pieces and dividing him up. First of all they
reserved for Moctezuma a thigh, and set forth to take it
to him.

And [as for] the captor, they there applied the down
of birds to his head and gave him gifts. And he summoned his blood relations, he assembled them, that
they might go to eat at the house of him who had taken
the captive.

And here they cooked each one a bowl of stew of
dried maize, called *tlacatlaolli*, which they set before
each, and in each was a piece of the flesh of the captive.

At the feast, the captor's relatives greeted him with

tears because they recognized that he, in turn, would eventually be killed in war or sacrificed by the enemy. Since this was done within the context of the feasting on the captive, it suggests that there was an implicit recognition that the ultimate fate of the warrior was to serve as food for the enemy. That this fate may have been seen as a reciprocal one may possibly be suggested by the fact that the captor viewed his captive almost as his son. Sahagún says:

And when [after sacrifice] he [the captor] had gone to and reached all the places, he took the insignia to the palace, and he caused [the body of] his captive to be taken to the tribal quarters, when they had passed the night in vigil; here he flayed him. Afterwards he had [the flayed body] taken to his house, where they cut it up, that it might be eaten and shared, and, as was said, to bestow as a favor to others. It hath been told elsewhere how this was done.

And the captor might not eat the flesh of his captive. He said: "Shall I, then, eat my own flesh?" For when he took [the captive], he had said: "He is my beloved son." And the captive had said: "He is as my beloved father." And yet he might eat of someone else's captive.

That to be eaten was the common fate of those captured in war is likewise suggested by the description of the hazards and difficulties of being a merchant or member of the *pochteca* traveling in the lands of enemies. Sahagún says:

In case they were besieged, enclosed, in enemy lands, living among others, having penetrated well within, they became like their enemies. In their array, their hairdress, their speech, they imitated the natives.

And if they came to an evil pass, if they were discovered, then [the foe] slew them in ambush; they served them up with chili sauce.

The question naturally arises as to the nutritional role the consumption of human flesh might have played in the Aztec diet. In his book *Daily Life of the Aztecs on the Eve of the Spanish Conquest*, Jacques Soustelle volunteers that the diet of the commoners included only "rarely any meat, such as game, venison, or poultry (turkey)." He similarly states, "The poorer people ate turkey only on great occasions," and also notes, "Poor people and the lakeside peasants skimmed a floating substance from the surface which was called *tecuitlatl*, 'stone dung'; it was something like cheese, and they squeezed it into cakes; they also ate the spongy nests of water-fly larvae." With an estimated 1.2 to 2.5 million persons dwelling around the lake, it is unlikely that the average consumption of fish or waterfowl was much more than one per person annually.

Despite the apparent scarcity of meat in the diet of the commoners, they theoretically could get the necessary nine essential amino acids from their maize and bean crops, the two foods complementing each other in their essential amino acid components. But one of the problems with relying on beans and maize was that they would have to be ingested in large enough quantities at the same meal in order to provide the body with the essential amino acids *in combination* in order for them to be used to rebuild body tissues; otherwise the dietary protein would simply be converted to energy.

Thus, in order for the Aztecs to obtain their amino acids from the maize-bean combination it would have been necessary for them to be able to consume large quantities of both plants together on a year-round basis. But according to Durán, poor people often could not obtain maize and beans in the same season of the year. Also, crop failures and famines were common among the Aztecs:

> Famines often occurred; every year there was the threat of shortage . . . in 1450 the three rulers of the allied cities distributed the saved-up stores of grain of ten years and more. But still there was always the need for stopgap foods, animal or vegetable, in an emergency. (Soustelle)

Under these conditions it is clear that the necessary maize-bean combination could not be relied upon as a source of the essential amino acids. Of course, the Aztecs had no knowledge of amino acids, but it should be parenthetically pointed out that the human body, like that of other organisms perfected under natural selection, is a homeostatic entity that under conditions of nutritional stress naturally seeks out the dietary elements in which it is deficient. If living organisms did not have this innate capacity, they would not survive.

Another dietary problem for the Aztecs was the scarcity of fats. While the exact amount of fatty acids required by the human body remains a subject of uncertainty among nutritionists, there is agreement that fats provide a longer-lasting energy source than carbohydrates, because of the slower rate of metabolism. It is noteworthy that fatty meat, by providing both fat and the essential proteins, assures the utilization of the essential amino acids for tissue building, since the fat will provide the necessary source of energy that must also be supplied if the dietary protein is not to be siphoned off as a purely caloric contribution. In this connection, it is interesting that the Aztecs kept prisoners in wooden cages prior to their sacrifice, and at least sometimes fattened them there. It should be noted that the prisoners could be fed purely on carbohydrates to build up the fat, since the amino acids are not necessary for such production. The confinement to the cages would also have contributed to the rapid accumulation of fat, given enough caloric intake.

A minority of the Aztec population seems to have been entitled to eat human flesh. According to Durán, "Commoners never ate it; [it was reserved] for illustrious and noble people." Sahagún may be implying a similar restriction when he speaks of the sacrifices at a particular temple: "And when they had cooked them, then the nobility, and all the important men ate [the stew]; but not the common folk—only the leaders." If we were to assume, for purposes of discussion, that the "illustrious and noble people" made up one-quarter of the population, then the annual ratio of victims to consumers would have been 20 per 100, a very significant contribution to their diet.

The point here is not to prove that cannibalism made a contribution to the diet of the total population; rather, it is to explain the extremity of the Aztec sacrificial complex. It is not essential for this argument that a majority of the Aztec population had to take part in human flesh banquets. What is essential is to demonstrate that the sacrificed captives typically were eaten; and this has been done. That the eaters of the flesh may have primarily been the Aztec elite is entirely consistent with the normal inequities of class-stratified society. While, during good times, this source of meat may not have been nutritionally required for the "illustrious and noble people," the privileges were undoubtedly good insurance against times of famine when they, as well as the commoners, could suffer significantly. For example, "[When] Moctezuma was lord, there was famine for two years, and many noblemen sold their young sons and maidens" (Sahagún). As is often the case in human societies, the rules for food distribution were probably forged under the extreme conditions of resource scarcity. Not surprisingly, the ruling class made the rules.

Superficially, it might appear that the Aztec prohibition against human flesh-eating by ordinary or lower class persons would cast doubt upon the potentialty of cannibalism to motivate the masses of Aztec society to engage in wars for prisoners. Actually, however, the prohibition was, if anything, a goad to the lower class to participate in the wars, since the right to eat human flesh could normally only be achieved by single-handedly taking captives in battle. Such successful warriors became members of the Aztec elite, and their descending lineage members shared their privileges. By hosting cannibalistic feasts to which their "blood relations" were invited and each given cooked human flesh (Sahagún), they appear to have effected a distribution of the meat beyond the traditional confines of the hereditary nobility. The distribution of the flesh, in other words, seems to have been done primarily within the framework of kinship and at the discretion of the captor, rather than through the state structure. While the captor could not eat his own prisoner, he could eat of another's, and we may assume that invitations to banquets were naturally reciprocated. Such reciprocity would have contributed to the reliability of this type of food supply. Beyond this, as in many other societies, such feast-giving would have contributed to the elevation of the host's status.

By encouraging the lower class to engage in war through the reward of human flesh-distributing rights and elevation in status, the Aztec rulers were able to motivate the bulk of their population, the poor, to contribute to state and upper class maintenance by participating in offensive military operations. It was in the interests of the ruling class and the state to prohibit the eating of human flesh by the commoners, precisely because they were the group most in need of it. By so doing and also by providing a path for obtaining meat, through war service, the Aztecs were assured of an aggressive war machine. And underlying the competitive success of that machine was the high population pressure of the Valley of Mexico.

The power of the priesthood in Aztec society, it is proposed, was reinforced by cannibalism. When the priests had seemed to fail in their supplications for rain or other weather changes to save the maize crops, they could simply demand sacrificial victims to appease the obviously wrathful gods. Thus, in the guise of satisfying gods, the priests actually were authorizing a hungry population to go forth and seize humans destined for consumption. Given the lack of beasts of burden, the seizure of captives would have also provided bearers to bring back whatever crop stores may have been looted. Thus, even those who might not have directly benefited from the ensuing cannibal feasts would have had their food supply augmented by the taking of captives for sacrifice. In a real sense, the priesthood had a fail-safe system: if the priests failed in their supplications to bring food in the form of local crop harvests, then with the aid of the nobility and the forces under their command, they almost automatically caused food to be brought from other regions. Either way, the gods could be seen as the benefactors of the population.

With an understanding of the importance of cannibalism in Aztec culture, and of the ecological reasons for its existence, some of the more distinctive institutions of the Aztecs begin to make sense anthropologically. For example, the long-standing question of whether the political structure of the Aztecs is or is not definable as an empire can be reexamined. A problem here has been that the Aztecs frequently withdrew from conquered territory without establishing administrative centers or garrisons. This Aztec "failure" to consolidate in the Old World fashion puzzled even Cortés, who asked Moctezuma for an explanation of why he allowed Tlaxcala to maintain its independence. Reportedly Moctezuma replied that it was done so that his people could obtain captives for sacrifice. In other words, since the Aztecs did not normally eat persons of their own polity, which would have been socially and politically disruptive, they viewed it as necessary to have conveniently nearby "enemy" populations on whom they could prey for captives. This kind of behavior makes perfect sense in terms of Aztec cannibalism. The Aztecs were unique among the world's states in having a cannibal empire. For this reason, they often did not conform to models of imperial colonization which were based upon empires possessing domesticated herbivores to provide meat or milk.

Similarly, an institution peculiar to Mesoamerica, the

Wars of Flowers, becomes understandable when one considers that it was revived by the Aztecs in response to the severe famines of the 1450s. These battles, designed mainly to procure prisoners, have been succinctly described by Soustelle as follows:

> The sovereigns of Mexico, Texcoco, and Tlacopan, and the lords of Tlaxcala, Uexotzinco, and Cholula mutually agreed that, there being no war, they would arrange combats, so that the captives might be sacrificed to the gods: for it was thought that the calamities of 1450 were caused by too few victims being offered, so that the gods had grown angry. Fighting was primarily a means of taking prisoners; on the battlefield the warriors did their utmost to kill as few men as possible.

Much more than just Aztec culture begins to become understandable when one keeps in mind that the ecological problems of the Aztecs were simply an extreme case of problems general to the populations of Mesoamerica. The pyramid-temple-idol complex found also among the Teotihuacanos, Toltecs, Maya, and Olmec, it is proposed, is very consistent with an emphasis on sacrificial cannibalism necessitated by the distinctive Mesoamerican ecological conditions.

Among those conditions, the uncertainty of maize-crop production contributed to the pyramid-temple-idol complex by providing an urgent and consistent reason for supplication and offerings to deities. Under such circumstances, human captives destined to be eaten were most naturally incorporated into the offerings made to assure crop production. The definition of the gods as human flesh-eaters almost inevitably led to the emphasis on the kinds of fierce, ravenous, and carnivorous dieties, such as the jaguar and the serpent, that are characteristic of the Mesoamerican pantheons. This, in turn, made it possible to rationalize the more grisly aspects of large-scale cannibalism as being simply a response to the gods' demands. Even such little touches as the steepness of the pyramids' steps become understandable if one keeps in mind the need for efficiency in rolling the bodies down from the sacrificial altars to the multitudes below.

What we can see in the Aztec case is an extreme development—under conditions of environmental circumscription, very high population pressure, and an emphasis on maize agriculture—of a cultural pattern that grew out of a Circum-Caribbean and Mesoamerican ecological area characterized by substantial wild-game depletion and the lack of a domesticated herbivore. Intensification of horticultural practices was possible and occurred widely; but for the necessary satisfaction of basic protein requirements, cannibalism was the only obvious solution. That cannibalism, disguised as propitiation of the gods, bequeathed to the world some of the most distinctive art and architecture developed by humanity. The ecological uniqueness of the situation led inevitably to unique cultural products, among them the famous Aztec sacrificial complex. From the perspective of cultural ecology and population pressure theory, it is possible to understand and respect the Aztec emphasis on human sacrifice as a natural and rational response to the material conditions of their existence.